Mike Ripley has twice won the Crime Writer's Last Laugh Award for comedy crime and his Angel novels have been optioned by the BBC. He has written for television and radio and is the crime fiction critic for the *Birmingham Post*, as well as co-editor of the *Fresh Blood* anthologies which promote new British crime writing talent. He lives with his wife, three children and two cats in East Anglia.

Also by Mike Ripley

Just another angel (1988)
Angel touch (1989)
Angel hunt (1990)
Angels in arms (1991)
Angel city (1994)
Angel confidential (1995)
Family of angels (1996)
That angel look (1997)

As editor (with Maxim Jakubowski)

Fresh blood (1996)
Fresh blood 2 (1997)
Fresh blood 3 (1999)

BOOTLEGGED ANGEL

Mike Ripley

Robinson · London

Constable & Robinson Ltd
3 The Lanchesters
162 Fulham Palace Road
London, W6 9ER
www.constablerobinson.com

First published in Great Britain 1999
by Constable & Company Ltd

This paperback edition published by Robinson, an imprint
of Constable & Robinson Ltd, 2001

ISBN 1 84119 299 6

Printed and bound in the EU

A CIP catalogue record for this book is available from the
British Library

Author's Note

'Two men were shot yesterday in what detectives believe could be a feud over bootlegged beer, as record numbers of day-trippers crossed the English channel to fill their cars with cheap continental alcohol.'

The Independent, 24 August, 1997

'Jim Bolton, senior investigations officer within the Customs and Excise said: "It's a case of dog eats dog."'

The Sun, 1 January 1998

In researching this book I am grateful to various honest (and brave) publicans in the Dover area, policemen, security consultants and Customs Officers who all prefer to remain nameless. One brewer must, however, be credited: Stuart Neame, who continues to fight the good fight against all odds.

To my wife Alyson for staying cool.

1

I could tell from the way the phone was ringing that I shouldn't have answered it. At best it would be somebody selling me a time share or double-glazing. At worst, it would be someone I knew.

'Yeah?'

'Hello, is that Angel?'

Oh no, not *her*.

'*Pronto! Pronto!*'

'Angel? This is the right number, isn't it?'

'*Che?*'

'I know this is the right number.'

She was talking to herself now. With a bit of luck she'd get as bored with that as everybody else did.

'Can I speak to Angel, please?' she persisted. 'This is Veronica. Veronica Blugden.'

I knew it was.

'*Ich bin ein Auslander, ich spreche kein Englisch ...*'

'Angel, is that you? If it is, just stop messing about, will you?'

I put my new birthday-present watch to the receiver and triggered the alarm.

'What's that?'

'Or you can send a fax right now ...'

'Angel! I *know* it's you and you're not going to put me off.'

'Or you can press zero and hash and an operator will take your call. Decide *now*!'

'There's no need to shout, Angel. That is so rude. I only rang you to offer you a job. An undercover job. Working for a brewery.'

She finished in a breathless rush and I let her hang for half a minute.

'Hello, Veronica, it's Angel. I'm listening.'

I should have pressed hash and hung up myself, right there and then. But then, I shouldn't have answered the phone in the first place. Actually, I shouldn't even have been in the house on Stuart Street as I didn't really live there any more. Well, not full-time. Springsteen did, though, so I had a perfect excuse for dropping by. Somebody had to visit him regularly to see how he was bearing up, make sure he was eating right, tell him the gossip, pick his brains on matters of national importance, smuggle him in some red meat and basically just make sure he hadn't killed anyone. I thought of myself not so much as a prison visitor as a one-man United Nations peacekeeping force.

Maybe the UN should have been called in anyway as I found a single sheet of paper taped to the door of my flat which was headed: CAT KILLS THIS WEEK. Underneath, in unmistakable finishing school copperplate, were listed: pigeons (2), sparrows (3), one yellow canary (missing from Number 27), one hamster (see card in window of Mr Patel's shop), mice (2), coypu (1).

A *coypu*? In Hackney? Well, I supposed it was just about possible, given global warming and all that, but probably I would have to take Fenella on one side and explain to her what a rat was. The recent mild winter had led to a boom in the rat population and there were now thought to be more rats than people in the country. It had always been true of London, though it was not something Fenella would ever have been able to get her head around. She had enough trouble with people.

For a start, she lived with Lisabeth in the flat below mine and Lisabeth was enough to cramp anyone's style, with the personality of a religious cult and the social skills of a Tiger tank. Still, you could have worse neighbours, I suppose. A Klu Klux Klan franchise gift shop perhaps, or an aerobics class line dancing to old Abba hits.

And they were good about Springsteen – mainly because they were, with justification, frightened of him – feeding him on a regular basis and letting him in and out whenever the whim took him, not to mention disposing of the bodies he seemed to be generating on an increasing basis. I put this down to the fact that he missed me. Others would be less generous.

And, to be fair, both Fenella and Lisabeth had been diamond geezerettes about me not actually living at Number 9 Stuart Street for the past year. It had cost me (chocolate for Lisabeth, aromatherapy oils for Fenella) but they had faithfully stacked up the junk mail, taken phone messages and, mostly, told the right people that I had moved to live with Amy in Hampstead and the wrong people that I was working abroad as a mercenary disc jockey in a maximum security holiday hotel on Ibiza.

Best of all they had kept that fact that I was no longer a full-time resident from our esteemed landlord, Mr Naseem Naseem. For years I had persuaded him that, thanks to a passing friendship with a great-niece of his, my rent on Flat 3 should in effect be frozen at round about the going rate for 1990. It seemed a reasonable price for him to pay on the condition that I had no intention of becoming a legal, or even permanent, member of his family. Likewise, he turned a blind eye on the 'No Pets' house rule even when I cut a cat flap in the flat door, and a deaf ear to the complaints about the music even when they came from two streets away. But I knew he had a 'non-resident' clause in the rental agreement – most landlords do to stop tenants sub-letting. If he found out I was living in Hampstead and only keeping the flat on as a bolt-hole in case of emergencies, then he would have me out and the rent up and four trainee solicitors in there before you could say 'house-warming'.

So I was grateful that Fenella and Lisabeth had not mentioned the fact that I had moved out to him.

But I was even more grateful to them for not mentioning that I hadn't to Amy.

I was only in Hackney to leave an envelope with the rent money for Naseem Naseem. As long as it was cash and it was regular, he wouldn't mind not actually seeing me for months at time; he probably preferred it that way.

I only answered the phone mounted on the wall by the front door because I assumed it couldn't possibly be for me. Anyone who needed to get me had the number of the smart new Ericsson cell phone Amy had issued me with, and because she knew I often turned it off, she had also made me wear a pager on my belt, to which she alone had the number. I had worked out how to switch it from 'beep' to 'vibrate' so that the experience, whilst often inconvenient, was at least pleasant.

Absolutely no one knew I would be in Stuart Street that day as I hadn't even decided to go myself until that morning. I hadn't seen anyone in the street who knew me and even parking Armstrong II outside hadn't raised an eyebrow or twitched a net curtain. But then, why should it? No one notices black Austin Fairway taxis in London; at least I hoped not.

Number 9 itself was devoid of legitimate residents, Springsteen included, though with him there was always a chance he was lying in ambush somewhere. Lisabeth would be out at work, though I never liked to ask what it was she did, and Fenella was still employed, for a second consecutive month now (a record), by a telesales company who liked her Home Counties accent and her totally innocent refusal to take 'No', 'Go away' or 'Piss off' for an answer. I had a theory that she sold things because the punters she called simply couldn't bring themselves to be rude enough to turn down whatever offer she was pushing.

Mr Goodson, the solitary civil servant who rented the ground-floor Flat 1, would be at work. He always was. Or maybe he wasn't. It was difficult to tell, he was so quiet. No problems on that score with the couple in the top flat: Miranda, still Welsh, depressive and bored with her reporter's job on a local newspaper, and her partner Inverness Doogie, still Scottish, still mad and now an up-and-coming second chef in one of South Kensington's trendier restaurants. Both of them were definitely out at work. I could tell that as soon as I opened the front door, because of the absence of (a) shouting, (b) cooking smells as Doogie experimented, or (c) the muffled sound of 'The Beautiful South' played with too much bass.

I only answered the damn phone because I thought I was doing one of them a favour, I never dreamed it would be for me. So much for helping out your neighbours. Okay, ex-neighbours. It might have been the first time I had done so. I was sure it would be the last.

And I only kept listening to dear old Veronica Blugden – bless! – because she said those intriguing words 'undercover for a brewery' and then I agreed to meet her and find out more.

So what happened subsequently was all a combination of me being in the wrong place at the wrong time, doing something innocent to help my fellow man, woman or Lisabeth, and being in a particular psychological state.

State of mind in question? I was bored.

Where I was *supposed* to be that morning was in a maximum security crypt the other end of High Holborn, surrounded by several million pounds' worth of hallmarked silver and at least six scantily clad models, all aged between twenty-four and twenty-six and all size 10.

It was all to do with Amy's expanding business empire, for which I had cheerily volunteered the Mission Statement (which every company has to have these days): 'Tomorrow The World'. But she'd replied, rather primly I'd thought, that she already had one: 'Quality, Choice, Variety, Value'. I still maintained that mine was the snappier.

When I first met Amy she was involved with two partners in designing and marketing clothes for female office workers. Their main item was a TALtop, the TAL standing for Thalia, Amy and Lyn, the three masterminds behind it, and their sales technique took the best ideas from the Tupperware parties of old and the naughty underwear parties still held in respectable homes up and down the country when the husband is down the pub playing darts. Using computer databases the TAL girls would identify offices in central London with a certain number of secretaries or junior clericals, then find the wine bar where they drank after work (usually Thursdays – payday – not Fridays, which were for boyfriends) and organise a mini fashion parade using the punters themselves as models.

To be fair, their main product, the TALtop itself, was a good product, an all-purpose top which by pulling the drawstrings around the neck could turn from long-sleeved to short-sleeved, round-neck to plunging V-neck. And the beauty of the deal was that they all came individually tailored with a very flattering label denoting the size. A size 10 TALtop mysteriously fitted a woman who could have sworn she was a size 12. A size 12 TALtop would mould perfectly around a woman who knew she was a size 14, even if she wouldn't admit it. In fact, ninety per cent of the production of TALtops were actually size 12, whatever they said inside the neckline. Once Amy moved production out of a Brick Lane sweatshop and discovered colour dyes which didn't run and stain the upper body parts in a light shower, then she was ripe for the big time.

She had promptly sold out to a big retail chain, though she retained various patents and rights and secured herself a position of power and a neat line in royalties.

Of course, having one of her original partners in jail and the other dead helped smooth the deal through, but she was never one to sit back on her laurels, take it easy and see out the century counting her money. Oh no, innovate and upwards was her motto, that's what she said. A pox on Chinese restaurants who gave out fortune cookies was what I said.

The latest must-have designer concept she had cooked up followed her discovery that there was now the technology to produce a silver thread – real silver – fine enough and strong enough for use with an industrial sewing machine. A nifty bit of designing ensured a single silver motif on the left breast of a black TALtop which gave the garment a uniqueness as no two motifs were exactly alike thanks to human error on the sewing machines. Amy swore this was the cleverness of a deliberately vague original design concept for the motif which allowed a certain amount of self-expression on the part of whoever was sewing it on. Not too much variation, though, this was real silver after all, just enough to give it a USP (unique selling point) and, naturally, a premium price. In fact the silver thread added less than a pound to the wholesale unit price, so it must have been Amy's design genius which accounted for the other £15 added to the retail price compared to a bog-standard TALtop.

Amy didn't see all of that extra margin of course, as she was always telling me, but she did get a percentage and as British women spent £1.002 billions a year on blouses and tops (I loved the '.002'), which was twice as much as they spent on tights and stockings, though less than they spent on shoes, even a small percentage was worth having. I had to agree there, saying I would drink to that – and I had.

The silver TALs were destined to hit the High Street shops in the autumn but to cater for the Sunday newspaper magazine supplements and their long lead times, the publicity photographs had to be taken now. It had been my idea to stage them in the Silver Vaults down Southampton Row.

I don't claim any divine flash of inspiration, in fact I was watching football on Amy's 48-inch flat-screen wall-mounted television (the ones that cost so much the BBC has to rent them) at the time. Amy had arrived home late, as was usual these days, from a high-powered planning meeting in Milan or Tooting or somewhere, and before I could ask her if she had remembered to pick up some more lager on the way back, she had started to moan and gripe and kick the furniture, growling a rosary of obscenities in the middle of which I managed to identify the words 'Bank of England'.

For a moment I thought she was improvising her own rhyming slang but when she calmed down to half speed I worked out that the Bank of England had actually refused permission for her to use it as a venue for her fashion shoot. So why not try the Silver Vaults, I'd said casually, without taking my eyes off the giant screen where a corner kick was about to be taken. And she'd asked me if I knew the place and I said I'd been there and, like most casual visitors, had spent a happy hour or two dreaming of how you could rob it – not because I wanted three tons of silver tankards, cutlery, plates, you name it, but just to see if it could be done.

'Does it have silver on show?' she had asked.

'Your photographer won't need a flash,' I had said, stifling a groan as eight million quid's worth of striker missed an open goal.

'Get it sorted for me, darling. A week Tuesday. There'll be six girls.'

'Why me?' I had shouted over my shoulder as she headed for the kitchen.

'Because that's your job,' she had shouted back.

So *that* was what I did to earn my wages as a 'management consultant'. I had often wondered.

Fixing up the gig at the Silver Vaults was easier than I had dared to hope. Having opened my big mouth and suggested it, I just knew it would be all my fault if anything went wrong but as it turned out, it couldn't have gone smoother. If anything, everyone I dealt with down there was glad to see me and fell over themselves to be helpful. Perhaps they just didn't get as many visitors as they used to and more than one of the dealers mentioned that silver 'wasn't sexy' any more, so the prospect of half a dozen nubile young ladies modelling lingerie (okay, so I blagged it up a bit) in and out of the silverware, seemed to go down well. The female dealers thought it would be good for the Vaults' image. The male dealers tried not to look excited and thought it would be cool.

For all their maximum security trappings, and the fact that they are underground, the Vaults have the atmosphere and layout of an indoor market just like you could find in Oxford or Leicester or Huddersfield or a hundred other places. The difference was that instead of the aisles and cross-streets being lined with open stalls, the Silver Vaults boasted closed-in shops each with more locks, alarms and closed circuit cameras than the average off-licence in Hackney. There was another difference, of course, as in most indoor markets you can buy fresh fruit and vegetables, fish, meat, second-hand books, clothes, hardware, offcuts of carpet, you name it. Here you could buy silver; that was it.

You could buy silver in any form imaginable short of pieces-of-eight with genuine pirate's teeth marks, though I never actually checked that you couldn't. I had no idea that there were so many things you could have made in silver, from a toothpick to a football trophy as well as a host of items you probably wouldn't give house room to. I knew that the old liveried guild halls in the City – Ironmongers' Hall, Saddlemakers' Hall, Brewers' Hall and so on – always produced their silverware for formal dinners. This was indeed 'the family silver' amassed over the centuries and you were expected to look at it and be impressed by the antique wealth of the sugar shakers and the mustard bowls and the things nobody was sure quite what they were for. You could look and admire and even have a guess at the value, but the one thing you could never do was touch.

I had gone down there to scope the place for Amy's photographic session and homed in on one of the shops in the centre of the Vaults which had 'Sloman and Son' stencilled ever so discreetly on its bulletproof glass door. The reason it caught my eye was that it was the only shop manned (and I do mean 'manned' as there wasn't a female in sight) by anyone under the age of sixty-five.

His name was Reuben and he was about forty-five years

14

under sixty-five and looked like a computer nerd rather than the great-grandson of a skilled silversmith.

'Models? Girls modelling clothes? Here?' he had said when I broached the idea with him. 'Oh, I don't know whether we do things like that down here in the Vaults.'

'A shame,' I had said, 'because it is all about promoting silver. The girls are really only there to show off the silver thread sewing. They just . . . fill things out.'

He had paused at that and his eyes had wandered to a small office, no bigger than a cupboard, at the end of the shop. The door was open and I could see a small desk and a high stool and on the desk were a pile of magazines, a can of Diet Pepsi and a packet of sandwiches wrapped in greaseproof paper. I could hear his mind working.

'They'll need somewhere to change, won't they?' he had said and at that moment he was mine.

When I got back to the Silver Vaults from Stuart Street, Reuben Sloman should have been cursing the day I had wandered into his shop. Half his stock had been piled in cardboard boxes and pushed to one side, Amy's photographer had set up lights which made the temperature in the place almost unbearable and there were a dozen people in a space where normally three customers would be a crowd. Amy was using a solid silver tulip vase as an ashtray and having a row with Nigel, her art director.

The six models stood around looking bored, but they were models so it came to them naturally. They were dressed uniformly in short houndstooth check skirts, black shiny tights and black shoes. They were also undressed uniformly in that above their skirts, they wore only their bras – two black, four white, one of them an uplift.

'Can I get anyone another drink?' Reuben was asking, moving in and out of the models like a bemused sheepdog. 'Hi again, Angel. It's going great.'

He seemed genuinely pleased to see me, not to mention grateful. It was nice to be appreciated.

'This is a farce,' hissed Amy, switching her venom from Nigel to me just because I was nearer. 'You never said it was this small.'

15

'I did. Well, "cosy" was probably the word I used.'

'Cosy is right. We could sell tickets.'

She was right about that. Most of the dealers from the other shops, several legitimate customers and a couple of security guards were loitering in the aisles outside trying to get a peek into the shop.

'Why the strip show? The tops not arrived?' I asked her, trying to show an interest in her career.

'No.' Her voice went down a half-octave, which meant sarcasm was coming. 'They're all allowed thirty minutes free boob-tanning under the lights before we shoot. It's in their contracts.'

'That's nice. Can I check, see if they're done?'

'Don't even think it. They can't wear them until we're ready to go because the lights make them sweat like pigs. Not the look we're after and Nigel's been having the vapours about it for the last hour.'

'He's not the only one,' I said, looking at Reuben, who gave me a big, cheesy grin in return.

'Yeah,' drawled Amy, 'I think we've got a hormone overload on our hands.'

'Don't even think it, darling,' I said sweetly. 'He's far too young for you.'

She flashed me a killer look so I tried to be helpful.

'Why not kill the lights? Use fast film and a flash?'

'Because,' she said slowly in full patronise mode, 'all this fucking silver bounces the flash and reflects everywhere. We took some Polaroids and it looked like the girls were standing in the Planetarium boldly going through hyperspace.'

'So why not go for that? Really do it. Get him to put two or three remote flashes on so you get a reflection in every piece of silver in the place. "All that sparkles really is silver." Something like that as a theme. Could work.'

She thought about this for all of five seconds but I knew it was going down well from the way the little vein in her neck throbbed.

'You might have half an idea there,' she said quietly. 'But I'll have to get Nigel to think of it.'

'Is that a problem for you?'

16

She grinned at that, looking at the back of Nigel's head as if it had a bull's-eye target painted on it.

'Nope. He won't feel a thing. Where've you been anyway?'

'Just popped over to Hackney, collect the junk mail, see if anyone was around.'

'And was anyone?'

'No, not a soul, but I did get a message.'

She gave me one of those looks which suggested that she still didn't trust me for some reason.

'From whom?' she asked primly.

'A woman called Veronica Blugden. I used to know her a couple of years ago.'

The *before I met you* hung in the sticky air along with the smell of sweat, tobacco and silver polish.

'She wants to see me and pick my brains on something.'

'Just your brains?'

'You don't know Veronica.'

'Yeah, well, get your appetite where you can, just remember you eat at home.'

'Yeah, yeah, yeah.' I'd heard that one before. 'It's purely professional. She just wants my help with a job she's got.'

'What does she do?'

'She's a private detective.'

Amy threw back her head and roared with laughter.

'*You*? A private detective?'

Suddenly I burst out laughing as well.

'You think that's funny? You should see Veronica!'

2

When I had talked to Veronica from Stuart Street, I had established two things before agreeing to meet her. Firstly, that she was still based in Shepherd's Bush in the office she shared with Stella Rudgard and secondly, that Stella wasn't around when I planned to call. I didn't mind Amy having suspicious thoughts about Veronica; all she had to do was see her and they would disappear immediately. Thirty seconds with Stella, on the other hand, would put the hairs on the back of her neck up and I could live without that.

Veronica had sort of inherited the detective agency from an ex-policeman called Albert Block who, if he hadn't exactly broken the law on occasion, had certainly bent it. I had met her on her first solo case when she attempted to hijack the cab I was driving.

Admittedly, 'hijack' is a bit strong. I was driving an Armstrong in those days, a black Austin FX4S London taxi; the sort you see on hundreds of postcards, tins of toffees and calendars issued by the London Tourist Board. That was the original Armstrong. Nowadays I drove Armstrong II (when I was allowed), a Fair-way, though only experts could tell them apart unless they noticed the word 'Fairway' in red script on the boot. Suffice it to say that the Fairway, with its improved engine, was the last in the line of the classic black cabs. Shortly after it appeared, we had the ugly and angular Metrocab and now the streets are crawling with the new generation of smaller, rounder TXs or 'Tixilicks' as they are referred to – though always behind the driver's back.

Veronica, in those days, could just about tell the difference between a black cab and a Number 13 bus. As it happened, there wasn't a Number 13 bus in sight but I was and she'd jumped in the back – whilst I'd been parked up on Wimpole Street, mind-ing my own business – and yelled, 'Follow that cab!'

There had been a time when I would have just gone for it and hoped she wouldn't notice that where the cab's meter should have been was a cassette deck. When that had happened in the past, I had always wheeled out the excuse: 'Sorry, guv, I forgot to put the meter on. Call it a fiver, shall we?' You'd be amazed at how many people coughed up, though there was always the wise guy who legged it, thinking they had put one over on a genuine cabbie. But the vast silent majority simply took things at face value. A black cab cruising London was a black London cab, part of the scenery, unremarkable, perfect camouflage. Or at least I hoped so. That was why I liked driving one although the hackney cab licensing authorities frowned on delicensed cabs being sold to civilians within metropolitan London, on the basis – heaven forfend! – that someone might take advantage of the situation.

18

The problem when I met Veronica was that I tried to play the stand-up guy and explain things to her. By the time I had got her to understand that I wasn't touting for a fare, the person she was supposed to be tailing had disappeared round the corner in a real cab and she had promptly burst into tears.

Even though it was the worst attempt at following somebody I had ever seen – she used the Homer Simpson Defence: 'It's my first day' – I took pity on her and helped her, one way or another, to solve her first case.

As far as I knew, that had been her *only* case but she said she was still in business and, even more surprisingly, still in partnership with Stella, the very person she had been trying to follow when, of all the taxis and all the minicabs in all the world, she had dropped into the back of mine.

I had always regarded Stella as at least one sandwich short of a picnic and only a healthy and totally amoral love of physical sex kept her just this side of psychotic. But then, I hadn't known her for long. Neither had Veronica when they had teamed up and formed Rudgard and Blugden Confidential Enquiries. I had been sceptical of them being able to work together and whether or not the business would ever turn a profit, but I had approved of the name. 'R&B Investigations' was just eye-catching enough to pick them out from all the other private detective agencies in the London phone book, most of whom thought that by calling themselves the 'A' or 'AA' agency, they would pick up business alphabetically. For most people, and in the absence of a *Which?* consumers' guide to private eyes, the name they hit first was the one they rang. At least 'R&B' sounded vaguely cool and, anyway, they discounted my other suggestion – 'Aardvark Enquiries' – as somebody had already done it.

Round in Shepherd's Bush Green, the plastic printed sign saying 'Rudgard and Blugden' was still on the door. Even if they had been doing well, there was no point in moving upmarket to a brass plaque in that area, it wouldn't have lasted a week. Most of the churches around there were technically classed as 'environmentally friendly' these days – lead-free, that is.

The push-button intercom was still there and still seemed to work, so I announced myself. A distorted voice answered:

'Angel? Come on up. You behavin' yourself?'

The voice, female, didn't wait for an answer and the lock buzzed and the door opened.

Even through the cheap electronic crackle I thought I recognised it. I knew it wasn't Veronica and she had promised me faithfully (and Veronicas don't lie) that Stella wasn't around. So it puzzled rather than worried me as I started to climb the stairs to the first floor where R&B had their offices. But not for long.

'Are you behavin' yourself? I asked if you were behavin' yo'self.'

'Doing my best, Mrs Delacourt,' I said as somewhere at the back of my head one of the few remaining unraddled memory chips snapped into action. 'Doing my best in a hard world.'

I could tell she didn't believe me.

Mrs Delacourt was certainly doing well, if appearances could be relied upon. I knew she must be pushing sixty but she had lost ten years thanks to a smart dark purple trouser suit, a frilly white blouse and a gold chain around her neck which matched the gold chain strung from her gold-framed glasses.

I used to knock about with her eldest son Crimson and once, when she thought he was in a spot of bother, she had approached Albert Block's (as it was then) agency for help. She couldn't pay to hire a detective so she offered to do a couple of days a week cleaning in the office. That was just the time when Veronica found herself inheriting the business and I recalled hearing that she had employed Crimson's mum as an undercover cleaner on jobs where there was petty theft going on from an office or the odd spot of industrial espionage. From the way she was dressed and the fact that she seemed to have her own office, that side of the business looked to be booming.

'You're looking well, Mrs Delacourt,' I said, turning on the smile at full wattage. 'In fact, you're looking well handsome. You behavin' yourself?'

'I intend to live long and prosper,' she said seriously, but her stern black face was letting the glint of a smile through.

'That sounds like a plan,' I said. 'How's Crimson?'

'Got himself married and two children in twenty months. You credit that?'

'Sounds like he's doing something right.'

'But at least he's got a steady job now. He's not done as well as you, though, Mr Angel. I hear you're –'

'Is Veronica in, Mrs D.? She said she wanted to see me quite urgently.'

She looked at me over her glasses and made a 'Mmmmm' sound deep in her throat. Then she looked at the digital switchboard/fax machine on her desk to check there were no lights flashing.

'She's off the phone now. You can go in.'

She nodded towards the end of the corridor. There were three doors to choose from but unless they had remodelled the building, I knew one was a kitchen and the other a toilet.

As I passed her, she said: 'Nice suit. I suppose you get them trade these days.'

I gave her trouser suit the once up-and-down and fingered the lapel of my jacket.

'You can't beat pure wool, Mrs D.,' I said bitchily, conscious of the fact that working in the fashion business was rubbing off on me. But it didn't cut much ice with Mrs Delacourt.

'You'll thank the Lord for Lycra when you get to my age,' she said, turning back into her office. And I couldn't argue with that.

But I wish Veronica had.

She was wearing white stretch leggings (never white, darling, they just scream 'fat') with the foot straps over a pair of red high heels (red shoes only in strobe lighting unless you're on the pull), but she had made an effort with a dark red TALtop rigged as a round-neck. I didn't know we did a size 16 (Euro 44) in that shade.

'Angel,' she said, businesslike, stepping from behind her desk, hand outstretched, 'thank you for coming so quickly.'

I ignored her hand and wrapped her in a hug so that she couldn't see me bite my tongue to suppress a giggle.

'Veronica, my dear, you're looking extremely well. Are you working out?'

'You can tell?' she whispered into my ear.

'It shines out, Von, shines out. You're looking well fit.'

I hadn't the heart to tell her I had spotted the Adidas sports bag on the floor behind her desk. She hadn't zipped it fully and

I could see the heel of a Reebok and more leopardskin leotard than my imagination could handle.

'I only do two sessions a week,' she said, disengaging delicately and putting the desk between us. 'It's difficult to find the time what with the amount of work we have on.'

'That's good to hear. Crime is one of the few growth industries left in this country, so cash in while you can.' I sat down in the low, metal-framed armchair reserved for visitors. 'Was this Stella's idea?'

'What?' She was genuinely puzzled.

'Having the client's chair lower than yours so they have to look up to you.'

'I didn't. . . . I never . . .'

No, you wouldn't have, but Stella would.

'I'm not complaining, Vonnie, I approve. Good psychology, especially when you tell them your daily rate.'

Even better if they could see Stella's legs through the kneehole in the desk. The last thing they would think about would be the daily rate. But this was Veronica.

'Contrary to the pulp fiction you read,' she recovered well, 'we mostly meet clients on site. The work of the modern confidential enquiry agent is more to do with security advice and systems for premises, to combat fraud or pilfering or shoplifting. That's why we don't usually quote a daily rate like you seem to think. Most of our work is tendered, full-contract installation or weekly or monthly rates for observational jobs, both overt and covert.'

'I'm impressed,' I said, and I was – very impressed that she'd learned that entire Mission Statement by heart without resort to prompt cards. 'So you basically sell people security cameras, closed-circuit TV, burglar alarms, that sort of stuff?'

'Mostly . . .' she said suspiciously.

'Which you get from where?' I said it as if I was genuinely curious.

'Out of Yellow Pages,' she answered too quickly. Then when she saw my eyebrows hitting the roof, she gabbled: 'But our clients are buying impartial, expert advice from professionals they can trust.'

'Of course they are, Veronica, that's absolutely right.'

I left the thought *Stella has trained you well* hanging in the air.

Her face darkened. 'There's no need to patronise me, Angel.'

'Hey, I'm not,' I said, palms up, all innocence. 'I think it's a great idea. You're like personal shoppers for the Neighbourhood Watch. Sounds like a business plan to me.'

She screwed up her eyes so they looked like a pair of seagulls coming at me head on.

'We do do *other* sorts of security consultancy as it happens.'

She shot the cuffs on her TALtop and opened a drawer in the desk, taking out a thin blue file. She laid it on the desk top in front of her and tapped it with a forefinger.

'This is why I rang you.'

She paused for effect.

'Why did you ring me at Stuart Street?' I asked, which she wasn't expecting.

'I keep in touch with Lisabeth and Fenella. They said you popped round quite a lot to rehearse.'

'Rehearse?'

'To play your trumpet. They said you kept them up until two o'clock one night last week.'

Yeah, well, it had been a good night out with some of the lads from the old days and I hadn't felt like going home when the pubs had shut and in truth I was getting out of practice now I didn't play in public and, anyway it had seemed like a good idea at the time. You had to be there.

'I do pop back occasionally,' I said.

'And I didn't have your new number. It's Hampstead, isn't it?'

Some detective.

'It's best to get me on my mobile,' I said casually.

'But I didn't have that either and neither did Fenella.'

Too right she didn't. I may be getting old but if you can still remember it's called Alzheimer's, you haven't got it.

'Anyway,' Veronica went on airily, 'I wasn't too sure about ringing you at home. I didn't know how your new . . . er . . . your . . .'

She had seen my expression change this time. Maybe she wasn't such a bad detective.

'Partner,' I completed for her.

'Yes, of course, partner. I didn't know how she would react to me contacting you.' She paused and stroked the sleeve of her TALtop. 'She makes nice clothes, though.'

'I'll pass on the official Veronica Blugden seal of approval,' I said keenly, almost as if I meant it.

'Please do. I've read about her in *Hello* magazine, you know.'

I remembered the day they'd come to interview her. She'd sent me to a factory in Leicester with an urgent delivery of colour swatches. By train. Second class.

'Next time I see her,' I said. 'She likes to keep the customer satisfied, stay in touch with the grass roots motivational driving force of the market – the consumer. That sort of thing. She might even ask you to join one of her focus groups.'

'Would she really?'

How would I know? I'd just made them up.

'Could do.' I made a point of looking all around the office before resuming eye contact. 'Wasn't there something else you wanted to say?'

For maybe two seconds she blanked me – the lights on but nobody home, her mind on another planet. Then she cleared her throat and flipped open the file on her desk in as professional a manner as she could muster.

'Seagrave's Seaside Ales,' she announced, as if making a presentation from a lectern.

'That's very kind, Veronica, but I've got to drive later, so how about a cup of tea?'

'No, no, I meant have you heard of them?'

She was more flustered than angry, but then she always had been dead easy to wind up. Too easy really. I should pick on someone my own size, even though she was bigger than me.

'Vaguely,' I said slowly. 'A small family brewery in Kent, with about half a dozen pubs in London mostly in the City or south of the river. Got their own hop farm, so they use a lot of hops. "A positive frisson of bitterness", I think the *Good Beer Guide* said of their premium bitter. Famous for their very strong winter warmers and they pick a new name every year, usually

24

something to do with the Church. I think it was Archbishop's Revenge last year. They also, though there's not many people know this, brew Mongoose beer – the lager you get in most Indian restaurants these days. Oh, and they've still got horse-drawn delivery drays which you see in virtually every BBC costume drama series. A private company, I think, so they're not quoted on the stock market. Apart from that, never heard of 'em.'

Veronica gave it a beat, then quickly closed the file in front of her.

'You've looked them up, haven't you? How did you know it was Seagrave's?'

'You said it was a brewery when you phoned.'

'Yes,' she snapped triumphantly, sharp as a pistol, 'but I didn't say which one.'

'No, you didn't. It was the other thing you mentioned that gave it away.'

'What other thing?'

'Smuggling.'

My father always used to say that he'd voted to join the Common Market, as it was then back in the early Seventies, for the cheap booze. To me, that was the one, best and only reason for going to the polls. Ever.

But twenty-five years on, it still hadn't happened even though we were now in the European Union and for five years had been in a Single European Market, with a single pan-Europe currency – the Euro – looming on the horizon. There was cheap booze all right, trouble was it was all in France.

With excise duty something like eight times higher in Britain, beer was a particular bargain across the Channel and since the Single Market came in allowing (supposedly) the free traffic of goods across borders, around thirty dedicated booze stores had opened up in Calais alone. Not that the good burghers of Calais did their shopping there; the vast majority of customers were British – day trippers, returning holiday-makers, lorry drivers on the home run and, as always, the wide boys out to make a quick profit.

The press called them Bootleggers at first, which made a

good headline even though it was totally inaccurate. Bootleggers were involved in the making of illicit booze, not just the buying and selling. The guys in Scotland who brewed up a counterfeit version of Stolichnaya Russian vodka a few years back, they were bootleggers and they would have got away with it for a lot longer if they had noticed that an honest Stoly bottle had 'Made in Russia Liquor Botle' embossed on the base. They just hadn't considered that a spelling mistake could be used to identify the genuine article rather than the fake, so they got caught. And there was the fact that their version, unlike the real thing, also contained 1.34 per cent methanol which, according to the Poisons Unit at the Edinburgh Royal Infirmary, gave rise to 'the possibility of permanent damage to vision'.

Those sorts of guys were bootleggers. Okay, not very good ones. They got caught, fortunately before anyone went blind.

The guys who hired a beat-up Transit van, drove down to Dover, threw up on an out-of-season ferry, bought (for cash) enough bottled beer to bend the axles on the van and then flogged it door-to-door round Woolwich or Barking, those guys were smugglers not bootleggers.

Just about anybody could do it, that was the beauty of it. You didn't need a Heavy Goods Vehicle licence, just a relatively clean driving licence and a local van hire firm who probably made you sign a waiver saying that you wouldn't do anything illegal in it, not that you would.

Nipping over to France to do a bit of shopping wasn't illegal. Buying booze there wasn't illegal; it had, after all, paid French tax even if the French idea of excise duty was somewhat cavalier compared to that of your average British Roundhead politician. And you could buy as much as you liked.

Sure, there were theoretical limits to what you could bring back but these were 'indicative limits' though no one was quite sure what they were indicative of. They were, in fact, the limits over which the Customs officers waiting at Dover could rightly have a suspicion that you were up to no good. Someone somewhere in authority had determined that 110 litres of beer (over 180 pints – not a bad night out), seventy bottles of wine and ten large bottles of spirits was indicative of an amount you might use for personal consumption. Funny that they never used those sorts of volumes when they talked about cannabis.

But you could get a lot more than 110 litres of beer in the back of a Transit van, maybe ten times that if you stuck to cases of beer and beer was where the bargains were to be had. Unless you had a doctor's note saying you were a registered alcoholic (and that had been tried), there might be some doubt in a suspicious Customs officer's mind that getting on for two thousand pints was indeed for 'personal consumption'. All you had to do then was give a good excuse. It was your fiftieth birthday party next week and you had invitations to prove it; the ones you'd had printed up on the £3-a-go business card machines in every train and underground station. Or it was your daughter's/sister's/cousin's wedding next month and you even had a booking form for the church hall which you'd hired for the reception; and which you'd cancel as soon as you got home to get your deposit back.

And so on. That was if you got stopped, of course. Her Majesty's Customs and Excise officers admitted that maybe they pulled one in ten suspicious vans. They did, after all, have other things on their mind such as drugs, guns and illegal immigrants. And even if they did pull you, all they could do was ask questions about why you had enough beer in the back of the van to keep a country pub going for a week.

If you had a semi-plausible excuse, and you would have because you would have rehearsed one, they had to let you go. After all, you were still not doing anything illegal.

It was when, a few hours later, you had unloaded the van and were selling the beer from the back of a car at a car boot sale, or delivering to the back door of an unlicensed drinking club in Brixton, or flogging by the bottle to school kids behind the bike sheds, *that's* when you were doing something illegal.

That was smuggling.

'So you're an expert on smuggling, are you?'

I assumed this was Veronica's attempt at sarcasm.

'I never said that. I know it goes on, sure. Who doesn't? I've probably bought a few pints which were smuggled at one time. Inadvertently of course.'

In fact I had a fridge full of 25-centilitre 'dumpies', the small, fist-sized bottles, of French lager back at Stuart Street as we spoke. I kept them there in case of emergencies, a bit like explorers in the Antarctic have depots of supplies stashed at strategic intervals.

'Oh, that's a pity,' Veronica sighed. 'I sort of assumed you would be.'

'Why?'

'Because you were the sort of person who was street-wear . . .'

'Streetwise. Streetwear is what Amy sells.'

'Yes, streetwise, wise in the ways of. . . .'

'The street.'

I tried to think of the opposite of 'streetwise' but there wasn't a word bad enough.

'Quite. You always seemed the sort of person who would know what was going on. You kept your eyes open, you were good at observing things others missed. You always used to see through people who weren't genuine. And you were always ready to help people when they needed it, just like you helped Estelle and I. We would never have set up this agency if it hadn't been for you.'

She was going out of her way to flatter me and she had obviously rehearsed what she would say, so I decided to sit back, enjoy it and let her say it. Then I realised she was talking in the past tense.

'Of course, that was a couple of years ago and things have changed. You've done very well for yourself and you're moving in different circles now. You're wearing suits – and very nice you look, too. You've got a stake in a very successful business. Maybe you've got commitments at home now that you're . . .'

'Veronica, when do I start?'

I knew when I was beaten.

3

'So what exactly are you supposed to do?' was the first thing Amy asked. It was the one thing I should have asked.

'First off I have to go down to Kent and see a man who owns a brewery, tomorrow morning.'

One of the silver thread TALtop models pushed between us facing me and proving that not all models were flat-chested waifs. I leaned back in case Amy got the wrong idea and almost sent a family-pizza-sized silver salver flying.

I was back in Sloman and Son's emporium in the middle of the Silver Vaults and Nigel the photographer seemed no further forward that when I had left. There must have been fifty Polaroid test shots scattered around the place, mostly on the floor, and at least three silver tankards and a specimen golf cup trophy had been pressed into service as ashtrays. Nigel had taken my tip and killed the floodlights but with him, six models, Amy and a couple of Nigel's assistants milling about the place, the temperature was nudging unbearable. To avoid sweatstains, the models were happily standing around in their bras, a can of deodorant in one hand, a Marlboro in the other.

It wouldn't have surprised me if young Reuben Sloman had thrown a wobbler and told us never to tarnish his silverware again, but he seemed to be loving it. He flitted around the girls like a moth round a bedroom lamp. I half expected to hear the hiss as he got his fingers scorched. He was explaining the beauties of an eighteenth-century cruet set to one of them, who looked about as interested as I would have been, when he saw me. He grinned inanely, gave me a thumbs-up and went back to his lecture on hallmarks. Even across the shop through the smoke haze, I could tell that his glasses had misted up.

'If Nigel doesn't get his finger out soon, we'll have the bloody cleaners in here with us,' Amy was saying. 'It's like something out of a Marx Brothers film as it is. Are you taking the BMW?'

'What?'

It never pays to let the mind wander (especially over a young model) when Amy is talking.

'Tomorrow, when you go to this brewery in Kent.'

'Drive the Beamer through south London? No way. I'll be picked up as a pimp.'

'You wish,' she said unkindly. 'So you'll take the Freelander?'

'Don't you need it?'

'No, I told you, I'm doing a marketing seminar out at Brocket Hall. They're sending a car for me.'

'Oh yeah, of course,' I said, trying to remember if she had told me or whether this was a test. 'But the Freelander might give the wrong impression out in the country. People might think I'm a farmer or something.'

'So to avoid being mistaken for a pimp or a farmer, you're going to take Armstrong and let everyone think you're a cabbie who's lost his fare?'

'A London cab blends in, nobody notices them,' I tried.

'Out in the sticks in Kent? In the middle of all those orchards and fields and things?'

'Come on, Amy, it's only Kent, for Christ's sake. It's commuter country, part of the stockbroker belt, it's like Woolwich with green bits in between the houses.'

'You'll stick out like a sore thumb. The locals will have you spotted in minutes. They'll probably stone you or shoot your tyres out for being an incomer.'

'Oh, don't be such a big girl's blouse. I'm talking about a drive down to Kent not a safari through Iraq.'

But perhaps I should have been.

As things turned out, that might have been safer.

I left Amy in the Silver Vaults promising to pick her up later and run her down to the River Café where she was due to have dinner with some clients, potential buyers from Estonia or somewhere. I wasn't actually invited along to the dinner but I was needed to chauffeur her there as parking was such a bitch in Chelsea. The BMW or the Freelander could have been ticketed or clamped or even nicked but Armstrong would have just blended into the background. It was nice to know he had his uses.

Before that he had another job on, getting me to Hackney and back in the rush hour as I had a vital piece of research to undertake: I had to go shopping.

In the days before the expressions like '7–11' or 'convenience store' were imported from America, any shop which opened early and closed late was either a garage or a 'Patel' after the owners who always seemed to be Mr and Mrs Patel. There were three Patels within walking distance of my old flat in Stuart Street and all, in their turn, had saved my life by being conveniently open when I needed them at short notice: for that desperate packet of cigarettes at 6 a.m. when I had run out at 5 a.m., for that vital herb or spice half-way through a recipe and, most importantly, for that essential bottle of vodka to take to a party after the pubs had shut.

The one where I had bought the French lager wasn't a Patel in the technical sense as it was run by a Sikh family, Mr and Mrs Singh, and it was Mrs Singh who was on duty by the cash register when I pushed open the door, activating the closed-circuit television cameras.

Mrs Singh had a black-and-white monitor behind her check-out counter, next to a portable television which showed Zee TV all the hours they were open. The closed-circuit system was there to cover the aisles of the shop, where everything from knitting wool to cat food to rental videos to Panadol (another regular on my shopping list at one time) was piled on shelves well above head height. The only items stacked in plain view of the counter were the sweets and chocolates and the alcohol. The confectionery was at risk from thieving school kids in the afternoon and both from drunks late at night, when they realised that they didn't have enough cash for a take-away because they'd just whacked back eight pints on an empty stomach. Mrs Singh obviously trusted her own eagle eyes rather than the closed-circuit for security, and even then the cigarettes and spirits were stacked behind her cash register. I wondered if she'd bought the system from Veronica.

Despite the suit, she recognised me, though I had not seen her for several months. I smiled and we exchanged Hellos and I drifted along the shelves of canned and bottled beer which were interspersed with bottles of alcoholic concoctions flavoured with lemons, oranges, cherries, passion fruit, ginseng, ginger, glucose, even hemp. (No, not that sort.) It took me a while to focus on those that were actually flavoured with beer.

I sneaked a look at the CCTV around the edge of Mrs Singh's sari to make sure that the shop was empty, then turned back to the beer shelves and spoke over my shoulder, dead casual, while running a finger across the shoulders of a row of bottles.

'Haven't you got any of that French lager, Mrs S.?'

When I didn't get a reply, I turned and saw that she was staring at me.

'You know, that cheap beer in the little bottles. Mr Singh let me have a couple of cases last month.'

'Don't know what you mean,' she said sullenly. 'We've got what you see.'

'I can't see it. You know, the stuff that comes from France in the dumpy bottles. Mr S. let me have a case for a fiver last time I was in.'

'Then come back when my husband is in,' she snapped. 'He's got his receipts for everything here. All the receipts. Come back later tonight.'

'Hey, it was never this difficult to get a drink when I lived round here,' I said with a big smile, but it cut no ice.

'Come back later. Tonight. After dark.'

I saw that she had taken a fold in her sari and was twisting it with both hands as if she was ringing water out of the material. It wasn't worth pushing it.

'Okay, Mrs S., I'll pop back. Take care.'

She said nothing but I felt her watching me through the closed-circuit cameras until I reached the door.

As I opened it, I noticed that the fingers of my right hand were filthy with dust.

I once had a old and distinguished friend (still have, if he's not in prison somewhere) who used to drive trucks across Europe for Heavy Metal bands. I'm talking serious articulated lorries here, not pick-ups or Transits or ten-tonners. It was a rule of thumb amongst Heavy Metal bands that you could never have enough trucks, for sound and lighting gear, and stage props, and a band on tour with less than three was definitely on the B-list.

On one trip he was driving through a village in a mountainous region of a certain Central European country when he had to slow to a crawl to avoid a flock of sheep blocking the road. The young shepherds, and he swears none were over ten years old, made obvious signs that they wanted cash hand-outs from the man in the big truck who was obviously richer than they were. Naturally, as any good 'transport tech' (they're not called roadies any more) would, he ignored them. In the next village, a couple of kilometres down the road, there were no sheep but there was a flock of young lads who shouted and gesticulated at him and threw things at the truck. Not noticing any physical damage, he kept going until the next village where he had to stop because the local cops were waiting for him. They pointed to the fresh blood on his hubcaps and headlights and, part in broken English and part in pantomime, accused him of running over a sheep, which was still a hanging offence in those parts. Despite pointing out that a fair number of hen feathers were lodged in his front bumper, where some unfortunate fowl had been whacked, it cost my mate a £200 on-the-spot fine instead of the loose change he could have got away with two villages back.

Nothing like that happened to me as I drove down through Deptford the next morning, not even in Greenwich, or 'Dome City' as it was known thanks to the Millennium Dome which, once complete, would bring everlasting prosperity to the area once someone could think of something to put inside it.

I don't know why I was letting Amy spook me. I was perfectly safe inside my London black cab even if I was venturing outside London and crossing the M25 which serves as a modern-day moat for the capital fortress, keeping out its natural enemies such as farmers, fox-hunters and all those vegetable smells the countryside generates.

It was only Kent after all; the garden of England, famed for Canterbury Cathedral, Romney Marsh (though I knew people who thought he was a footballer), the young Charles Dickens, hops, orchards and probably lots more.

Oh yes, I remembered, it was maidens. That was the other thing it was famous for, Kentish maidens. Or at least I was pretty sure that was right, but then I hadn't taken even a recreational drug for months, so what did I know?

By then I was on the M2, a beautiful, scenic piece of motorway which bypassed all the boring places like Rochester and Chatham where nothing of interest had ever happened, and I was on a clear run to Canterbury. This was usually about the place where decent, law-abiding citizens realised that they had got on the wrong motorway and they should actually have been on the M20, not the M2, which takes them straight to the Channel Tunnel. Unless of course they were actually going to Canterbury, say they were an archbishop or something.

I wasn't – going to Canterbury, that is. At the end of the motorway I turned off towards the north coast, Whitstable and Herne Bay and the steely grey mirror of the North Sea. The local tourist bodies probably called it the Kentish Riviera or similar. Londoners called it the mouth of the River Thames.

It's a coastline of islands, or 'isles' – of Grain, of Sheppey, of Thanet – some of which are islands, some of which aren't – famous for its bird sanctuaries and its oysters. Maybe it was the oysters which attracted the Romans and explains the fact why you can't walk far without tripping over the remains of Roman pottery or pottery kilns, iron works and even a fort, at Reculver. Or maybe the Romans brought the oysters with them as a sort of take-away in case they didn't like the native grub. I forget.

I found Seagrave sandwiched between Whitstable and Herne Bay, which was something the Romans hadn't done as it hadn't been there then. The town – and it was just about big enough to be called a town – was basically nineteenth-century overspill, perhaps, given its name, as a place where people from Whitstable and Herne Bay went before they died. With a name like Seagrave it should have been a natural for a Charles Dickens novel but even he seemed to have missed it. There were no oyster beds there, it didn't have a harbour as such, it could not boast miles of golden sand, there wasn't even a funfair. There was no obvious sign of heavy industry and the bungalows which dotted the sea front were desperately in need of a coat of paint. The place didn't seem to have a lot going for it; but then it did have Seagrave's Seaside Ales.

The fact that there was a brewery there at all was not that

surprising given that the Victorians went through a spell of building breweries designed to be solid enough to last a thousand years. They found that, as in politics, a thousand years is a long time.

Victorian engineers thought they had the technology to build just about anywhere and deep, thickly insulated wells to get at the local water table were not seen as a problem even at the seaside. Sadly, they underestimated the power of the sea and, within a generation, many brewery wells had been breached and contaminated with salt water. Unless it had access to other sources of water, the brewery was doomed, which is why only a handful of them survive on the coast itself.

It was not the fact that there was a brewery in Seagrave that was surprising, it was that there was *still* a brewery there, and still there since 1849 according to the date woven into the wrought-iron gates of the main entrance.

The gates were probably original. Certainly the main entrance into the brewery yard was. No company would have been allowed to build a brewery from scratch there today, shoehorned as it was between a supermarket and a library on what passed for the town's main drag, Seagrave's High Street. But then the Victorians probably built the brewery first, then the town around it.

I could always have asked the white-haired old man who opened a window in the gatehouse and yelled at me. He looked old enough to know.

I slid down Armstrong's window and cupped a hand to my ear.

'I'm sorry?'

His face seemed to fill the open sash window and his white moustache bristled impressively. I wondered what rank he told people he had held in the war. I wondered which war.

'No one here's called for a taxi,' he shouted although we were only about two feet apart.

'I'm not collecting, I'm visiting,' I shouted back.

He consulted a green clipboard, then waved it at me.

'No brewery tours booked for today.' He was going a lovely shade of rose pink as he yelled. Maybe I shouldn't have been revving Armstrong's engine so much. 'You have to make an appointment.'

'I'm not here for a tour and I do have an appointment.'

'Whom with?'

I let the pedal up from the metal.

'With Mr Seton,' I said smugly.

'Which one?' he snapped back.

'How many have I got to choose from?'

I only said it to wind him up. I didn't think for a minute he would rise to it, but he did.

'Well, Mr Wilfred only comes in on the second Friday of the month these days.' He held up a hand and began to count them off. 'Mr Hubert is in court today . . .'

'Oh dear, how sad,' I said.

'He's a magistrate,' he replied, glaring at me. 'And Mr Edgar is on his annual skiing holiday.'

He put his head on one side, his mouth twisting into a smile, waiting for me to make my move.

'So that just leaves Mr Murdo,' I said, nodding as if agreeing with him on some fundamental piece of philosophy. 'And I think you'll find he's expecting me. The name is Angel and I'm representing Rudgard and Blugden. I was told he liked people to be punctual.'

I had been told no such thing but it sounded impressive, or at least I hoped it did to the gatekeeper.

Something worked. With reluctance, he looked at his clipboard, then he looked at me and then he looked over the length of Armstrong then he looked back at his clipboard. Then he shook his head and levered himself to his feet. When he emerged from the gatehouse he was wearing a peaked cap to go with his brown uniform jacket and trousers. I had just known he would be.

He rattled a couple of bolts and pulled on the gates until they swung open on small iron wheels which had worn grooves in the concrete yard, but he himself remained smack in front of Armstrong's radiator.

'Park over there,' he shouted, pointing to a corner of the yard, 'in the space marked "Visitors". Health and Safety regulations require me to tell you that if you park anywhere else you could put yourself and your vehicle at risk. This is a working area and our dray lorries are constantly loading and

36

unloading. The company can accept no responsibility. Someone will come and collect you from your . . . vehicle.'

I gave him a big smile as I accelerated by him, missing his toes by at least an inch, and aimed Armstrong across the brewery yard to where an ancient Citroën Safari was parked in one of two painted rectangles labelled 'Visitors'.

I swung Armstrong round and reversed into the space next to the Citroën on the basis that it is always safer to park facing the direction of departure in case you need to make a quick exit.

I turned off the engine and looked at my watch in disgust.

I had been in a brewery for almost thirty-five seconds and nobody had offered me a drink yet.

There were two flat-backed lorries and a real dray, a horse-drawn one (though no horses), in the brewery yard. All were standing empty and there was no sign of anybody working anywhere though there was a distant hum of machinery from somewhere inside the brewery buildings and a really quite comforting smell of sweet, warm malt in the air.

As I locked Armstrong, I scoped the place to try and get a feel for the layout and locked on to a sign on a thick oak door across the yard which read: 'Sampling Cellar'. That seemed the obvious place to start, but I had taken no more than three steps when a voice behind me growled:

'Mr Angel? The offices are this way.'

It felt like the first time you are caught browsing the Erotica section in the bookshop; by your mother.

She was old enough to be somebody's grandmother and formidable enough so that you didn't feel like mentioning it. She wore a cardigan around her shoulders like a cape and a double string of large fake pearls so long she could strangle you without taking them off. Only a very short, black leather skirt and black tights and high heels belied the image of 'Miss Prim, the Secretary' from a pack of Happy Families cards. But then, she had pretty good legs, so why not show them?

I didn't mention that either. I just said:

'Oh, thank you. I'm here to see Murdo Seton.'

'Yes, I know. Mr Murdo is waiting for you in Reception. This way.'

I followed the leather skirt up half a dozen stone steps and through a door which could have come from any Victorian suburban villa. It even had a brass knocker and a letter box.

Once inside, it felt like a Victorian villa. There were gas mantles on the wall, a long wooden high-backed bench like a church pew and a wrought-iron fireplace in one wall which had a coal fire in it. I mean like burning, with heat and smoke and flames. Not something you saw in London these days, outside a museum.

The walls were decorated with a series of posters advertising beer. I could have quenched my thirst in a long hot summer with a 'Golden Harvest' pale ale, seen the harvest home with a 'Hazel Nut Brown', put my feet up at Christmas with an 'XXXmas Barley Wine' or sipped a 'Seagrave Oyster Stout' whenever there was an 'r' in the month. From the style of the artwork, I guessed all the posters dated from the 1930s and judging by the yellowing and crinkled edges, were almost certainly authentic originals.

The message they transmitted was a crude, sentimental image of an England that had long gone: healthy young bodies playing ball on the beach, threshing machines and skylarks at harvest time, red-faced old codgers knocking back barley wine under the Christmas tree. Who, even then, thought such images would actually make people thirsty?

I looked at my watch: two and a half minutes and still dry. Unbelievable.

The rest of the Reception area was dominated by a telephone exchange and a giant lectern. The telephone exchange was exactly that, one of the old fashioned exchanges with wires and plugs and flashing lights which told you a line was open or a call was coming in. There was even a headset with a bakelite microphone resting on a rack of switches.

The woman who had shown me in saw a circular light flash on the board and said 'Excuse me.'

She put on the headset, sat down behind the wooden-framed board and inserted a plug.

'Seton and Nephew, Seagrave's Seaside Ales. Good morning.'

It was spooky. As she sat down and pushed her chair in, it was impossible for a visitor to see the short skirt and her legs. The only view was of her top half, complete with cardigan and string of pearls, and if you didn't look too closely at her make-up and the hairstyle, she fitted in perfectly. It was a good trick. Visitors suddenly felt they were in a time machine rather than a brewery and it took their minds off the fact that they had been there over five minutes and still not been offered a drink.

'I'll put you through to Telesales,' she was saying, though if she'd received an order by carrier pigeon I wouldn't have been surprised.

I looked again at the lectern and realised that it wasn't a lectern as it was too big, too wide and tall-backed to have ever fitted in a church or a lecture hall. I then twigged what it was – it was a post desk, the stand-at sorting desk where a Scrooge or a Marley or a Uriah Heep would open all the post before anyone else in the firm got a look-in. Not only did the person opening the mail get first crack at any incoming cash or cheques, they also knew exactly what was going on and were thus in a position of power.

Recognising the post desk for what it was would have got me an automatic place on the panel of experts on *The Antiques Roadshow* were it not for the give-away that there was a very tall man standing behind it opening the morning's post with a long, ivory-handled letter knife which was attached to the desk by a long brass-link chain.

He was hypnotised by what looked like a bank statement but he eventually noticed me standing there. It was probably the sound of my tongue swelling at the back of my parched mouth which attracted his attention.

'Oh, Mr Angel, do forgive me. How rude. Sorry. Welcome.'

He took a pace towards me, holding out a hand and not realising that he still held the letter-opener in the other. The brass chain ran its length and snapped before he got to me, the chain whipping behind his left leg.

'Ow! Dammit! Oh, not again.'

The woman on the switchboard raised her eyebrows and shook her head as she plugged into another call.

'Seton and Nephew, Seagrave's Seaside Ales. How can I help you?'

The tall man – and he was tall, at least six feet six if not seven – rubbed the back of his leg with his bank statement and hobbled towards me, still holding out his right hand. In that position I was able to make eye contact with him.

'I'm Murdo Seton,' he said.

'Roy Angel. Are you the Seton or the Nephew?'

I said it for the sake of making polite conversation, but he took it like a question on *Mastermind*.

'Er ... no ... well, not the original one of course. The Founding Fathers were brothers, Othniel and Ezra Seton, and the firm was supposed to be called Seton Brothers but Ezra died in a tragic accident when a vat of porter burst and flooded the cellars.'

He saw the look in my eyes and mistook it for interest.

'He drowned. In the brewery's test brew. Quite tragic.'

But at least he got a drink, I thought.

'So Othniel Seton brought his brother's son into the firm, even though he was only ten at the time. It's been called that ever since and the present board is actually descended from that nephew. My uncle, both cousins and myself are all from Ezra's side of the family, not Othniel's.'

'They died out?'

From thirst, probably.

'No, they were all girls.'

The woman on the switchboard was shaking her head quite violently now and looking at her watch. I had the bizarre thought that maybe she'd been working here for thirty years and still hadn't been offered a drink.

'I see,' I said, wondering how to get out of this. 'Fascinating.'

'Yes, it is. Or I find it so.' He tried to reconnect the letter-opener chain to the desk but failed. He wrapped the dangling chain around it and placed it on top of the desk.

'Yes indeed. Brewery history is a fascinating subject.'

He looked around for somewhere to put the bank statement, then screwed it into a ball and stuffed it into the pocket of his coat.

'It's about time for my daily tour,' he said, looking at his

40

watch. 'Beatrice here can hold the fort. Have you ever been round a brewery, Mr Angel?'

'No, I never have,' I said, brightening and totally forgetting to add: *Not legally.*

4

I don't know how tall the average Victorian brewery architect was, but he was either six inches shorter than Murdo or he had a warped sense of humour. On the climb up the brewery there were no less than eight doorways and archways which I could get through with ease, but for which Murdo should have ducked. Should have, but didn't. Hit every one with his forehead. Got the lot.

But it didn't stop him talking and the second thing I learned about Victorian Tower breweries was that when they said Tower, they meant it and that involved climbing narrow staircases until we reached the Malt Store on the top floor.

The view through two leaded windows which wouldn't have looked out of place in a church was spectacular if you liked dark grey seascapes and weren't worried about the fact that the seagulls were flying below you. The state I was in, I wouldn't have been surprised to see some of them wearing oxygen masks.

'So here we are, at the top of the Tower system and these are the three sorts of malt we use: a basic pale ale, a crystal and a chocolate.'

Murdo spun around on his heels, pointing at a platoon of dumpy sacks slumped against the walls. He wasn't even out of breath. He might be concussed but he wasn't out of breath.

'Let me get this right,' I wheezed. 'You drag the heaviest thing you use all the way right up to the top here?'

'We use pulleys and winches of course,' he said, 'and if you want to be picky, the water we use is actually the heaviest ingredient.'

'And that,' I pointed a finger down the spiral staircase I had struggled up, 'is way down there under the ground, right?'

41

'Well . . . yes,' he pondered and I got the feeling that normal brewery tours didn't give him this much trouble, 'but the beauty of the Tower system is that from here on gravity takes over.'

He skipped over to an ancient red metal box which looked like a giant coffee grinder – and I wasn't far wrong.

'This is our mill, our original mill.'

He said it with pride. I wondered if Beatrice down on the switchboard was an original fixture too.

'Where we grind the malt into a fine powder which we call grist.'

He paused for dramatic effect.

'As in . . .'

'. . . grist to the mill,' I completed.

'Why, yes.' He seemed genuinely crestfallen, then he recovered. 'The grist goes down to the floor below where we mash it with hot water, which we call liquor for some reason. Don't ask me why.'

What did they call thirst?

'After mashing we boil with hops – good Kentish hops, of course, we use no other – which gives the beer its bitterness.'

'So there's beer one floor down?' I asked.

'Sort of. It's still green beer in a sense, not that I mean organic or anything. Though it probably is as we use only natural ingredients and we try and avoid pesticides and suchlike.'

He tried to describe 'organic' with his long, thin hands. I'd never seen anybody do that before. Well, not anyone who actually knew what it meant.

'But there's no alcohol in the beer yet. We call it wort, which I'm told is a good old Anglo-Saxon word.'

I know another, I said to myself.

'Hopped wort to be accurate,' he went on, 'which is cooled and run into fermentation tanks and then we add yeast and the wort ferments happily for a few days then we let it condition itself and then we transfer it through pipes across the yard to the racking lines where it goes into casks or kegs or bottles. But I'll show you all this.'

I had drifted away and was looking out of the window down into the yard, where Beatrice was click-clacking in her high heels towards the door marked 'Sampling Cellar'. Two men in brown brewery logo overalls were heading for the same place from a different angle. The ancient security guard came out of his gatehouse, rattled the gates to make sure they were locked and marched that way too.

'So you don't actually get to sample the stuff except way down there?' I had my nose virtually pressed against the window by now and found myself eyeball to glassy eyeball with a passing seagull. He seemed to be smirking at me.

'That's right. And all our employees are expected to have at least three halves a day and fill in a sheet of tasting notes so that we can make sure our Head Brewer is keeping his hand in.'

He flapped a hand at the stairway. 'Shall we hurry along?'

'Oh yes,' I said. ' Let's hurry.'

Thirty-eight minutes so far and still not a drop.

We eventually made it down to the brewery yard. By this time – one hour and nine minutes after crossing the threshold, but who was counting? – I was an expert on brewing. I could spot a 'rocky head' on a fermentation vessel at fifty feet and I could appreciate the aromatic properties of hops. (The trick was not just to sniff them, but rub them between the balls of your thumbs to release the full aroma. What they don't tell you is that way the aroma stays on your hands for days.)

Across the yard someone in the Sampling Cellar had turned on a light, giving its leaded windows a warm, welcoming, orange glow like a church in autumn. I thought I could hear the tinkle of happy laughter and I strode out towards the sound.

'I see you take your undercover work seriously,' Murdo Seton said behind me.

'What?' I stopped and turned.

He was standing admiring Armstrong, reaching out a hand, stroking a wheel arch.

'Miss Blugden said you were one of the best undercover operatives they used and I can see why now. No one would suspect a cab driver.'

I would, I thought, but said:

'It's delicensed of course, but it is ideal for London. Never any problem parking and people usually get out of your way, even buses. Did Veronica really say that?'

He had his hand on the driver's door handle now.

'Oh yes, she did. She said undercover infiltration was the second biggest segment of their business after security and risk assessment.'

Brilliant. After all this time and within fifty feet of the Sampling Cellar, he decides to talk shop.

'I've never driven one of these,' he said dreamily. 'What's on the clock?'

'130,000 miles, or that's what it says. I wouldn't put money on it being accurate.' I looked at the battered Citroën Safari next to Armstrong, noting the three-inch fringe of rust around the lower bodywork. 'I see you go for the classic cars yourself.'

'What? This thing?' He was genuinely amazed. 'This is just the old family run-around I inherited from my father. One of the doors doesn't open any more and I put my foot through the floor last week but she still starts up every morning. I really ought to take the old warhorse in for an overhaul. Marvellous car: one of the few you can get skis inside. Don't see many of them on the road these days, though.'

'They haven't made them for about thirty years,' I said. 'You don't even see them in France much.'

'Really? No wonder the garage charges me so much for spares, but I like the old Safari. Everyone round here knows it and when they see it coming they know it's me.'

I'll bet they do – see you coming, that is.

'You should take it across to France for servicing,' I said seriously. 'You'd find it cheaper and you are near enough, for heaven's sake.'

'Cheaper, you say?' He was thinking about it.

'Much. And you could fill up with cheap beer on the way back,' I added casually. 'You could get a fair few cases in the back of that thing.'

He stared at the Citroën as if estimating its cubic capacity and I waited for it to sink in. I had fed him the words 'France' and 'cheap beer' virtually in the same sentence. Surely the cartoon light bulb above his head would flash on sooner or later.

It did.

'Funny you should mention that, because that's what I wanted to talk to you about.'

He looked over my shoulder – over my head actually – and noticed the Sampling Cellars as if for the very first time.

'Shall we do it over a drink?'

One hour and twenty-two minutes.

Bingo.

I warmed to young Murdo as the afternoon wore on, though to be honest after my second pint of Triple S (Seagrave's Seaside Special) I would have struck up a conversation with a tax inspector or hugged a traffic warden.

Murdo's problem – if he had a problem – was that he had been a gangling youth who had left boarding school to become a gangling undergraduate at Cambridge and then had strolled, bashing his head all the way, into the family business. Along the way, he simply hadn't got out much.

He had probably looked forty-two since he was eighteen, may even have practised at it, but he was, he said, only twenty-seven, which was a little bit sad. He had absolutely no idea why I went into a fit of giggles and spluttered into my beer when he said, airily:

'It was only four years ago, when I came down from Cambridge, and I was wondering what sort of a career to follow . . .'

For goodness' sake, I wanted to scream, *your dad owns a brewery!*

Where was the problem?

Given that he seemed to have inherited an extra clumsy gene, I could understand why the family firm might not have wanted him working too closely with hot liquids, dangerous machinery or substances open to abuse, such as alcohol. (I didn't think it wise to tell him that hops were related to cannabis. Information overload can be an ugly thing.) So a career in the brewery was not actually a foregone conclusion. It had, however, given him a summer vacation job during his years as a student – starting with mucking out the stables and moving up to supervising the bottling lines – so, when he finished his degree, it seemed sensible to 'help out' in the brewery until he found his vocation.

Surprise, surprise, he was made an Area Manager within a

year; Tied-Trade Director (looking after the company's own pubs) within two; and a member of the Board six months ago. And none of this had anything to do with him being called Seton?

'No, not really. I don't think so,' he had said seriously.

I had been tempted to ask how many people on the Board were *not* called Seton, but then he was behind the bar pulling the drinks.

The Sampling Cellar was not actually a cellar, it was a miniature pub with an in-built advantage: no customers. Or, at least, no *paying* customers as there were no cash registers. It had scrubbed wooden tables and chairs, a dart board, a bar billiards table, even a shove-ha'penny board, and a long bar with two pumps of each of the brewery's beers making sixteen handpulls in all.

Murdo explained that one pump of each beer was the latest brew whilst the second would be the same beer but an earlier batch, so the trick was to guess which was one day old and which was up to thirteen days. The only person who could tell for sure, especially after the first three samples, was the Head Brewer. He, I was told in a whisper, was the short, bearded man in a white coat, smoking a pipe at a table by himself with eight glasses and a clipboard.

Beatrice, the gatekeeper, the draymen and a couple of other staff drifted off after Murdo and I entered and when only the Head Brewer was left, minding his own business, Murdo suggested we see if they had left us any lunch. I was grateful on the basis that any more of this professional sampling on an empty stomach and I would be in no fit state to get Armstrong out of the brewery yard let alone back to London.

At the end of the bar was a glass-fronted electric hot cabinet in which was a large joint of roasted beef, half a dozen soft bread rolls and a carving knife which could have doubled as a pirate sword.

'Help yourself,' said Murdo. 'We have a different roast on every day.'

'You don't employ many vegetarians, then?' I asked cheerfully, making myself a sandwich.

'We have salmon on Fridays,' he said hesitantly.

'Those are Catholics, not vegetarians.'

He waited a good half-minute before he laughed.

'Oh yes, very good. Miss Rudgard told us you were. . . . Now, what was the expression she used?'

'A chopsy little git?' I offered.

'Yes!' He was wide-eyed. 'That was exactly it.'

'Shot in the dark,' I said modestly, munching on an inch-thick slice of beef and surveying fourteen beers as yet untried. Life suddenly seemed good.

'Your glass is empty,' Murdo said, not for the first time. 'Let me try you with something else.'

He took my glass without much of a fight and marched around behind the bar, selecting and grasping a pump handle like he was sizing up an opponent at Olympic arm-wrestling.

'Have you worked for the Misses Rudgard and Blugden for long?' he asked as he pulled.

'I've never heard them referred to as that before. Thanks.' I took a full glass from his hand. The pump he had used had a brightly painted bird on it, a swan or something. Then the words 'Seagull Special Bitter' came into focus. 'You not having one?'

'I'm taking it easy. I have to go up to town tonight to a brewers' dinner. Very boring. Tell me about the R&B agency.'

'Well, you hired 'em.' I toasted him with my glass. 'And they hired me, so wouldn't it be better if you told me what exactly you want me to do?'

Murdo flipped his eyebrows then jerked his head and I automatically looked behind me, but there was only the old Head Brewer sitting in the corner sipping beer.

'Later,' Murdo mouthed without a sound, so I went along with it. After all, he was buying.

'Well, I'm only a freelance, you understand. A specialist, working on a job-to-job basis. The agency's main business is security systems.'

'Yes, I know,' he said, leaning over the bar and resting his elbows on it. He was so long his hands jutted out way over the edge. 'What's Miss Rudgard's speciality?'

Stella's speciality? Oh God, could I get into trouble here.

'I think she's the brains of the outfit, the business brains that is. Veronica is more the muscles in the partnership.'

'Sort of good cop, bad cop, eh? She jolly well frightened me.'

I nodded in agreement as I sipped my beer. Then I realised he was talking about Veronica and I was thinking about Stella.

'Do you know her well?' Murdo asked quietly.

I must have been going down with the 'flu or something because I only just realised that Murdo was sniffing around the subject personally, not professionally.

'We don't exactly move in the same social circles,' I said carefully, 'and of course she doesn't get involved in my side of the business. You know, the covert, behind-the-lines, get-your-hands-dirty side of things.'

'Oh, obviously not. You couldn't see Stella rubbing shoulders with criminals, could you?'

No, that was true. Sleeping with them, yes, but not rubbing shoulders.

'She leaves the sordid end to people like me,' I said.

He nodded in agreement at this, then did a double-take.

'Oh, I say, I'm sorry. I didn't mean to imply anything about your role in the operation.'

'Don't fret it,' I said generously, waving my glass in salute. 'We all have our specialities.'

'And yours is?'

'Didn't Veronica tell you?'

'She may have done . . .' He hesitated.

But I bet myself he had been too busy looking at Stella's legs.

'She was probably being deliberately vague,' I said reassuringly. 'Sometimes it's best if the client doesn't know *exactly* how we get results.'

He tapped the side of his nose. Honest to God, he tapped the side of his nose like he'd seen Cockney wide boys do in black-and-white films shown on Sunday afternoon television.

'I'm with you. Say no more.'

I was glad one of us knew what we were talking about. I noticed my glass was empty.

'What's that one?' I pointed to the pump at the end of the bar.

'Ah, that's the last of our special Christmas brew, Noel's First. It's a really quite powerful barley wine. Try a drop.'

He took my glass and started to pull.

'You don't get many barley wines on draught these days but my Uncle Edgar always has a pin at home over the Christmas holiday. He keeps it near the fire in the drawing-room and puts a heated poker into his tankard before he drinks it.'

'Why?'

Murdo paused, mid-pull.

'I don't honestly know.'

'Still, nice name for Christmas,' I said, 'First Noel and all that.'

He looked slightly stunned.

'It's named after our Head Brewer, Noel. It was his first Christmas brew. The Christmas carol had never occurred to me. Makes sense now you think about it.'

Behind me I heard a snort, and then a chair scraped back across the floor and footsteps stomped out of the door. The Head Brewer had taken his leave of us. He probably had made the connection, and heard it a million times.

Murdo looked positively relieved that he had gone.

'Ah, good, he's gone. That's a relief,' he said and because I had been thinking that, it seemed quite amusing and I think I giggled into my new beer.

'Listen, Mr Angel – or can I call you Roy?' he asked, walking round to my side of the bar.

I had just taken a mouthful of Noel's First and seemed to have lost the use of several motor neurones. As far as I was concerned, he could call me Rafael Sabatini. I think I mumbled something to the effect that it was cool by me.

'I know it looks as if I've been messing around for the last couple of hours, but I really need to brief you in private. Now we're alone, I suggest we stay here as this is just about the most private place in the brewery, but I need to get something from my office. Something to show you. It'll only take me a few minutes to get it but I'll be right back. I'm afraid I'll have to lock you in while I'm gone. It's company rules. Do you mind awfully?'

Did I mind being locked *in* a brewery sampling cellar? There was a poser.

'No worries,' I said.

He was gone about five minutes, or it could have been two hours, I really didn't mind, and when he returned he was carrying a thin grey case under his arm.

'My laptop,' he said proudly, setting it up on the bar. 'I'd be lost without it. It does absolutely everything for me.'

'Can it pull a pint?' I asked, thinking that was just about the wittiest and most charming thing anyone could have said in the circumstances.

'Er . . . no.' He looked around, flustered for a moment. 'Please, help yourself.'

'Thanks, I will.'

I already had.

'Grab a bar stool,' he said, settling on one himself, but even when he was sitting down I still had to look up to him. Maybe that was because my legs had started to turn to rubber.

When I had a full pint glass, though I couldn't remember which beer it was, I pulled up another bar stool next to his and tried to make out the graphics appearing on his computer's screen. The image was of a mosaic design and the colours were oddly soothing.

'This is a map of the European Union,' said Murdo.

And so it was. I closed my left eye and it became clear.

'Sixteen countries from Portugal to Finland, all living in unity, peace and harmony under the provisions of the Treaty of Rome, and all with their own systems of tax – income tax, value added tax and, most importantly for brewers, excise duty.' Murdo hit a button on his keyboard, and on the map all the borders between the countries disappeared. 'Then came the Single Market in January 1993 and – in theory – all obstacles to trading between these countries disappeared. It was supposed to be a Europe without borders, without Customs officers, without restrictions. If you want to buy a German washing machine, go do it. You want an Italian car or a Spanish video recorder, the choice is yours. But of course this only makes

50

sense if the goods are taxed the same in all the member states.'

'Harmonisation,' I slurred into my beer.

'Quite right. Harmonising taxes must be the logical outcome of a Single Market, otherwise the thing doesn't make any sense and there would be little point in being in it. But all the member countries have their own tax regimes and they guard them very fiercely, so much so that even with twenty years' warning, they couldn't agree to do it before the Single Market came in.

'On some taxes, though, they at least agreed to move towards a band or range. Value added tax, for instance. There are still different rates of VAT in the different countries, but they're all in roughly the same ballpark.'

'Ah yes, ballparking,' I murmured. I had heard Amy talking about 'ballparking' on wholesale prices of TALtops. I still didn't have a clue what it meant.

'And the same stop-gap measure should have applied to excise duties, where the discrepancies are even more pronounced.' He hit another key and his Powerpoint program hummed and began to colour in the countries on the map. France, then Italy, then Spain began to turn blue whilst Denmark, Sweden and Ireland were the first to go red. Eventually, the European Union was split red and blue, the red countries mostly the northern ones: Ireland, the UK, Denmark, Sweden and Finland.

'The red countries are the high tax ones, blue is low tax and here's the nub of the problem.'

Murdo typed something on his keyboard and, on the graphic, borderlines began to flash in yellow between Ulster and the Irish Republic, between Germany and Denmark, and Sweden and Finland, and in the Channel between England and France, and in the Kattegat between Denmark and Sweden.

'In these places, you have high tax countries next door to low tax ones when it comes to alcohol – especially beer – and, in theory, no border controls or restrictions on how much you can buy. This isn't like the duty-free booze you bring back from holiday; this is duty-paid but paid in a country with a very low rate of tax. For example,' he began to point a long, thin finger at the screen, 'beer tax in Denmark was about eight times higher than in Germany at the start of the Single Market, so any sensible Dane would have driven across the border to buy their beer. Sweden came in, with a much higher beer tax than Denmark, so nipping over to Copenhagen on the ferry to load up the Volvo was the obvious thing to do. Same story with Finland and Sweden, and, of course, the classic one – us here in Kent only twenty-two miles from France where the beer tax is eight times *lower* with regular ferry crossings and now we've even got a tunnel and high-speed trains.'

'What about Ireland and the border between the North and the South?' I asked, very proud that I could think of something to ask. Indeed, I was quite pleased I could still speak.

'Well, in theory there ought to be a fair bit of cross-border shopping there, but it doesn't seem to have become as much of a problem as elsewhere. I think it must have something to do with the Irish attitude to tax. They don't seem to take it very seriously.'

'Maybe they have a point,' I said wisely.

'Perhaps they do, but down here near the Channel, we have to take things seriously because the problem's going to get a lot worse before it gets better. Look at this, and remember what I said about value added tax.'

I nodded enthusiastically but in reality I couldn't remember which beer I was drinking let alone what he'd said about VAT.

The screen dissolved and reformed into a bar chart with sixteen columns each with the flag of a member state of the Single Market. Some filled the screen, some were very small and there were two dotted lines horizontally near the bottom of the screen. Each column had an arrow pointing towards the dotted lines. The colours were really cool.

'This shows the beer duty in pence-per-pint in all the EU countries and this line would be a harmonised rate.' He pointed to the lower dotted line. 'Now that's only a couple of pence per pint and look where we are.'

His finger rested on one of the flags on the screen and by holding a hand over my left eye I could see that he had picked out the Union Jack, way up near the top of the screen, flanked by the Irish tricolour and the flags of Sweden and Finland.

'Now that's a long way to come down for these high tax

countries so, as with value added tax, Europe agreed a target *rate* which countries could at least aim for. The low ones, like France and Spain, would put their beer duty *up* to get to near that target, which is about 7p a pint, whilst the high tax countries should come *down* to meet the others coming up. Guess what?'

Oh God, I hate the quiz part and he never said he would be asking questions afterwards.

'What?'

'It didn't happen. Well, not here. It did everywhere else.'

'You surprise me.'

'I share your instinctive cynicism about pragmatic politicians.'

Did that mean I'd got something right? I tried to look world-weary and philosophical, rather than just weary.

'Even worse,' Murdo went on, 'the gap is getting wider. Look closely. I'm sorry it's a bit small but it really stands out when I do a presentation with a big screen.'

'You do this as a . . . a . . . presentation?'

I was gripped with an image of Murdo boring the pants off the Seagrave Women's Institute in the church hall on a wet February night.

'Oh yes, it's my party piece. I'm a bit of an expert on the subject, though I say it myself. Of course, you're only seeing a bit of the whole thing. When I showed it to the Treasury Select Committee last week I concentrated on the failings of their macro-economic model when it came to disposable income and the positive effect of a duty cut on the Gross National Product. Not to mention the Retail Price Index.'

'Right,' I said slowly, trying to remember not to mention the Retail Price Index. 'So what am I supposed to be looking at?'

'The UK column. See? Every other country is moving towards the target rate for beer duty except us. The Irish, the Danes, the Swedes are all coming down and the French and Spanish and so on are all coming up. Every single country is moving towards that line except Britain. We're going *away* from it. Our government is continuing to put our beer duty up when it should be reducing it. So now we're not just out of line with our partners in Europe, we're *way* out of line. That means a big differential in tax which gives the smugglers more incentive and more profit and makes smuggling one of the fastest growing businesses in the UK. There.'

At the flick of a finger the screen dissolved and turned into a cartoon graphic. One half of the screen was a line-drawing or print depicting eighteenth-century pirates, complete with hooks, eye-patches, cutlasses and flintlock pistols, off-loading wooden casks from a beached longboat and rolling them up a beach to a cave. It could have been ripped from an illustrated edition of *Treasure Island*. The other half showed a scanned-in colour picture of a procession of white Ford Transit vans rolling off a car ferry docked under the White Cliffs of Dover.

'On the eve of the twenty-first century,' Murdo said portentously, 'we have reinvented the eighteenth-century crime of smuggling.'

'But if they go round looking like that, even the cops should be able to spot them. Maybe they could get one of the parrots to grass them up.'

Murdo frowned and I had the distinct feeling that my credit at the bar was in jeopardy. Then his face brightened.

'Oh, I see. Yes, an excellent point.'

What was?

'If only it was that simple. But you're quite right, the smugglers don't go around shouting 'Yo-ho-ho' and delivering brandy to the vicar and 'baccy to the clerk.' What was he talking about? 'Well, actually they do smuggle tobacco, quite a lot of it, but that mostly comes in from Holland and goes through Harwich or Felixstowe. But your basic point is correct and a very astute observation.

'Not only do today's smugglers not look like that,' he pointed to the pirates, 'but they don't look like that much either.' This time he pointed to the fleet of white, unmarked vans.

'As you rightly say, Mr Angel, the smugglers are becoming more sophisticated – more organised. The "van trade" as we call it is simply too obvious these days, in fact the anonymous white van has become something of a symbol of the beer smuggler, almost a what-do-you-call-them . . . like a trademark . . . a . . .'

'Logo,' I supplied.

'That's it. It's almost shorthand for the newspapers. They

show a picture of a white van and slam the word "Bootlegger" underneath it, though "bootlegging" is inaccurate. The crime is smuggling.'

'Most people don't think so,' I said, though even I could hear I was slurring.

Murdo looked horrified. This time I had gone too far.

'Exactly! You've put your finger on it again!' He slapped his hand down on the table, rattling his laptop and almost sending my empty glass flying. 'Miss Blugden said you were sharp, that you cut right to the quick. You're just the sort of man we're looking for.'

I tried to look humble and smile at the same time. I don't think either worked.

'It'll be your round, then?' I asked, offering my glass.

5

I hadn't been back in the safety of London for more than twelve hours before I was beaten up, tortured and left for dead.

When I came round I could see a weak and watery sun climbing over the rooftops, which told me it must be morning. My spine and kidneys hurt as if they'd been speared and twisted with a corkscrew and my head felt as if an anvil had dropped on it and was still resting there. I could only open my right eye, the left seemed glued shut with something thick and sticky, and the back of my left hand throbbed with a three-inch diagonal burn.

I was wearing only a T-shirt (a 'Somebody Killed Kenny' Christmas present) which explained why I was cold and starting to shiver. A plastic bag drifted by my face and I could see empty take-away food cartons, an old shoe, a pile of cigarette butts, empty beer bottles and, from the corner of my good eye, something sleek and furry scuttling away.

Various smells assailed my nostrils; rotting, vegetable smells like . . .

'Angel? Was that you falling out of bed? Are you awake?'

Oh, *bloody hell*.

From the knees down, my legs were still on the bed. My bed. My old bed, in the Stuart Street flat. The rest of me was face down on the floor, which explained the bend and incredible pain in my spine. I was facing the bedroom window which was wide open, which was why I was so cold. The second-degree burn on the back of my hand fitted exactly the corner of an aluminium food box on which the word 'Rice' was written in green pencil. Who'd have thought they could hold so much heat? My eye seemed to be gummed with a prawn curry of some description and the flattened box told me that's where my face had landed when I had rolled off the bed. The fact that there was no sign of any prawns any more explained the sleek figure of Springsteen, who was circling me in the hope that I was dead and therefore suitable for lunch. All the empty bottles – and some full ones – bore Seagrave's Seaside Ales labels.

'Angel? Are you sure you're all right?'

Oh bloody, bloody, *bloody* hell.

It was Fenella, clumping up the stairs. I must have left the door open as well as the windows. Why didn't I just get a neon sign saying 'Burglars Welcome'?

I tried to get off the floor, or off the bed. Either one, I wasn't proud, but everywhere I tried to put a hand or a foot down, there seemed to be cold food or a rolling empty bottle. Eventually I found room to put my feet down.

I pulled my T-shirt out and wiped my face with it. It came away with unspeakable orange stains but at least I could see out of both eyes. What I couldn't do was work out why my kidneys hurt.

'What a sight!' shrieked Fenella from the bedroom doorway. 'You look absolutely awful!

She put her hands to her mouth to hide her giggles.

'Didn't you make an exhibition of yourself last night, young man? I hope you feel as bad as you look. *Half* as bad as you look! You should be grateful we were here to look after that nice Mr Seton and get him a minicab. And you should say thank you to Lisabeth for putting you to bed after you fell down the stairs ...' She paused for effect. '... the second time.'

That explained the bruised kidneys.

I touched my hair and found food there too, so I pulled my

T-shirt off and towelled my head with it. That gave me a brilliant idea: I needed a shower. Right now. Nothing else mattered. Speech would come later.

Fenella shrank back into the living-room as I staggered by her, heading for the bathroom. I could see her nostrils quiver as the scent of prawn curry – a korma perhaps? – wafted towards her.

'Is there anything I can get you, Angel? Seriously, you look like something the cat dragged in.' Then, over my shoulder, she said: 'Sorry, Springsteen.'

I stopped in front of her and waited until she stopped giggling at her own joke, then I held three fingers up in front of her face.

'Three things?' she asked innocently, like it was a game of charades.

I ticked off the fingers one by one.

'Para. Ceta. Mol.'

I found small words came easier.

I slouched under the shower long enough to put a dent in the water table, then raided my emergency stash of spare clothes for clean underpants, socks and a T-shirt which read 'My Other T-shirt is a Paul Smith'. One of these days Amy would notice that I came home in clothes she'd never seen before.

Amy.

I rushed to the door of the flat which Fenella had thought-lessly left open and yelled down the stairs:

'Fenella! Have there been any messages for me?'

'Just a couple,' she said from somewhere close behind me, shredding what few nerve endings I had left.

'Jesus! Don't ambush me like that! What the hell are you doing anyway?'

She had bright yellow rubber gloves on and was carrying a plastic bucket in one hand.

'I'm soaking the curry stains out of your carpet,' she said primly and then waited, practising her lemon-sucking expression, for me to say something like: *Oh, you didn't have to do that.*

'Why don't you just run the hoover over it?' I said.

'Then the stain would stay and it doesn't match the pattern.'

It didn't? Oh come on, who knows what colour their bedroom carpet is?

'Whatever. My messages?'

She breathed heavily down her nose then pulled off a glove and reached into the back pocket of her jeans to produce my mobile phone.

'It says "Five Missed Calls" but I think they're all from Veronica,' she said, then she unclipped my pager from her belt. 'And this says you have to call Amy on her mobile.'

'Thanks,' I said, taking the mobile from her and holding out my hand for the pager.

Fenella's lower lip jutted out and she glared at her feet.

'Lisabeth said you wouldn't let me keep them,' she said under her breath.

'I gave them to you? Last night?'

She nodded. 'Twice.'

'Hmmm. Look, Fenella my dear, I'm going to put some coffee on. When you've finished with the carpet, come and have a cup and you can tell me everything that happened last night. OK?'

'I suppose so,' she sighed, turning back to the bedroom and pulling on her rubber glove with an elaborate *thwack*.

'Oh, and can I borrow some milk?'

'Yeah, yeah,' she said over her shoulder.

'And some bread? And orange juice? Oh, and you haven't got any Corn Flakes, have you? I've got a distinct touch of the munchies. I must have missed dinner.'

From the bedroom she shouted:

'No, you didn't.'

Ooh. Sharp.

She was getting good and I felt a twinge of pride. It had been me who'd taught her everything she knew.

The pieces began to fall into place but it wasn't the sort of jigsaw you'd give your aunty for Christmas.

I remembered being in the Sampling Cellar down in Seagrave and suggesting to Murdo Seton that as he'd always wanted to drive a real, live London taxi (or as near as damn it) and he was going 'up to town' that evening, why didn't he drive Armstrong back – as I sure as shooting wasn't in any fit state to do so.

Naturally, he'd loved the idea and said it was perfect because he could finish briefing me on the way, but would I mind staying in the Sampling Cellar for an hour or so while he nipped home to change into his dinner jacket? I had agreed to this, reluctantly of course, I convinced him that I could work my way through the rest of the Powerpoint presentation on his laptop while he was gone, so I could get up to speed. (For some reason, bringing yourself 'up to speed' really impresses people in business.)

He hadn't been gone five minutes before I was into his Jazz Jackrabbit 2 program and, fuelled by another pint of Seagull Special or whatever, had made it to Level 3 before the killer tortoises cornered me in a treasure cave and zapped me to pieces. Or at least I think that was what happened. Either way, I managed to shut down the laptop just as Murdo returned, fairly confident that he would have saved his economic presentation somewhere in the memory.

Murdo, thankfully, didn't ask what I thought of his presentation. He wanted to continue the briefing as he drove and could he have the keys, please, as he was really looking forward to this?

So was I. I'd never been driven by a man in full evening dress before.

Somewhere between the Sampling Cellar and Armstrong, I acquired a crate of bottled beer which fitted neatly on the floor of the cab while I stretched out on the back seat. Murdo even gave me a metal opener embossed with the legend 'Seagrave's Seaside'. I do remember asking him why the word 'Ales' seemed to be missing and he muttered something about it being faulty stock, but I didn't mind: it worked fine.

I was grateful for Murdo's souvenirs of my visit for the way he drove I certainly needed a drink. I began to work my way through the crate as Murdo talked, keeping my head down so I didn't have to see either the road or the speedometer.

Amazingly, some of it went into my fuddled brain and stayed there, because even the morning after, with four out of the five voices in my head telling me to call in sick, I could still remember the gist of it.

Murdo was obviously the moderniser in the family firm. Not only was he getting the business computerised but he was trying to be environmentally friendly along the way. Where possible, he had enrolled his pubs in a scheme called Bottleback, which basically involved a large plastic bin in the carpark so that people could recycle their empty bottles. Country pubs helping to keep the countryside tidy was the tag line and it made a lot of sense, with a truck coming round once a month or so to take away the full Bottleback bin and leave an empty one.

Some bright lad down at the local waste recycling plant (though I remember when they were called rubbish tips) noticed that one of the Bottleback bins was crammed full of small, French lager bottles and nothing else. When it happened again he phoned the brewery and reported it, having checked which collection route it had come from. Murdo investigated and identified the actual pub where the bin had been parked, one of his small country tenancies called the Rising Sun at a place called Whitcomb about ten miles south of Canterbury.

Finding empty French beer bottles in recycling bins wasn't, of course, that unusual. As Murdo pointed out rather ruefully, the biggest selling beer in Kent was now French and it was one which was not officially imported. But finding nothing else, not even a jam jar or an empty sauce bottle, was unusual, especially when it was happening once every ten days or so since the brewery started monitoring it and when all the bottles came from the same batch.

I failed to see why Murdo needed an undercover detective, and I said so, shouting from the back of Armstrong trying to make myself heard over the screaming engine. It was an exercise in the blindingly obvious: the Rising Sun was flogging smuggled French beer instead of Seagrave's Stunning Ales but at least had the decency to recycle the empties or just assumed that once in the Bottleback bin they were out of sight and out of mind.

That was the easy explanation, Murdo had said, and I think he was a little disappointed in me for suggesting it. But he knew that the landlady of the Rising Sun would never do that.

It was just unthinkable. In any case the bottles all had French labels and even one of his brewery's regional managers would have noticed if the pub had them on display. But just to be sure, Murdo had checked back on the pub's orders and deliveries and there was no obvious drop in the amounts it was buying from the brewery. So either the pub had found some new customers and a new sideline in French lager or someone was dumping the bottles in the pub's Bottleback bin as a bit of a sick joke.

And I was supposed to do – what?

Go down to the Rising Sun and hang around keeping my eyes open. Go and see some people in Dover, people who were experts on the smuggling industry. Find out who the main runners were these days – that's what they called them in Dover, beer-runners. Keep an ear open, as well as an eye. Listen to the gossip, spot the drivers and the 'mules' – the innocent ferry passengers who were carrying booze and cigarettes for the smugglers. Be prepared to write it all up in a report, from the front line so to speak.

But why me? What on earth could I bring to the party?

Because I was an outsider and in Dover, a town swamped with transients, I would fit right in. And I obviously didn't look like a Customs officer or a private detective, did I? And, anyway, I had a Heavy Goods Vehicle driving licence, didn't I? Miss Blugden had said I had.

I admitted she was right there and then it dawned on me. Murdo wanted me to become a runner – infiltrate a gang and find out where the booze was going.

'Oh, I couldn't possibly ask you to do anything to break the law,' he had said. 'Could I?'

'He seemed like a really nice man,' Fenella said as she spooned scrambled egg on to my plate.

'I introduced him to you? Pass the Tabasco, would you?'

'Oh yes, when we had to come down and let you in because you'd forgotten how to use your key. Mr Seton was sort of holding you upright. Then he brought all that beer in for you, so we had a little chat. Where's the Tabasco?'

'Cupboard above the fridge. How did Murdo get to his dinner party?'

'Banquet, actually,' she shouted from the kitchen. 'He was going to a banquet at the Brewers' Hall. It's in the City, near St Paul's.'

'I know where it is, it's just behind Love Lane police station. How did he get there?'

'You phoned for a minicab for him.'

'I did?'

'Well, Lisabeth actually spoke to them, but you dialled the number all by yourself. Is this it?'

She held a small red bottle in front of my face.

'No, that's Kickin' Ass Salsa, but it'll do. So, you had a nice little chat with Murdo, did you?'

'Not for long. It was a bit difficult with you playing the music that loud.'

I paused between forkfuls.

'Music?' I flashed a look to where my ancient B-flat trumpet was still in place, balanced on top of one of the hi-fi speakers.

'No, you didn't play,' she said, 'you spared us that. But you wanted Murdo to hear one of your old CDs – some African stuff about a taxi driver.'

I noticed the green light blinking on the CD-player where I had left it on all night.

'Turn off the stereo, would you?' I said, pointing with a piece of toast.

'Hey, don't ask me to touch it. You know Lisabeth won't let me, not since you used her Chris de Burgh record as an ashtray.'

'All right, I'll do it myself,' I said wearily. 'So what did you and Murdo talk about?'

'Oh, this and that,' she said coyly. 'But only for a few minutes, really, whilst I got him a bandage.'

'Springsteen?'

''Fraid so. Murdo said he had three dogs at home and the secret with all animals was that if you treated them like humans, they would respond like humans.'

'Poor Murdo, but it's a common error. Dogs think they're human, but cats believe they're God.'

'To err is human, to purr divine.'

I looked at her in amazement.

'That was very good, Fenella.'

'Thank you. I've been thinking about that one.'

I wondered for how long.

'So where did Springsteen get him?'

'Back of the hand. There was quite a bit of blood but he was very brave. Tell him I hope it's healed up.'

I didn't like the way she said that.

'What do you mean?' I asked, suspicious.

'You have checked your messages, haven't you?'

'Yes.'

Well, I had responded to Amy's pager call, only to get a recorded message saying: 'Not going to make it home tonight and one of our Italian buyers wants me in Milan tomorrow so if I get a flight I'll just pick up a few things on the way to Heathrow. Should be back by Friday. See you when I see you.'

'Your messages from Veronica,' Fenella persisted like she was talking to someone whose IQ test had come back negative.

'Oh, them.'

'Yes, them. All the messages she left this morning about your meeting.'

'Meeting? What meeting?'

'This afternoon at her office at two o'clock, with Murdo.'

'Why didn't you tell me?' It was 1.15 p.m. by my fancy new watch and I didn't think I could make it to Veronica's office before Murdo did.

'I told you she'd left messages. I just assumed you were ringing her while I was forced to make you lunch.'

'Look, I told you, I needed the protein. Strewth, you just can't get the staff these days, can you? Where's my jacket?'

'Behind the sofa, where you threw it.'

'Don't worry, I'll get it,' I said, resigned to the fact that if I wanted anything done right, I would have to do it myself. I just couldn't rely on Fenella for anything.

'Where are Armstrong's keys?' I asked, going through my pockets.

'In the freezer compartment in the fridge,' she said smugly.

'Why?'

'You wanted to put them out of temptation's way in case you fancied nipping out for a curry later. Even you said you weren't in any fit state to drive.'

'Yeah, well, that was then and this is now. Make sure Springsteen's got some food before you go, won't you?'

I was half-way down the stairs before I had to stop, about-turn and march back into the flat. Fenella hadn't moved, had just stood there looking at her watch, timing me, tapping her foot impatiently.

'Fenella, sweetie,' I said.

'Yes?'

'Where exactly *is* Armstrong?'

I found Armstrong at the end of Stuart Street and he seemed to be intact although the fuel tank was nearly empty. By the time I'd filled up with diesel and cut all the way across town to Shepherd's Bush, I was running at least half an hour late and I had to suffer the full wrath of Mrs Delacourt's pursed lips and eyes which made a shark's look compassionate as she waved me through into Veronica's office.

Veronica didn't seem to mind, though. She was getting on with Murdo almost as well as Fenella had, in fact she seemed a bit annoyed that I had turned up at all.

'Nice of you to make it, Angel,' she said, all businesslike in a pin-stripe trouser suit.

'Absolutely amazed you made it,' said Murdo with a grin.

He stood up and towered over me. I had forgotten how tall he was and it gave me altitude sickness just making eye contact.

'Oh, your driving wasn't that bad,' I said, shaking his hand – the one without the gigantic sticking plaster.

He seemed genuinely puzzled.

'Actually, I meant I was amazed at how much of our ale you managed to put down yesterday. That was quite impressive for someone not used to it.'

'You should have stuck around last night,' I said confidently. 'Fenella and I finished off the crate you left.'

'Really? I got the impression she was a game on sort of lass –'

'Could we get on, Mr Seton?' Veronica interrupted. 'Find yourself a chair, Angel, we're just finalising the details of your surveillance operation.'

I dragged a chair in from Mrs Delacourt's office, avoiding her killer look and making as much noise as possible. The effort of doing it almost exhausted me and I was relieved to sit down, but I was determined not to nod off as I might miss something.

'Surveillance,' I said knowledgeably, as if I knew what I was talking about. 'You want me to watch a pub, or rather the litter bin in the pub car-park.'

'It's not *quite* as simplistic as that, Angel,' Murdo muttered. 'We need a fresh pair of eyes and ears on this one, on the ground in this country. We've never done that before.'

'We?'

'Brewers, pub operators, publicans, farmers, suppliers – all of us in this country who are losing out to the beer-runners. Oh, we've complained to the government and we've complained in Europe and we've had people in Calais watching the trade grow for five years now. Did you realise that one in five beers drunk at a party last Christmas were smuggled?'

'Good heavens,' I breathed, thinking of what was in my fridge back at Stuart Street. 'They're probably stocking up for the Millennium New Year parties already.'

Murdo turned towards Veronica and grinned broadly.

'I told you he was on the ball, Miss Blugden.' Murdo turned his teeth on me. 'That's exactly what I suspect they're doing and there's a man down in Dover, a Customs and Excise man, who thinks the same.'

'So why isn't he doing something about it?'

It must have come out stronger than I had intended as Veronica hissed: 'Angel . . .'

Fortunately, Murdo came to my rescue.

'No, Miss Blugden, that's a good question. The Customs man is called Lawrence, Nick Lawrence, and he'll explain things to you personally, but his main problem is he has other fish to fry.

If you think about it, it's quite ridiculous that Her Majesty's Customs and Excise should be chasing booze-runners on the eve of the twenty-first century. The Customs men should be watching out for drugs and guns, not nasty French lager. They've doubled the number of Customs officers in Dover in the last year or so but they're still only dealing with the tip of the iceberg. Go down there, talk to Nick Lawrence and see for yourself. It's rife down there, quite rife.'

'And the connection with this pub, the Rising Sun?' Veronica asked to prove she had been listening.

'Nick Lawrence has a theory about that, but I want him to tell Angel himself. I've given you his number, haven't I?'

Veronica nodded and held up a business card to show she hadn't lost it.

'And you're sure it couldn't just be that the pub is on the fiddle and is selling the stuff?' It still seemed the obvious answer to me.

'Oh no,' Murdo said emphatically, 'no way. It simply isn't in character. Once you meet Ivy you'll see why.'

'Ivy?'

'The landlady of the Rising Sun. She's a diamond. An absolute diamond. You two will get on famously.'

Why did that sound bad?

6

Amy rang me from Milan the next morning to say that her Italian job would take longer than she expected and involved a return at the weekend via Paris after a photo-shoot there on Saturday. And did I fancy joining Nigel the photographer and three of the TALtop models on the Eurostar to make a party of it? What she meant was would I chauffeur Nigel around, get him on the right train and to the right location without him losing any of his cameras or any of the models, as had happened in the past.

When I said no, I was going to be busy, there was a deathly silence at the other end of the phone then she said OK, if that was my attitude.

I didn't like to remind her that not only did I have attitude, but I knew how to use it.

Before leaving the Hampstead house I packed an emergency sports bag with some clean clothes and a British Airways First Class toiletries pouch. (I get Amy to steal them for me. Their razors are excellent and the revitalising foot spray is almost as effective as a Mace spray if you get close enough to the eyes.)

I also took a camera and a dictaphone recorder because I figured no well-dressed private eye should be without such things. The camera was an Olympus 2000 Zoom and the dictaphone was a Grundig. Both were Amy's, but she wasn't using them. She also wasn't using either of the cars and I ended up juggling three sets of keys trying to make the right choice.

The Freelander I ruled out almost immediately as it looked like a posh company car version of a Land Rover, which is what it was. Down in Dover I would look like a Hampstead reject nipping over to Calais for some cheap Chablis and a camembert for a dinner party. In Armstrong, I'd probably get beaten up by genuine Dover taxi drivers who thought I was a London musher stealing their trade. I didn't know if they ran Austin black cabs down there but I didn't want to risk it. (Manchester and Birmingham, I could blend in and one or two other places too, but black London cabs were still a specialised beast most suited to their natural habitat. A bit like a mole, really; supremely at home tunnelling under a suburban lawn but at a bit of a loss swinging through the canopy of a rain forest.)

The BMW, a Series 5 convertible, therefore chose itself. It was a respectable four years old now and thus had slipped down the Most Wanted list of cars stolen to order in London. Being a convertible, it had suffered the odd knife slash to the roof proving that amateur thieves still fancied it even if the professionals no longer considered bending a coat hanger for anything less than a brand new Series 7. And it hadn't been washed or valeted for a couple of months, so the ashtray was full and the passenger seat and floor were littered with screwed-up tissues and empty Diet Coke cans. Just the sort of image I wanted to project.

Rather than struggling through the West End and crossing the river into Brixton and Lewisham, where BMWs were known as 'Bobs' after Bob Marley and the Wailers, I cut north through Hendon and on to the AI until it hit the M25 orbital at South Mimms. In the morning, the M25 clockwise is always quieter than anticlockwise so I made good time, putting my foot down on the early stretch through Hertfordshire and easing off once I got into Essex, where the traffic cops were known to be more active.

I have always enjoyed going over the Dartford Bridge, with its panoramic views of oil storage tanks one way and the fins of the Thames Barrier the other. It is worth the £1 toll whereas crossing south-to-north you have to use the Dartford Tunnel and you pay for a lungful of the exhaust fumes of the car in front.

Half-way over the bridge, I passed a white Transit van. On the rear doors, written with a finger in the dust and grime, was the legend: IF DRIVEN PROPERLY, PLEASE REPORT STOLEN.

I liked that. You saw far too many of those prissy 'Like My Driving? Then ring . . .' notices on the back of big corporation trucks these days. What sort of person likes driving behind an articulated lorry carrying frozen fish fingers enough to admire the trucker's skills? A sad one, that's who. And what sort of person would bother to phone a corporate PR answerphone to record their gratitude? The one who would buy the T-shirt saying 'I'm Upholding the Highway Code' when everybody else was wearing one saying 'I'm Pissed and I've Got a Gun'.

I wondered if the Transit van was beer-running, but I could tell from the way it sat on its suspension and swayed in the wind going over the bridge that it was empty.

There, I congratulated myself as I threw my pound coin into the Auto Toll basket, I was an expert already.

Immediately after the toll booths, something like ten lines of traffic do a Grand Prix start to get back on to the M25 motorway. There's nothing much to it, the trick is point yourself roughly towards the middle, go like hell and don't look to either side.

After that I took the M20 exit and followed the signs for

Maidstone, Ashford and the Channel Tunnel entrance outside Folkestone. Almost immediately the traffic dropped away enough to allow the Beamer to hit a respectable cruising speed. Even the sun came out, but not enough to make me put the roof down. I might have been tempted if Amy had had any decent music cassettes in the car but I had forgotten to pack any of mine and so I made do with some re-released BBC Sessions of Led Zeppelin. So what if they were over twenty years old? At least I knew all the words.

I stopped at a service station to buy a couple of maps, one of the North Downs area and one a town plan of Dover itself. Next to the local maps was an entire shelf of road atlases and guides to driving in Europe and, in particular, the Calais area. I picked one at random called 'A Shopper's Guide to Calais' and opened it up. On one side was a street map of the town itself, surrounded by adverts for local French businesses. On the other side was a much bigger map which showed only the main roads and the locations of the cheap booze warehouses and hypermarkets, around thirty of them. Nothing else, it would appear, was of the slightest interest to the visitor to France.

Outside the service station shop I dug my mobile phone out of my bag and made a call.

There was a time before the phones were digital when you could really freak out the electronics on the petrol pumps if you used a mobile near a garage. There would be an innocent businessman ringing his girlfriend telling her he was going to be late because he had to go home first, and down the rank an irate trucker would be trying to turn off a jammed pump as diesel spilled out of his full tank and over his boots. Ah, those were the days.

I punched in the number of Nick Lawrence the Customs man, from the card Murdo had left with Veronica, and entered it in the memory just in case I needed to call him again. It was his direct line and he answered on the second ring with the single word 'Lawrence'.

I said who I was and who had sent me and he told me he'd been expecting a call and would be free at one o'clock. When I asked where, he suggested a pub called the King Louis and, with the town plan stretched over the bonnet of the BMW, I got him to direct me through the one-way system. He told me to head for a multi-storey car-park as there was no parking at the pub, but it was just around the corner so I'd find it.

I asked if we'd find any beer-runners there and he said no, not there, and then hung up like he had something more important to do.

Somehow I managed to refold the town plan without ripping it and climbed into the car before consulting the tourist map of the North Downs area. I found the village of Whitcomb up what was called the Elham valley and worked out a route which would get me off the motorway and across country so that I could do a drive-by of Murdo's pub the Rising Sun and then pick up the A20 to Dover the other side of Folkestone.

It was still too early for the pub to be open, but I had plenty of time before the meet with Nick Lawrence so I might as well check it out. If nothing else I could keep a private eye on the Bottleback bin in the car-park, which might give me a clue.

A clue to what was another matter, but I was sure I would spot one if I saw one. And what finer way was there to spend a couple of fresh spring days? It beat going to Paris with a trio of scantily clad models, didn't it?

Didn't it?

The village of Whitcomb was nothing to shout about. Technically it was probably a hamlet with no more than thirty houses strung out either side of a narrow B-road almost as if they'd fallen off the back of some gigantic lorry as it careered down the lane.

If there was a church I didn't see it, nor a village shop. The houses were not thatched or timber-framed or anything cutesy, giving Whitcomb a pretty low rating on the picturesque scale.

The Rising Sun was tacked forgetfully on to the northern end of the village a good half-mile from the last house, set back from a bend in the road. I slowed down to a crawl to get a better look, keeping one eye on the mirror in case I was blocking the road, though I hadn't seen a single other vehicle on it.

Like the village, the pub would never be a contender for a Kent County Tourist Board calendar but a picture of it could have featured in an advertisement for exterior paint, though only as the 'before' shot, not the 'after'. It was probably seventy or eighty years old, which is nothing in country pub terms, built of brick which had been painted sunshine yellow at some time but now looked like bleached custard and had a tile roof.

A weathered inn sign depicting a sun with a beatific, fat smile peeping over a green meadow swung precariously on a free-standing pole from which most of the white paint had flaked. A long rectangular board in a reasonable state of repair broadcast the legend 'Seagrave's Seaside Ale' above the door, which was firmly closed.

To the left of the pub was the car-park, which seemed huge to me but then I was used to London pubs, few of which had them. At the far end were two green plastic bins about five foot high and shaped like beehives with a porthole in the top. I could just make out the words 'Green glass' on one and 'Clear glass' on the other.

That was it. No sign of life anywhere. No clues.

I reversed into the car-park and turned the BMW towards the Dover road.

There are two ways of driving into Dover. Both are spectacular.

You can come in round the castle and think: why did they build that there? Or you can come in, as I did, from the A20 and see the White Cliffs and then the natural harbour below you and think: why only one castle? For God's sake, we're only twenty miles from the enemy, we need more defences than this. You think Land's End is where England stops. That's not the point; Dover is where Europe starts. Dangerwise, this is the direction we should be looking.

The road dives down the famous White Clifs into the town. I spotted a Hovercraft out at sea and a car ferry coming in to dock at the ferry terminal, but there wasn't a bluebird in sight. They had probably been put off by the exhaust fumes of the solid convoy of trucks creeping up the hill out of the port. It really did look like a continuous stream of traffic and almost all were lorries. From their registrations, most were Dutch or French but there was the old German, Dane, Swede, Italian and something I guessed was either Serb or Croat. The sheer number of them made me think the port must be bigger than I remembered, but it was still the same size, it was just that it was incredibly busy.

I thought of something to ask Nick Lawrence when I met him: how on earth can you control what is coming in this constant flood of traffic? I knew the answer already: you can't.

Once down in the town proper, with the old Western Docks and the Hovercraft Terminal on my right, I followed the instructions Lawrence had given me against the town map I had open on the passenger seat. The one-way system wasn't half as difficult as he'd said it was, but you always get that when locals give you directions to where they live. 'Oh, you'll never find it', they say, as if living somewhere easy to find was a bit down-market.

I eased the BMW through the congested High Street and found the old London road. Every other shop seemed to be a Chinese take-away or a kebab shop. I almost felt at home and figured that this beer-running lark must give you an appetite.

Following the map, I doubled back through the one-way system until I saw the signs for a multi-storey car-park. I took a ticket from the machine and zipped up to the second floor, as the first level was jammed solid, to find I had it entirely to myself. That was not a good sign. The earlier arrivals had squeezed uncomfortably into every inch of space on Level 1 rather than drive for an additional ten seconds to get up to the second or third floors. That meant at best that the lifts didn't work or that no one wanted to leave their car out of sight of the pensioner who manned the exit barrier and collected the money. I locked the Beamer and tried the door handle out of sheer paranoia, making a mental note to tell Veronica she should pitch for the job of supplying the car-park with video cameras.

The rear exit to the multi-storey brought me out on to a back street behind a shopping precinct and at the end of that I could see the King Louis pub on the corner of the street opposite.

I hadn't thought about it until I saw the sign above the door but the pub was named after Louis Armstrong and the sign was a painted reproduction of a photograph of old Satchelmouth himself. A sun-faded notice in one of the windows claimed there was live jazz there every Sunday night. I should have brought my trumpet and busked a few quid.

It was still twenty minutes before noon, the magical hour

which most Englishmen think is the official start of the drinking day, though it doesn't seem to worry the French or the Germans or virtually anybody else. But I thought, what the hell. Somewhere on the world wide web it was after noon and that was good enough for me.

The pub wasn't empty, but you'd have needed heat-sensors to detect that there were six or seven customers in there from the outside. They were fairly evenly spread throughout the one bar, which dog-legged into an L shape ending in a raised stage area decorated with old posters and photographs of jazz musicians. All were reading newspapers and most were smoking, trails of smoke from their ashtrays snaking up to the ceiling, mingling with the dust motes in the sunlight from the windows. Not one of them looked up as I entered and moved to the bar.

There was a single bar stool and I nodded towards it. The man behind the bar said, 'Good morning' and shrugged at the stool to indicate that it wasn't anyone's favourite seat, or at least nobody important or at the very least nobody coming in today with cash money.

I ordered a pint of Seagrave's Top Mild in a tone of voice which I hoped sounded as if I knew what I was talking about. The barman looked surprised, but didn't say anything and reached for the beer pump. I looked around rapidly as I settled my buttocks on the stool. I was the only one drinking the Top Mild and there was a good reason for this: I should have looked first. It was the same situation as when I was once touring Scotland (driving a very bad, but very loud, Heavy Metal band) and had asked a Scot, one Slasher Carmichael, which whiskies to drink in the pubs on the tour. He'd told me to watch what the locals drank and follow suit, as that would be the best value on the premises. It was good advice I should have remembered. There was a Rule of Life in there somewhere.

The barman was a big guy with a beard worthy of an American Civil War officers' call and his short-sleeved shirt held arms as big as Parma hams except that Parma hams don't normally have tattoos saying 'Do NOT start with me, you will NOT win'. He also had several anchors and what I hoped was a torpedo covering one bicep. With that beard he could have passed for a retired merchant seaman. This was Dover; he probably was.

He gave me my beer and change and shuffled off to the other

end of the bar to go back to the *Daily Mirror* crossword. So much for conversation, but that seemed to be the norm. Maybe this bunch didn't mind drinking before noon, as long as they didn't have to talk to anybody. I felt as if I should have brought a book with me, or knitting. To keep myself occupied I tried to read all the jazz posters dotted around the pub and it was only then I noticed that most of them had nothing to do with jazz at all. A fair proportion were notices, some of them handwritten. Among them were: 'Don't ask for cigarette papers, we don't sell them', 'Runners touting for business will be shown the street' and 'All spirits in this establishment are legal'. I got the impression that the people who ran the pub had something on their minds.

'The reason they don't sell cigarette papers,' said a voice behind me, 'is that there's no legal rolling tobacco sold in the town any more, so if you've got some it must be smuggled. It's a form of protest. You must be Roy Angel.'

'And you must be early,' I said as I turned my head.

He was about my height but chunkier, with light brown hair cropped very short. Under an open reversible storm coat he wore a light blue suit, a four-button Italian cut with high lapels, neither of which he had bought in an Oxfam shop. I guessed he was about forty but you can never be sure these days.

'Nick Lawrence,' he said to me, then, to the bearded barman: 'Usual, Bob.'

The barman took the top off a bottle of Coke and placed it on the bar. Lawrence picked it up without waiting for a glass, making no effort to pay. He tipped it towards me then took a swig.

He seemed to be settled where he was, leaning against the bar next to me, but I thought he might prefer a seat so I asked; 'Are you OK to talk here?'

Lawrence chose to misunderstand.

'We're fine here, aren't we, Bob?' he said loudly and the barman bobbed his beard twice. 'This is a runner-free zone, this pub is, just about the only place in Dover where you pay full whack for everything. Right, Bob?'

There was a grunt from somewhere inside the beard.

'Bob's had his car vandalised and his windows smashed but he still chucks 'em out if they come round touting for orders.'

'Orders?'

'Oh yeah, they take your order and do your shopping for you, whether you want them to or not.' He saw me looking at my pint of beer. 'Not beer, though, not in a pub. A publican would have to be really stupid to sell French beer across the bar. The beer goes to the corner shop, 'specially the ones run by Asians who take it rather than risk a petrol-bombing. But a pub could be tempted by some duty-free spirits or cigarettes at Belgian prices.'

He produced a packet of Benson & Hedges and offered me one but I declined.

'No, look,' he said.

On the corner of the flip-top of the pack was a paper seal which carried a price in francs – F118,00 –and the description '20 Sigaretten'.

'I bought these last night out of a ciggy machine in a pub in Folkestone. The landlord of the pub knew nothing about them. Genuine. He wasn't on the fiddle, the guy who filled the cigarette machine was though. Buys his own stock at £2 a packet and retails them through a pub machine for £4, pockets the difference. Nice work if you can get it.'

He lit one of the cigarettes with a disposable lighter and exhaled blue-grey smoke in my face, keeping eye contact, almost willing me to complain.

'I'm told you're the man to ask about beer-running,' I said, not allowing my eyes to water just to show him I was tough too.

He waited a beat before answering.

'Ah yes, Murdo. I try and help him when I can. Feel sorry for him in many ways, but he should have seen all this coming. If I'd've been him, I'd've sold up and gone to live in Switzerland five years ago. There's so much smuggled beer in Kent now I don't know how he keeps his pubs open. He won't beat the runners.'

'Can't you?'

'You mean the full might of Her Majesty's Customs and Excise?'

'I suppose so.'

He shrugged his shoulders.

'Other priorities, I'm afraid. It all comes down to money, to budgets. We get more officers, we have to justify them by increasing our results, increasing our productivity. We have targets now, comparisons with industry, all that fucking bullshit.'

I tried to look sympathetic for the plight of a tax-collector. It was a first.

'And beer-running doesn't count for many Brownie points, is that it?'

'Our number one priority: drugs. Has to be. Big problem, big villains, big result every time we score, lots of good press and public approval. Priority number three: guns. Not as sexy a story as you might think but the politicians love us for it. Good for law and order and keeps the Police Federation quiet.'

He was on a roll so I didn't interrupt.

'Four: tobacco. Easy to smuggle, dead easy, and mega-profits. Mega tax-loss for the government too, and nobody's going to stick up for smokers these days, are they? So we've got to be seen to be hot on the ciggy-runners and sometimes you can score heavily. We did a lorry two weeks ago, supposed to be carrying rolls of newsprint. One of them was hollow. Contained one and a half million cigs. Whammo! One pull and that's £4,000,000 to the good on the revenue accounts, or at least it looks that way.

'And then, number five, you've got beer and essentially two crimes. You've got the carousel operation, which is big time. For that, you need capital and a warehouse and you buy your booze in England, pretend you're exporting it so you get the duty back. We bust a carousel operation and it's worth a coupla million and somebody goes down for six or eight years. But your average beer-runner is small time. A vanload of beer is worth what – five hundred quid in lost revenue?'

'But it's worth more than that to the smuggler,' I said.

'Sure, but we have to catch them reselling it, or the police do. Frankly, there's more chance of doing them for overloading a van, a traffic offence, than nicking them red-handed when they sell it on.'

'And number two?' I asked.

'What?'

'You never said what your priority number two was.'

'Oh, yeah, right. It's pornography, mostly gay porn and paedophile shit and all Triple X rated, heavy stuff. And most of it is legal in Europe. Funny thing, really, if it hadn't been for the beer-runners we wouldn't have got the extra officers and we wouldn't have found half of what was coming in.'

He took another pull on his bottle of Coke.

'Some people were really looking forward to us going into Europe, for the porn. They saw it as one of the benefits of the Single European Market.'

'One of the benefits the government didn't tell us about,' I said.

'That's not for me to say, Mr Angel, I just nick 'em.'

'If you can find them,' I offered.

'Oh, we know where they are, or most of them. Come on, I'll show you where they live.'

The first thing that unnerved me was the obvious surprise on Nick Lawrence's face when he saw where I had parked the BMW and the fact that it still had a wheel at each corner. When I asked him if this was a bad area, he said, no, that was where we were going.

That was the second thing.

I followed Lawrence's directions through town and out on the old Folkestone road to an area known as Clarendon, which turned out to be a rabbit warren of houses turned into bedsit apartments. Lawrence told me to take a left, then a right and then slow down.

'That one,' he said, pointing to a terraced house with a faded green door.

I slowed to a halt ten feet beyond it. Lawrence was holding out a £10 note.

'Take this and go down the alley to the back door and buy me a carton of cigarettes.'

'Just like that?'

'Just like that.'

I switched off the engine and climbed out of the Beamer, taking the keys with me.

The house Lawrence had pointed out didn't look out of the ordinary unless you looked closely. The front door wasn't really a door, well, not a normal door. There was no letter box, no street number and no handle, though there was a concave dent in the wood where one should have been. The windows, downstairs and up, all had thick net curtains which made it impossible to see inside. The only thing which distinguished it from the house next door was that there was a seagull perched on the roof.

I walked down the alley and round the back and spotted the seagull from the rear. For no particular reason he let out a loud 'Caw!' which scared the hell out of me and I realised then what Hitchcock had seen in them.

The back door of the house was through a ten-foot square piece of dirt which had once been a garden but had been stomped flat so that not even the weeds could force their way up. The back door itself was another solid piece of wood, almost certainly not the door the house came with originally, with a newish Yale lock. The bottom half of the kitchen window had been painted out white with the same stuff people paint on greenhouses. Apart from the seagull, there was no sign of life.

I knocked on the door and nothing happened although I thought I saw something flash by the upper half of the window. I decided to count slowly to ten and then wander back to Lawrence but I only got to four when the lock snapped open.

The young boy who stared at me was maybe eleven years old, thin and sunken-cheeked. He had greasy black hair and a sallow complexion which suggested jaundice or that he never left the house. He stared at me with dark brown eyes and didn't say a word.

Then I realised he wasn't staring at me, but at the £10 note I was holding in my left hand. To be sure, I moved it from side to side and his eyes followed.

'Cigarettes?' I tried and his head moved up and down.

'Zigaretten,' he said, or something like it and moved over to the sink.

There was a chair there, which he had stood on to look out of the window at me. He pulled it aside and opened the cupboard under the sink and stuck his hand in, pulling out first one then another pack of Benson & Hedges.

Suddenly they were in my hands and the note was in the pocket of his jeans.

'Beer?' he said and I tried to figure his accent. 'Pilsner?'

While I hesitated he stepped to a pantry door and pulled on the plastic handle. The cupboard was far from bare, it was crammed floor to ceiling with bottles of French beer, twenty-four to a case.

'Just these,' I said holding up the cigarettes, 'for the moment, thanks.'

He didn't seem to understand, but didn't seem worried about the fact either, he just held the back door for me until I stepped out and then he clicked the lock.

Before I got to the end of the alley the hairs on the back of my neck told me something was wrong. The thought flashed through my brain that Lawrence had somehow set me up to buy smuggled cigarettes, but that was crazy as it was only four hundred and he had given me the money to do it.

I stuffed the smokes under my jacket as I turned on to the street.

Lawrence was out of the BMW, leaning on it, his arms folded. Three houses down the street two middle-aged men wearing leather jackets were standing in the doorway, hands in pockets staring at Lawrence. Something made me look behind me and at the other end of the street, on the corner, were three more men under a lamp post, all of them giving Lawrence – and now me – the evil eye.

'Done deal?' Lawrence asked me, dead calm.

'Yeah, no problem.'

'Let's go, then.'

But instead of getting in the car, he pushed himself away from it and stood in the middle of the pavement. He held both hands out in front of him, clenching them into fists, his arms straight. Then he moved both arms to his right and swung them across his body as if he was holding a battering ram to thump something.

Which was exactly what the pantomime was all about.

Back in the car I fumbled the key into the ignition. Lawrence got in and slammed his door. The five guys watching us hadn't moved but I found I was sweating.

'Just leaving them a message,' he said. 'Telling them the next time I'm round here, I'll be bringing the old masterkey with me.'

I realised what the dents in the front door were, the result of a Customs raid or 'knock' with one of the hand-held rams they had bought in from America after watching one too many episodes of *NYPD Blue*.

I pulled the BMW away from the kerb and headed down the street, passing the two guys in the doorway who watched us without blinking.

'Get the fags?' Lawrence asked, lighting up one of his own.

'Yeah.' I dug into my jacket and flipped the packs to him. 'There wasn't any change.'

'Can't argue at those prices. See any beer in there?'

'Some. About enough for an Irish wake.'

'Welcome to Dover. Take a right here. Let's get something to eat.'

I turned as he instructed and we headed back towards the town centre.

'You shop there regularly?'

'No, but I go calling on them from time to time.' He made the battering-ram movement he had out on the street. 'Knock, knock? I've got the masterkey! Who served you?'

'A kid. Probably should have been at school.'

'Somebody has to keep an eye on the stock while Dad's at the office.'

'The office?'

'Well, in his case, the twelve o'clock ferry coming in from Calais. It'll probably be the fourth run he's made today since he clocked on about 2 a.m. One of those other oiks on the street will take over from him this afternoon. They like to offer a twenty-four-hour service.'

'The kid is Czech, isn't he?' I said, without really knowing why I thought it might be important.

'Very good, Roy, very observant,' said Lawrence, looking at me as if genuinely impressed. 'Yeah, he's Czech. So's his dad. So is everybody who lives on that street. Interesting that, isn't it?'

Yes it was, and worrying.

But not half as worrying as the realisation that Lawrence was setting me up.

7

'It's not local, you know,' said Lawrence, his hand negotiating an octopus of chips towards his mouth. 'The fish. Oh, it's probably caught just up the coast but then it goes up to London and gets filleted and frozen before being sent back here.'

'Mmmm,' I said through a mouthful, trying to give the impression that he was talking to someone who gave a toss.

His idea of taking me to lunch was that I drove as he directed to a fish and chip shop he knew, I handed over a £10 note and he hopped out of the Beamer to 'get them in' and, incidentally, keep the change. Then he had me drive on to the Marine Parade and he selected a bench seat with a sea view in what appeared to be the municipal gardens. It gave you a great incentive to eat your fish and chips quickly, before they congealed into a single lump.

'So what's with the Czech connection?' I asked, if only to get him off the topic of fish. I half expected a lecture on the historical significance of the Dover sole.

'They're a gang, that's all,' he said, spraying flecks of batter over his chin. 'Flavour of the month, sure, but next year it'll be somebody else, Bulgarians, Croats, who knows?'

'What are they doing here?'

'We didn't even know they *were* here until a couple of months ago when the Social Security people did a swoop. There are four or five extended families, a coupla hundred of them, all living in the same street or bedsits within sight of each other. Only about three of them speak English. You going to eat that cod?'

'Help yourself.' I offered him my paper parcel and waved the chips away as well. 'What brought them?'

'What brings anybody to a port? Boats or contraband. Europe has stuff we want but can't have or can't afford. Beer from France, drugs from Holland, ciggies from Belgium or Spain. How does it get here? On a boat through a port. Just needs somebody to bring it in. Every lowlife on the Continent knows they can make a fast buck on the Channel run. They come, they sign on at the Benefits Agency, they work the beer runs for a month, they go.'

I wiped my fingers on a tissue, Lawrence used the bottom corner of his storm coat and continued to eat chips.

'How do they manage if only three of them speak English?'

'The kids pick it up first, usually from the television or films. It's the kids who take dad down to the signing-on office –'

'No, I meant how do they sell the beer and the tobacco?'

Lawrence shrugged.

'Not round here, that's for sure. Oh sure, they'll sell you the odd carton of fags or a coupla cases of lager round the back door like you saw, but the bulk quantities end up in London or up north, Manchester, Sheffield, Huddersfield, places like that. The West Midlands police did a road check on the motorway just before Christmas and pulled enough smuggled booze to fill two warehouses in Coventry. They called off the operation after three days because they'd run out of storage space.'

'Were your Czechs involved?'

'They're not *my* Czechs. And no, they weren't. They rarely leave Dover.'

'So there's a middle man somewhere, buying the stuff off the beer-runners and distributing it.'

'Seems to be. It's the best way if you think about it. Let somebody else run the risk of crossing the Channel and getting clocked. If our boys don't spot them, we at least get their vehicles on closed-circuit TV and the brewers have their own people on the other side, in Calais, logging the overloaded vans, spotting the frequent flyers. That's what we call the guys who do four or five crossings a day, usually with a different vehicle every trip.'

'Then there must be a base or a distribution centre somewhere nearby,' I reasoned. 'You can't get up to Sheffield and back four or five times a day.'

'Exactly.' He scrunched up his fish and chip papers and for a moment I thought he was considering throwing them out to sea.

'But you haven't found it?'

'Nope.'

'Are you looking for it?'

'Nope.'

'Other priorities?'

'Yep.'

Nick Lawrence didn't have much more he could – or would – tell me, so he walked me back to Amy's car, dumping his chip paper in a litter bin on the way. A lone seagull landed on the rim of the bin, sniffed once then flew off. Lawrence hadn't left any pickings.

I gave him the cartons of cigarettes I had bought with his money and he stuck them under one arm, shook my hand and said, 'Good luck with – whatever' and he wandered off along the sea front.

I estimated that I still had several hours to kill before anything interesting happened at the Rising Sun, so I decided to head north out of Dover on the A2 and then swing down into Whitcomb from the other side of the Downs. As you do that, you drive down Marine Parade, heading straight for the cavernous entrance to the Ferry Terminal at the Eastern Docks. At night, lit up, it really can look like the gateway to hell or at least the overspill car-park for hell if they've got a busy night on.

At the last minute, though, you realise there is a roundabout in the road and by following round to the right you are suddenly on the Jubilee Way and the A2 itself and you are, literally, up and away as the road goes up on stilts and sweeps around the cliff to bring you out on the other side of Dover Castle. It is a spectacular piece of road and gives you great views of the harbour if you are coming down it into the port. If you are leaving the town, well then you get a different angle on the castle and a cheap laugh at the expense of the foreign tourist as by the time they see the first sign saying 'Remember to Drive on the Left' they have already travelled nearly a mile and are well confused.

I had driven this way before and it was a quiet time of the afternoon with little traffic, not even a confused Belgian to watch out for. That was probably why I noticed the two figures hunched in brightly coloured rainproof ponchos sitting in an otherwise deserted picnic area to the right of the road, on the edge of those famous White Cliffs. They were obviously watching for something, perched on camp stools with what

I guessed were binoculars on tripods in front of them. I didn't peg them for birdwatchers as not only was there no sign of a bluebird, there wasn't even a seagull in sight. And anyway, their binoculars were pointing downwards into the Ferry Terminal, not up into the sky.

Just for the sheer devilment of it, I pulled off the main road and followed the signs which said 'Picnic site', parking the BMW in a crunch of gravel about twenty feet behind the pair of them. They didn't seem to have a vehicle anywhere in sight but they had several bags and two metal suitcases, the sort photographers carry their cameras in. They didn't seem worried that a car had parked close to them when it had an entire empty car-park to choose from, and neither of them even turned to look in my direction. Or at least not until I had got out of the car and zipped up my jacket against the wind and walked up behind them and said:

'Hi there. On the look-out for beer-runners?'

The figure on the right, dressed in a red waterproof with matching sou'wester, turned her head and looked up at me.

'I beg your pardon? Can we help you?' she said in an accent which would have cut glass, at range, in any of the Home Counties.

Her partner, in a green plastic poncho and hat, didn't move from her bent position. Her eyes glued to a pair of tripod-mounted binoculars which could have graced the conning tower of a U-boat, she said:

'Is he from the National Farmers Union, Daphne?'

'Are you?' asked Red Hat or Daphne as it seemed she was called.

The question had thrown me, I admit, but not as much as what I was seeing now I was up close if not personal.

The one called Daphne had a folded tartan rug at her feet. Laid out on it in the way a surgeon lays out his scalpels and clamps, were a Nikon with the longest telephoto lens I had ever seen, a short wave radio which looked suspiciously like police issue and a digital camera of the sort which doesn't come cheap (£1400) even when fenced (£900). In her right hand she held a mobile phone with a wire running up the sleeve of her water-proof to a neck mike and then an ear-piece, a state-of-the-art hands-free version. Her thumb was poised over the Send button. I guessed she had an armed response team on speed dial.

'Er . . . no . . . I'm not from anybody,' I said. 'I was just curious when I saw you spy . . . er . . . watching the ferries down there. I'm interested in beer-runners, you see. Smugglers, boozecruisers, that sort of thing.'

Daphne smiled at me, but then I think she smiled at everyone and that made it just that little bit more difficult to lie to her face but I thought she would go along with the story that I was a prize-winning investigative journalist for one of the respectable papers.

'I hope he's not a journalist,' said Green Hat, still using the binoculars like she was tracking a convoy.

'Of course I'm not,' I said quickly. 'I'm working for a local brewery doing a survey of smuggled beer. Seton's Brewery at Seagrave, you may have heard of them.'

'Oh yes,' said Daphne still smiling, 'my husband owns shares in them.'

That put me in my place. I tell the truth and I'm already reduced to a mere employee.

'But you won't spot many beer-runners these days, not here,' she went on. 'Well, not at this time of day. Most of them use the ferries at night, say between 1 a.m. and 6 a.m., at least the traditional white van trade does. But you don't see half as many as you did two or three years ago. It's the Tunnel, you know, the beer-runners are using flat-back trucks and estate cars on Le Shuttle these days. I think they must get a cheaper rate or something. We used to see the white vans all the time coming up the hill here. They were terribly slow some of them because they were so overloaded, and the drivers used to wave to us. One of them even gave us a bottle of vodka one Christmas. The good stuff, Stolichnaya.'

I think I remembered to close my gaping mouth at that point. I was certainly tempted to ask her if she had a spare folding stool so I could sit down and take notes.

'But you're not here watching for smugglers, are you?'

'Oh no, not smugglers. We're not interested in what's coming *in*, only what's going *out*.'

Forget the stool, I needed to lie down but there wasn't a psychiatrist's couch in sight.

'Going out?'

'Exports – of animals,' she said slowly as if she was explaining which was the soup spoon to a particularly slow grandchild. 'Live animals. They are transported in the most appalling conditions. We have leaflets on the subject if you are interested.'

I'll bet they had. I remembered the protests when crowds of middle-aged women, students and a fair sprinkling of the usual Rent-A-Mob suspects just out for a punch-up had blockaded ports like Dover and smaller, private ones such as Brightlingsea in Essex, to stop the export of live animals to the Continent. The animals were mostly calves – all long tongues and wide, brown eyes – destined for the Dutch veal trade, or occasionally sheep and little woolly lambs, all squashed into trucks, unable to move or eat for days on end. There was no doubt it was an unpleasant trade, but I had often wondered if the export of live pigs would have garnered as much sympathy. Not as photogenic, you see, and nowhere near as cuddly.

Things had got out of hand, as you should have expected if you put middle-class Britain on a crusade involving animals. The police had been called by the port owners, then the police had called in the Riot Squad and even used horses for crowd control. Now there was a moral dilemma for the protestors. Assaulting a policeman was one thing, handbagging a police *horse* was a matter of conscience. It had all turned ugly and got quite violent. People had got hurt; mostly kids and innocent bystanders, as usual. The government had promised to do something or other, as usual.

'I thought the Government had done something about that?' I said, then added: 'Because it was a disgrace, wasn't it? The conditions those animals had to endure, I mean.'

Daphne softened visibly and slipped the mobile phone into a pocket.

'Oh, they brought in some regulations, quotas and things, and tried to make the lorry drivers stick to schedules with rest periods and things, but they still have to be watched – to make sure.'

'So that's what you're doing, is it? Watching for cattle trucks?'

I pointed to her set of binoculars, a flash single-lens, very modern pair on the tripod in front of her.

'That's right. Constant vigilance, that's what we call it. Round the clock surveillance. Spying, I suppose. We are the private eyes of the animal kingdom. Say it like that and it sounds quite exciting.'

'There seems to be plenty to spy on around here,' I said under my breath. 'So you spot 'em and snap 'em do you?'

Daphne looked down at the cameras at her feet. Her friend in the green hat snorted as if it was the stupidest question she had heard since a canvasser had called at the last election asking if she would consider voting Liberal Democrat.

'If it's at night we have to rely on infra-red and the night shift has one of those cameras developed by that nice David Attenborough so he could film badgers during the dark. What we do during the day is photograph the licence plate and if there are obvious signs of overcowding or cruel conditions, then we use the digital camera. We have a friend in Dover who can feed it straight into a computer and e-mail the image to the Ministry of Agriculture in London. The best we've done is having an e-mail to the Minister in eight minutes.'

I was impressed. I was very impressed.

'I'm impressed,' I said to prove it.

'Somebody has to do something, ' said Daphne. 'If you could see what those poor creatures have to go through ... it's a national disgrace. Would you like a mug of soup?'

She reached down to one of the canvas bags at her feet and unzipped it. Inside were half a dozen shiny steel Thermos flasks.

'They're all home-made. We have tomato and basil, Scotch broth with pearl barley –' so they didn't mind the little lambs once they were dead –'and a clear borscht – that's beetroot – spiked, I think they say, with vodka.'

This was getting ridiculous.

Here were two wonderfully nutty English ladies old enough to have been snogged by Philip Marlowe spending their retirement on the wild and wet White Cliffs over Dover pretending to be private eyes. Fair enough, I was pretending to be one too, but the point was these two old dears were better informed about booze-running than I was. And they had better equipment. Their cameras were better, they had state-of-the-art communications and I didn't have any binoculars at all. They were even better fed than I was, and they probably weren't on expenses.

'He's had lunch,' said Green Hat gruffly.

'Oh yes,' said Daphne, blushing. 'I forgot.'

'Excuse me?' I said when the penny finally dropped.

'We . . . saw you,' said Daphne, bending over to zip up her bag to give her something to do so she didn't have to look at me. 'Eating your fish and chips with your friend down on the Promenade.'

Like an idiot, I stood on tiptoe and looked over the cliff down into the town below.

'Through these.' She patted her binoculars. 'We get bored when there aren't many trucks.'

'So you watch people,' I said sternly. 'You pick them at random and try and guess what they do for a living, or who they're meeting or what they'll do next. Is that the game?'

'Why, yes. You've played it yourself?'

No, but I've bet on it.

'And you've been watching me?'

'Only when you were near the Marine Gardens with your friend. We can't see much further than that into town. Not into bedrooms or anything like that.'

Well, that was a relief. With all the security cameras around these days (ones that work, not necessarily those from Rudgard and Blugden) you could also be under constant surveillance from little old ladies who suspected you of being unkind to animals. Was nowhere safe?

'He's still there,' said Green Hat.

'Excuse me?'

'Your friend. The one you had fish and chips with. He's still there walking up and down Marine Parade.'

For the first time she unglued her face from the eyepieces of the binoculars and looked at me. She had a jawline I wouldn't argue with.

'See for yourself,' she said, standing up and putting a hand into the middle of her back as she stretched.

Daphne waved at Green Hat's vacant seat.

'Go on, let's have a look. It'll be fun,' she said and began to adjust her own tripod.

I nodded to Green Hat – not totally convinced that she wasn't going to cosh me from behind – and sat down.

'Nice glasses,' I said and she seemed impressed that I had used the right jargon.

'My husband took them personally from the commander of U-265 in May 1945.'

I might have known. I sat down and leaned in to the eye-pieces. The rubber surrounds smelled of lavender.

'There he is,' Daphne was saying, 'just down from where you had lunch. He's talking to those two men.'

I had to make only a minor adjustment to see what she was talking about. Yes, it could have been Nick Lawrence, or someone wearing a similar coat, but it was difficult to tell at that distance. The two guys with him were equally minuscule and all I could tell was that they were wearing leather jackets just like the guys in the street where I had bought the cigarettes. The guys that Lawrence had implied were part of a Czech gang. But then, I was wearing a leather jacket too.

'That could be him,' I admitted, 'but it's difficult at this –'

''Course it's him,' Green Hat snorted behind me, 'I've had him in view since you left him. Bugger all else happening on the sea front, so I kept him in my sights.'

Thank God she was an animal lover. No grizzly bear would stand a chance.

'I don't know . . .'

But then I did, because the figure I was now convinced was Nick Lawrence was suddenly holding a gold package, which could just be two packs of cigarettes purchased not two hours before, and then he was handing them over to one of the leather jackets.

'You might be right,' I said, which was greeted with another snort. 'It's funny, isn't it, how everyone seems to be watching someone in Dover. Crazy town, eh?'

'We're not the only ones,' said Daphne to my right.

'Pardon?'

'Down and across the street, about four o'clock from where you are now. A blue Volvo estate car, one of the flashy new designs, a V70, parked on the right.'

She was good. She was very good. I wondered if she and her

mate fancied a job with an all-girl snooping firm in London I knew.

I moved the heavy *Kriegsmarine* glasses as she instructed and focused on the Volvo. If it had been there when I had been talking to Lawrence, then I must have driven right by it without noticing it.

The passenger side window was down and I could make out the shape of a shoulder and an elbow and something protruding which could have been a rifle or a lens or a telescope or a microphone or an umbrella for all I knew.

Whatever it was, it was pointed in exactly the same direction I had just been looking, towards Lawrence and the two guys he was talking to.

Like I said, everybody was watching somebody.

I parked in the main street of Whitcomb – the only street in Whitcomb – but no one minded. There wasn't anyone around to mind.

I locked the BMW knowing that Amy would kill me if it got stolen down here in Sleepy Hollow after touring London and the seedy side of Dover. I would be so embarrassed I'd probably offer to help her.

Hands in pockets, I wandered down the road towards the Rising Sun. The Bottleback beehive bins were still there in an otherwise deserted car-park. The Seagrave sign was still roughly above the front door. Nothing had changed since that morning. How the hours dragged in the countryside. I knew pubs in London that had been turned into Seattle Coffee Houses in less time.

A hundred yards beyond the pub and round the bend in the road I got bored with staring at hedgerows, turned on my heel and walked back to see if the pub looked any different or gave me any more clues from that aspect. Nothing sprang into view, but something almost creamed me from behind.

It was a bicycle and of course I realised that immediately – well, as soon as my heart started beating again – ridden by an old man but at a speed which wouldn't have been out of place at a mountain bike trial. The rider was balding on top but with long white hair flowing in his slipstream. He wore black wellington boots, brown cord trousers and two short-sleeved pullovers one over the other. He was hunched over the handle-bars, head down, aiming for the front door of the pub like a bullet.

He had come up behind me without a sound and cut close enough to have picked my pocket. As he reached the pub, he braked in a scrunch of gravel and dismounted by swinging a leg over the crossbar and letting go of the handlebars. The bike rolled forward for about three yards under its own momentum and then fell sideways, propped up against the pub wall. It was a neat trick and one he had obviously been practising; for about fifty years from the look of him.

The old guy stared with approval at his parking technique, rubbed the palms of his hands down the front of his trousers and reached for the latch on the pub door.

I stood there at the entrance to the car-park watching this and wishing that Daphne or her friend Green Hat had been with me.

They would have noticed that the pub was already open ages ago.

'Oh yes, we're open all day, but there's not much call for it.'

The sign above the door was a home-made job, not the sort the local magistrates would have approved of, which read: 'IVY BRACEGIRDLE, Licensed to sell beers, wines, spirits, cider and victuals at reasonable prices and unreasonable times.'

At first I thought Ivy was sitting on a bar stool behind the counter, but she was standing up. When she moved to pull me a pint of Seagrave's Special Bitter, the top of her head came no more than half-way up the ebonied hand pumps.

I didn't even want to guess at her age but beside her the mad cyclist, the only other customer, standing at the end of the bar sipping from a metal tankard, looked like a reject from a Boy Band.

She wore enough make-up to shore up the average garden wall and blood red lipstick to match her nail polish. Her thin arms, already weighed down with thick gold bracelets, looked as if they might snap as she lifted the pint glass around the pumps towards me, but she didn't spill a drop.

I had smiled my best smile at her and ordered a beer and remarked that I hadn't expected the pub to be open.

'Not much call at all these days,' she went on, friendly enough. 'It's a bit like Angostura Bitters. It's always there behind the bar but you don't get much call for it.'

I wasn't too sure about the analogy but I kept smiling.

'I always keep it near the gin.' She looked around at the back fitting on the bar. 'Well, I used to. Just there. That's funny. I can't remember being asked for any for ages. What's this?'

She picked up a large brown bottle and read the label.

'Lovage. What on earth is Lovage? I didn't even know I had that. And I'm not sure I would know what to do with it.'

'It's a herbal cordial,' I said helpfully. 'You put a splash in with brandy, same as you'd put ginger wine in whisky. If you look you'll probably find one called Shrub, they usually come in pairs. Lovage for brandy, shrub for rum. They come from the West Country, down Cornwall. When they used to smuggle brandy ashore the casks sometimes got damaged and seawater got in, so they added lovage to kill the taste. They used shrub for rum and people got to like it.'

If I thought she appreciated my little nugget of gastronomic anthropology, or thought she might just be grateful for a second human being to talk to, I couldn't have been more wrong.

Her face clouded, even under all that make-up.

'Smugglers?' She almost shrieked it. 'Don't talk to me about fucking smugglers! Those bastards are not fit to lick my toilet bowl! Shits and fuckers, all of them!'

I took an involuntary step backwards, taking my beer with me in case she spat in it.

And to think, she probably kissed grandchildren with that mouth.

8

So Ivy had a thing about smugglers. It was understandable and I hadn't been expected to know, being a stranger to the area. And if I thought her language had been a trifle ripe, then I should have heard her a few years ago when the vicar from the next village had asked her to sell raffle tickets for the Harvest Festival and one of the prizes was a case of French beer. Not to mention the lecture she'd given to two families in the village, just before banning them from the pub for life, when she'd discovered they had shopped in Calais for the beer for a Sunday afternoon barbecue.

I got all this from the psycho cyclist, who turned out to be called Dan. He had been a regular for thirty years and there was no danger of him doing a beer run across the Channel. He couldn't swim so there was no way he was getting on a ferry and he was claustrophobic, so the Tunnel was out. No wonder he had never bothered to apply for a passport.

Dan told me all this for the price of a pint, along with a potted history of Ivy's tenancy at the pub and how she had buried two husbands, was determined to leave the pub in a box herself and how she refused to let him make an honest woman of her. He told me in a very loud voice with Ivy standing there behind the bar not three feet away. She sniffed and sighed occasionally as if she had heard it all before, which she certainly had, shaking her head as Dan's story got gradually more outrageous and she pretended to be embarrassed.

It was a double act they had obviously performed many times in front of the customers. That's why there were so many of them.

'What do you do for customers around here?' I asked when I had their trust, or at least when they had run out of things to say.

'Oh, we have our regulars,' Ivy said without much conviction. 'The Major will be in at six, always is.'

'You barred him,' Dan muttered into his beer.

'Yes, but he never listens. Then there's Melanie and her mum, they look in all the time, not as much as before the accident, though. There's Joe and Freda Dyson ...'

'They're barred,' said Dan.

'Frank Osmond and his wife. They drive over from Folkestone every Sunday.'

'Not since he lost his licence.' Thanks, Dan.

'Maybe not. There's the Taylor brothers. They used to come in and play pool twice a week.'

'Doing eighteen months for smuggling cigarettes.'

Ivy looked shocked.

'Are they? The little *fuckers*. They're barred, then. What about the Fowlers?'

'They moved to Ashford last year.'

'Oh.' She seemed pensive. 'I thought I must have barred them.'

'Face it, Ivy, love, the pub trade's dead around here. Marry me and we'll lock the doors and have no more truck with bloody customers.'

'You watch your fucking language, Dan Dexter. I'm not that desperate yet. We've got customers. There's those lads who've started to come in and play darts in the week, they fill the place up.'

'They don't drink much, though, do they?' Dan chipped in helpfully.

'I rely on you and the Major for my wet sales,' Ivy snapped back. 'And talk of the devil, here he comes.'

She must have recognised his tread on the gravel as she couldn't possibly have seen over the bar and out over the frosted lower half of the windows.

'He's not driving tonight,' said Dan, 'so your takings'll be up.'

The door latch clicked and I felt the early evening air cool on the back of my neck.

''Evening Ivy, 'evening Dan,' came a clipped, military voice. 'Had to hoof it tonight. Some damn wide boy's parked a bloody great Panzer at the end of my drive. Couldn't get the old motor out.'

'Er ... back in a minute,' I said, diving for the door.

By six-thirty the pub was humming, the sound of merriment and laughter bouncing off its oaken beams, horse brasses and ranks of pewter and silver tankards hanging from hooks above the bar. There were seven of us in the place now and I had to resist the temptation to look around for the jukebox. There wasn't one, but if there had been it would have played 78s.

Dan was still at his corner of the bar and the character

known as the Major had settled on to a bar stool into which his buttocks had made grooves.

In a corner of the bar were a middle-aged couple who had parked a Ford Mondeo at the back of the car-park so it couldn't be seen from the road. I had noticed that, but I didn't think the others had. It wasn't anything seriously suspicious, they were just meeting for a drink after work as married (though not to each other) couples do every day before going home.

I had switched to bottles of Seagull Low, which might have sounded like a Battle of Britain call sign but was in fact the brewery's version of an alcohol-free beer. The label told me it probably contained less alcohol than tomato juice. It certainly had less taste. I doubted if it was one of Murdo's best-selling lines.

The switch was necessary for two reasons. Firstly, I hadn't decided what I was going to do with Amy's car and didn't know whether I would have to drive it back to London or not. Secondly, I decided five minutes into the Major's company that after a couple of Seagrave Specials I would probably have clocked him one.

He had opinions on every subject under the sun and was anxious to share them. All the problems of England on the eve of the Millennium were down to socialists, sociologists, illegal immigrants, graduates in media studies, the lack of policemen on the beat, spin doctors and women priests. He made the 'Major' character in *Fawlty Towers* look like a cross between Einstein and Bertrand Russell.

He also had the really annoying habit of deliberately mispronouncing things. For some reason, he started to describe his Sunday lunch of 'swoop' (soup), 'roasty beef and Porkshire Goodings' and 'Saucyradish', which I guessed was horseradish sauce. When my sides stopped splitting, I wondered how he had made the rank of major, and in which army.

The other two passing customers were more interesting. They were Ted and Marion and I could tell from the obvious clues – the way he looked along the bar at the levels in the spirits bottles and the amount of jewellery she wore – that they were licensees. It turned out to be a professional call and they exchanged 'Evenings' with Dan and the Major. That doesn't mean to say they knew them. Maybe every pub round here had a Dan and a Major.

'Good evening, Ted, Marion,' said Ivy. 'Usual? Or would you prefer a brandy and lovage?'

'The usual, please, Ivy. Brandy and lovage, eh? Haven't heard that one for a while,' said Ted.

'Ivy hadn't heard of it at all until this young fella told her what it was.'

Dan was unlikely to get Brownie points for mentioning this but it had been a while since anyone referred to me as 'young fella' so he was going up in my book.

'You in the trade?' Ted asked me in a friendly enough sort of way, although Dan and the Major leaned closer to hear my answer.

'No, no, just a customer. But I've been in a few pub quiz teams. You pick things up, you know, trivia. You've got a pub?'

'Oh yes, the Old House At Home, down in Rye. Do you know Rye?'

Before I could answer him, the hand pump Ivy was pulling made a rude squirting noise.

'Oh, fiddle!' exclaimed Ivy on best behaviour. 'The bitter's gone. Won't be a minute.'

'Don't worry, Ivy, I'll have a bottle of something,' said Ted with something close to alarm in his voice.

'No, you won't. It'll have to be changed sometime and better now than when we get a rush on.'

All five of us at the bar exchanged glances at that, but said nothing as Ivy disappeared behind the bar. And I mean disappeared. The others had probably seen it before, but it was new and magic for me so I leaned over the bar to watch.

Ivy was bent over as if touching her toes, using both hands to haul back a large metal bolt in the floor. With a squeak and a snap it slid open and a square yard of trap-door fell away with a crash as it hit the cellar wall. Ivy dropped to her knees and poked one of her thin arms into the gloom until there was a click and a light came on below. I could see a set of wooden steps descending at an angle which would not have looked out of place in the last reel of *Titanic*. With one hand clutching her skirt, Ivy started down, smiling regally at us as she did so.

'I won't be a moment,' she said gracefully.

'You be careful, Ivy,' Marion said with genuine concern. Then to Ted, in a whisper: 'Those stairs'll be the death of her.'

'I know, I know, but she won't be told.'

From the cellar came a metallic crash followed by:

'Fuck! Damn! Shit! Where's that bastard hammer?'

'In the box with the soft spiles,' Dan shouted down the trapdoor.

A banging noise told us she had found it.

'You should get the brewery to do something about that cellar access,' Marion said to her husband.

'Pah!' spluttered the Major. 'Get the brewery involved and next thing you know they'll be turning the place into one of those theme pubs.'

I wondered what theme the Major had in mind. A *Fall of the House of Usher* pub perhaps.

'Look, she's a member of the Association but that doesn't mean I can interfere in her business,' said Ted, wincing at another clatter of metal from below.

'Would that be the Licensed Victuallers Association?' I asked him.

'Yes, but she doesn't attend much.'

'Does the Association have much to do with the beer-runners?' I tried and he seemed relieved to talk about anything to take his mind off the banging and crashing in the cellar.

'Oh, we're suffering. Maybe not as bad as some, because we're a big eating house. We're sixty per cent food to forty per cent wet sales, but we've noticed the dip in the last few years. Oh yes, we're hurting. All pubs in Kent are.'

He looked longingly at the unused beer pumps as more crashing and cursing echoed up from the cellar.

'Is it a problem in Rye? Smuggling?'

'Not directly. It's a small port, not like Dover where you've got – what? – nine thousand vehicles a day landing. That's where most of it comes in. Everybody knows that.'

Everybody did.

'So what can you do about it?'

He shrugged his shoulders.

'It's up to the government. They keep putting the tax up, it just makes more sense to buy your beer in France. More bargains for the beer-runners.'

'We should make the Froggies put their tax up,' the Major butted in. 'That would stop the smugglers in their tracks. Or we should just pull out of Europe all together. Leave them to stew in their own juices.'

'Here we go again,' sighed Dan.

Fortunately, we didn't as a final thump from the cellar followed by a victory cry of 'Gotcha yer bastard!' meant that Ivy was ready to ascend from the underworld and normal service was about to be resumed.

I leaned over the bar to watch, fascinated, but before anything happened I had time to whisper in Ted's ear:

'Any chance I could get any food here?'

He reached into the top pocket of his jacket and silently handed over a business card. It was for his pub in Rye. I nodded a silent thanks.

Through the trap-door I could see the sheer staircase had a thick rope running at the side of it, serving as a handrail. Ivy's tiny hand made it go taut as she started up and I could see that she was holding a second, thinner rope as well, one with some sort of toggle at the end.

She hauled herself into the bar and smiled angelically at Ted.

'Not long now, Ted. All good things are worth waiting for.'

'Retirement, f'r'instance,' Ted whispered under his breath.

Ivy hauled on the thin rope she held and the trap-door swung upwards. When it was in place, Ivy kicked the bolt shut and let go of the rope. It snaked down through a knot hole in the woodwork until the toggle hit the floor. The toggle, I could now see, was a wine bottle cork and Ivy tipped it into the knot hole and tamped it down with a dainty toe.

She grapped a pump handle and began to work it furiously.

'Just draw the first couple off,' she confided to Ted and Ted nodded professionally, if thirstily.

'You had anybody round looking at your tankards, Ivy?'

Ivy grinned and her eyes sparkled.

'Is that rhyming slang for something rude, Ted Lewis?'

Ted's wife Marion laughed loudly in a voice which surely came in handy when it came to closing time. Dan spluttered into his beer. The Major sniffed haughtily. The married (but not to each other) couple decided to leave.

'I'm serious, Ivy. There's a couple of rich Americans in the area, doing the rounds buying up antiques and especially silver tankards.'

Ivy looked up at the forest of tankards hanging from hooks above her head.

'What's the catch?' she said as she eventually handed Ted his drink and waved away the offered £10 note.

'No catch, they seem dead straight.'

'Don't like the sound of it meself,' said the Major as if someone had asked him. 'Yanks buying up the country's heritage? Bad news.'

'Well, say what you like about that, but these two seem genuine. Downright honest actually. They came into my pub and bought an old silver mug I'd been keeping pencils in. Gave me £250 for it and then came back a few days later and told me they'd made a mistake and they'd dated it wrong.'

'Oh yes?' Ivy nodded knowingly. 'Wanted their money back, did they?'

'Yes, they did, Ivy,' said Marion, 'but it's not what you think. They said the tankard was actually worth £2500 and they didn't feel right about taking it so cheaply so they sold it back to us.'

'How much for?' Ivy and I said in unison, then we looked at each other.

'Two hundred and fifty,' said Ted. 'Just what they paid. I thought that was a really nice gesture. They could have legged it and we'd have been no wiser. See, there are some honest folk left in the world.'

'None of them use this pub,' cracked Ivy and roared with laughter. Then she slapped a hand over her mouth. 'Except for this young gentleman here. I'm sure he is. Sorry, love, I don't know your name.'

'Roy,' I said and bit my tongue, leaving it there.

'Please to meet you, Roy. You working locally?'

'No, just driving through,' I said, thinking rapidly. 'I'm in the fashion business.'

'What, like a travelling salesman?' asked Ivy and the others all leaned in to hear the answer. Maybe they had a thing about travelling salesmen. One had probably called at the pub and sold them all nose hair clippers or run off with their Christmas Club fund round about 1930.

'Oh no. I'm an assistant to a fashion photographer. I help the models get dressed and undressed.'

They blanked me, all of them.

'It's only thirty quid a week but it was all I could afford.'

More blank looks and half a minute of dead silence then they all laughed out loud, except the Major. I was just grateful they never watched old Woody Allen movies and for the old adage that the best comedian is one with a longer memory than his audience.

'The Major here had you pegged as one of those computer boffins,' said Dan, toying with his empty glass.

'Computers? Wouldn't know how to turn one on,' I said. 'Get you another? How about you, Major?'

'Wouldn't say no. Jolly decent of you. Never really had you down as one of those wide boys, y'know.'

Ivy was already filling their glasses.

'Shouldn't judge a man by his car,' the Major was saying.

'But you always say that,' Dan exclaimed. 'You can always judge a man by the car he drives, that's what you always say. That's why I ride that old bike of mine. You can judge a man by his car, but you can't judge a man by his bicycle!'

'Nuff and sonsense, Dan,' blustered the Major, hiding his face in his pint.

'No, it's not,' Dan protested, not letting it go. 'You've been on and on like a nun's knickers for weeks about wide boys in BMWs tearing up the village shouting into their mobile phones.'

'Well, they do. Shout that is. Some of them don't need a phone. Just because one is retired, it does not mean one is deaf,' said the Major primly.

'Tosser,' said Dan quietly and the Major gave no sign of hearing.

'You got tearaways in the village, Ivy?' Ted asked her, and he seemed genuinely concerned. 'You're pretty isolated here, you know.'

'Nothing to worry about, Ted, unless you're the Major here. I reckon they're running raves somewhere round here. Secret locations and all that. That's why they need the mobile phones.' Ivy thought about it. 'Little buggers never ask me, though. I could show them a thing or two.'

I wondered whether to laugh or not, but no one else was and that was sort of spooky.

'Anyway,' Ivy went on, 'the Major's only got the hump because they've got better cars than he has and they're young and some of them are black.'

'Now, Ivy, I've never held the colour of a person's skin against them,' said the Major, blushing.

Dan's eyebrows shot up and stayed up.

'I wouldn't mind holding the one I saw last week against me,' said Ivy, putting a glass under the gin optic. 'Fit as a butcher's dog, that one. All muscles. He could have me in the back of his car any time. 'Course I'd have to wear some flat shoes. Wouldn't want me stilettos ripping the lining of his roof, would I, Marion?'

'Ivy, behave yourself!' laughed Marion and this time it was safe to join in.

'It's not them, it's their attitude,' the Major persisted. 'Driving up and down, music blaring and always on their bloody mobile phones. They give you cancer, you know.'

We all looked at him.

'Mobile phones. It's been proved. They're radioactive and it sets off something in the brain which makes them addictive and then they give you cancer. Should be banned. Ruining the art of conservation – conversation.'

'Really, Major, you do come out with some twaddle.' Ivy shook her head in despair. 'Are you all right, Roy?'

'Er ... yes, fine. Where's the Gents?'

'Out the door, turn right and right again. I'll put the outside light on for you.'

She flicked a switch behind the bar and I shuffled gratefully off my bar stool.

My pager had started vibrating over my right buttock and I didn't want to answer it in front of the Major. God knew what he would have made of that.

* * *

The toilet block was basic to say the least and open to the stars and the dark night sky, which made sure the visitors didn't linger.

Out in the car-park the pager told me Amy wanted me to call her on her mobile so I rescued mine from the glove compartment of the BMW, relieved that I hadn't taken it into the pub.

I punched her up in the memory and said, 'It's me, where are you?' when she answered.

'I'm in Paris where I'm supposed to be. Where are you?'

In the background I could hear a not half-bad jazz band playing. She was probably on the eighth course of her dinner. The models would be sitting there watching, not eating. I hoped she was getting a feel of where I was, just downwind of the Gents' toilet.

'I'm on a stakeout down in Kent.'

'Is that half as exciting as you're trying to make it sound?'

'Not really. I'm in the car-park of the Pub From Hell trying to decide which flavour crisps I'm going to have for dinner.'

'Then I won't tell what we've just eaten but the duck was outstanding and we've been promised a really special pudding wine.'

Pudding wine. She had to rub it in.

'Great. What am I, some sort of Foodies Anonymous? Are you ringing just to read me the menu?'

'I just wanted to tell you that we've wrapped here already. Nigel worked like a demon and we got some really good shots, everything we're going to get anyway.'

'Bully for Nigel.'

'So we're heading back early,' she ignored me. 'We'll be back tomorrow. Any chance you could pick us up?'

Here we went again. Funny how people love you when you've got a taxi.

'Tell you what,' I said, thinking on my feet. 'I'm only a few miles from Ashford. Get off the Eurostar there and I'll pick you up. We could even have a day at the seaside. Go for a paddle if you fancy it.'

'Have you been drinking?'

'Not yet.'

'Don't worry, we'll go into London and –'

'You can drive the BMW back,' I said, knowing the reaction.

'You've got my car there while you're playing private detectives?'

'You said I could borrow it.'

'I did? When?'

'Sorry, dear, you're cracking up on me. What was that?'

'Don't try that on me, Angel, I know you. And I know that that is one of the best digital phones in the world. So you take care of that car, I've had it longer than I've had you. I'll give you a ring in the morning and you can pick us up from the station. Is there anything you want bringing back?'

'A nice pudding wine?' I suggested.

'We'll see,' she said and switched off.

I put the phone back in the BMW and locked it and I was walking back to the door of the pub when for the second time that evening somebody tried to run me over.

This time the vehicle did at least have lights and the driver did sound a warning.

She shouted 'Beep! Beep!' just before her nearside wheel clipped my heel.

I had no idea wheelchairs could corner so well.

9

I had no idea that wheelchairs came equipped with headlights either.

Actually, they don't. They were a refinement which Melanie had added herself – in fact they were battery-powered bicycle lamps – so that she could get down to the Rising Sun in the evening. She liked her nights in the Rising Sun as there was sod-all on television these days and the Rising Sun didn't have any steps, so there was automatic wheelchair access. And anyway, it was the only bloody pub in the village, wasn't it?

I got all this just by holding the door open for her and keeping my toes out of the way as she rolled herself inch-perfectly through the doorway and into the bar, where she was greeted by the regulars with a cry of 'Mel!' just like they used to shout 'Norm!' in *Cheers*.

She gave one flick on the wheels of the chair to get her across the floor then did the wheelchair equivalent of a handbrake turn, switching off her cycle lamps as she did so, ending up side-on to the bar dead opposite Ivy.

"Evenin' all. Usual, please, Ivy.'

Ivy cracked the top off a bottle of Beck's and handed it over the bar. It was a bizarre sight. Ivy could only just see over the bar, Melanie could only just reach it.

'Keeping well, Melanie dear?' Ivy asked as she scrabbled for change.

'Well as expected, Ivy. Almost got a speeding ticket in Folkestone this afternoon.' She drank beer from the bottle while Ivy laughed politely. 'And I almost creamed one of your customers just now, outside. You get extra points if they've got their back to you.'

'You'll have to get a bell put on that thing, young Melanie.'

'You can ring my bell any time,' leered Dan.

'And you should eat cheese late at night,' she toasted him with her bottle.

'What did she mean by that?' Dan hissed in my ear.

'Dream on,' I hissed back.

Ted and Marion downed their drinks. Now another customer had arrived, protocol was served and they could leave with a clear conscience.

'You take care, Ivy love. You know where we are if you need anything,' said Ted, already half-way to the door.

'I'll pop over for a meal one of these nights,' said Ivy, waving and blowing a kiss to Marion.

'You do that, dear,' gushed Marion. 'You do that soon.'

'Only if I win the lottery,' Ivy muttered under her breath.

'Pricey is it, their pub?' Melanie asked her.

Ivy levered herself on the bar with her elbows so she could look over and down.

'You'd have to drink a lot more bottles of Beck's before I could afford a prawn cocktail at Ted Lewis's Grill and Carvery,' she said emphatically, then let herself drop back to earth with only the slightest of wobbles on her high heels.

'You can't beat crawn pocktails and beef from the Cravery,' the Major mused, smacking his lips.

'*Cravery*?' Melanie mouthed silently, shaking her head.

'Which reminds me, I have to get home to my rot poast. Goodnight children, one and all.'

He finished his beer and then wiped a forefinger along the line of his moustache. Then he stood up, pushed his bar stool up to the bar and nodded to each of us in turn before turning on his heel and marching, stiff-backed, out of the door.

'Pot roast?' Melanie rolled her eyes. 'More like a Sad Person's single portion TV dinner.'

'I have to ask,' I said, moving down the bar to her chair, 'where was the Major a major?'

'You mean like what regiment?'

'Like which army?'

'Oh, he wasn't ever in the army. We call him the Major after that stupid old git character in *Fawlty Towers*.'

'And he doesn't mind?'

'Don't think he's ever seen it. Don't care if he has. Can I buy you a drink to make up for running over your foot?'

'Sure, I'll have a shandy, though. I'm driving.'

'That your BMW out there?'

'Yes, well it's my . . .' I bit my tongue to stop myself saying the 'w' word. 'It's the firm's.'

'So what do you do then?'

I tried to remember what I had told the others. It was probably one of the rules of being a private eye: try and keep your stories relatively straight, or at least only slightly curved.

'I tell people I'm in fashion photography, but really I just drive the photographer's equipment around.'

'That sounds cool.'

'It's not really.'

'For round here, it's life in the fast lane, trust me.'

She put her bottle on the bar and unzipped her coat, a black padded storm jacket with enough pockets to accommodate a crate of hand grenades, and began to ease it off her shoulders. I put out a hand to help her, but gingerly, knowing that being disabled doesn't mean being incompetent. She didn't seem to mind. Under the coat she was wearing a blue TALtop. I hoped it was one of the later models where the dye didn't run. She had

105

arranged it V-neck style to emphasise her cleavage. Both she and the TALtop were doing a grand job.

'You hang that up and I'll get the drinks,' she said, edging forward in her chair so I could pull the coat out from under her. 'Oh, get my darts out first, though, will you . . . ?'

'Roy,' I said reaching into one of the coat pockets and producing a plastic case containing three brass darts with large green feather flights. 'You looking for a game?'

'You looking for a hiding?' she said without looking at me.

'So you're good, are you?' I growled back, putting on the tough-guy act.

Ivy placed a pint of shandy and another bottle of Beck's on the bar.

Melanie pointed a dart at them and said:

'Those are the only drinks I'm buying tonight.'

'Game on, then.'

After the first game, I realised that the darts Ivy had loaned me were faulty.

After the second game, I was sure that the dart board was hung too low. It was certainly not at eye level. After the third game I remembered that I hadn't played for at least two years so no wonder I was rusty.

'Best out of seven?' Melanie asked sweetly as I pulled her dart out of double sixteen again.

Whilst we had been playing I had managed to get a good look at her. She was about twenty, with straight shoulder-length blonde hair tied back in a pony tail with a single red hair band. She wore no make-up, not even lipstick, to spoil a clean, freckled complexion and her hair smelled of a mint shampoo.

She put her chair at right angles to the board when she threw her darts but made no protest when I pulled them out for her each time after chalking the score on the blackboard.

'I'm not in your league,' I told her. 'You must practise a fair bit.'

'I played a lot at university, but since the accident I only play down here to hustle drinks.'

I hadn't dared ask up until now and I still wasn't sure how

to ask, or whether I should. Was she giving me an opening here?

'You get three guesses,' she said.

'Excuse me?'

'Three guesses as to how I got into this wheelchair. I know you're dying to ask and somebody's bound to tell you when the lads arrive. So let me make you suffer. It's one of the few pleasures I have left.'

Lads? What lads?

'OK then, if you insist. A car accident – you said it was an accident.'

'Nope.'

'Riding then; a riding accident.'

'Like the guy who played Superman? Nope, 'fraid not. Last chance.'

She fluttered her eyelashes at me, I swear she did. It was more than cute.

'You were involved in some bizarre sexual experiment and it all went horribly wrong?'

She threw back her head and laughed at that.

'Good call. I'll use that one, but unfortunately it's wrong. You lose, your round.'

'Story of my life,' I sighed. 'Was I close?'

'Sadly, no. I was a mouse and I fell off the battlements of the Enchanted Castle.'

She put her Beck's bottle to her lips but kept looking at me, checking or maybe timing me, to see if I could work it out.

I waited until she'd finished drinking, wiped my chalky fingers on the leg of my jeans then held my hand out for the empty bottle.

'Dangerous place, that EuroDisney,' I said.

The 'lads' arrived about thirty minutes later but by then I knew that Melanie (you can call me 'Mel' but any reference to Spice Girls invokes serious shit) was indeed twenty and heading for her second year of a law degree at Southampton, or would have been had it not been for the holiday job in France. And yes, she had played a mouse, one of several, in the daily parade and had fallen off a motorised float right in front of a family from Birmingham and a pimply youth had pointed at her and yelled: 'Look, Dad, pissed as a rat!'

That sort of thing, I agreed, could scar you for life not to mention putting a damper on your career prospects within the Disney corporation. I also told her I thought she must have made a very sexy mouse and did she fancy having dinner with me somewhere? After all, mice had to eat.

'Ivy'll do something for us, she always lays on breakfast when the lads pop in to play darts,' she said straight-faced. 'Don't you, Ivy?'

'Oh yes, Mel love. I'll do one of my specials if the boffins turn up,' Ivy said, just to prove she had been listening.

I was slightly relieved, not that I had been planning anything special. After all, I was making this up as I went along. But the prospect of leaving Ivy with only Dan as a customer seemed a heavy responsibility and one not to be undertaken lightly. Pubs shouldn't be empty, it was against the law of nature. Or it should be. Hang on a minute; had Melanie said 'breakfast'?

'Who are the boffins?' I asked Mel. With my luck they would turn out to be the local chapter of Hell's Angels.

'Computer programmers or software jockeys as they like to call themselves. They're all my age but they're not a bad bunch.'

I wasn't sure how to take that 'my age' reference but I was beginning to like Mel so I decided not to let her tyres down just yet.

'Where do they come from? I wouldn't have thought this place was on the regular circuit for a lads' night out.'

'Oh, they work in the village,' she said airily.

'What? You got some sort of silicon valley hidden away here?'

The question was genuine. I had driven through the village twice now and not caught a glimpse of anything which could provide gainful employment unless it involved a scythe or a hoe.

'I'd hardly call it that. They've just converted a few of the outbuildings from the old hop farm.'

'You mean like an oast house?' I was showing off, proving I knew the term for what is the unofficial logo of Kent, the tall conical brick buildings which tourists think are windmills that have had their sails stolen. 'I don't remember seeing an oast house in the village.'

'There isn't one,' said Mel, chinking her bottle against my glass. 'The nearest oast was turned into a stockbroker's country retreat about twenty years ago. We just had a farm here, only a couple of fields, and that went bust. The boffins work in the old stripping sheds and storehouses. And before you say anything, the stripping shed was where they stripped the hops off the bines.'

'Does everybody in Kent grow hops?'

'No, we just have to pretend we do. Did you know the hop was related to cannabis?'

Of course I did.

'No, really?'

'Scooter said he could go into big time Ecstasy production there and the Drug Squad wouldn't find them because the sniffer dogs would have a snootful of hops.'

'Sounds a bright guy. Scooter, did you say?'

I was getting into this asking questions business, just like a real private eye. I wondered if there was a teach-yourself CD-ROM out on it yet.

'Oh, Scooter's sharp enough. So sharp he'll cut himself, as my mother would say. Lots of big ideas, not much staying power.'

'You've known him for long?' I tried.

'We were at uni together, until he dropped out.' She looked up at me suspiciously. 'Why are we talking about Scooter? We should be talking about me.'

'Just checking out the opposition,' I said, showing teeth.

She laughed at that.

'Scooter's not opposition, but there *is* opposition. It's just he works during the week.'

'He's not one of the Seven Dwarves or anything, is he?'

'Oh no,' she said, catching on immediately, 'he works in London, not EuroDisney.'

'Your other boyfriends are here,' said Dan from the end of the bar, proving there was nothing wrong with his hearing except when it came to his round.

'Hey, some of them are mine, you know,' Ivy chipped in,

109

putting four empty pint glasses and six half-pint ones on the bar. 'Mel can't handle all of them herself.'

'You behave yourself, Ivy Bracegirdle,' snapped Mel, flicking her hair behind her ears. 'I don't need you to show me up, I can manage well enough myself.'

'You can say that again,' Dan came back.

As they exchanged banter I drifted over to one of the windows and stood on tiptoe so I could see out of the top half of unfrosted glass, over the yellowing net curtains.

In the car-park, a 4 x 4 Jeep had pulled up near Amy's BMW. The interior light showed me two figures climbing out and one of them walking round from the driver's side. They both took a good look at the Beamer and then the one who had been driving shook his head, closed the door of the Jeep and activated the central locking so that the indicators and side-lights flashed once and then went out.

More light appeared, silhouetting the new arrivals, from the headlights of two vehicles turning into the car-park from the village road. They pulled up alongside the Jeep and killed their lights. One of them was some sort of pick-up truck, the other an estate car. Doors opened and half a dozen shapes gathered, all looking at Amy's BMW.

A mobile phone trilled and startled me into reaching for my pocket even though I knew I had left mine in the car. It was a purely Pavlovian reaction and I should have known better. I would never own a phone which was programmed to ring the first six bars of 'When I'm Calling You'.

It was Mel's. I hadn't noticed the mobile in a leather holster which she had stuck to the side of her wheelchair with Velcro strips.

As she answered it, Dan moaned: 'Bloody things, they drive the Major mad.'

I moved nearer to him and away from Mel, who turned her chair through an arc, so that it didn't look as if I was ear-wigging.

'He mentioned it,' I said. It was about the only thing the Major had said which I had taken notice of. 'Driving BMWs and talking loudly into mobile phones. Must be a red rag to a bull.'

'That's only part of it,' said Dan, anxious to make conversa-

110

tion as his glass was almost empty. 'They always play loud music, you know, that dance music stuff. And they've usually got the windows down. You can hear them coming a mile off.'

'That gets the Major too, does it?'

'That –' Dan dropped his voice – 'and that fact that they're black.'

I made an O with my mouth and nodded wisely.

'Is that why he went? Before they turned up?'

'Oh, I don't mean those computer boffins. Those lads are all right. It's the others that get the Major's goat.'

I was about to ask what others but never got the chance.

Mel had finished her call without me noticing and was packing the phone away as the door opened and a procession of young guys entered, each one flapping a hand and nodding and saying: 'Mel! Ivy!'

Ivy was pulling beer into the pint glasses and pouring orange juice into the smaller ones and saying: 'Now who's driving tonight, lads?'

Mel was acknowledging them individually although at first it sounded as if she had taken me seriously and was trying to summon up the Seven Dwarves. But once I tuned into her wavelength, the names did make some sort of sense, relating to what the guys looked like or what they were wearing.

'Hi, Combo.'

(Blue denim jeans and jacket.)

'Hi, Ginge!'

(A redhead.)

'Elvis!'

(Because he wore glasses like Elvis Costello does.)

'Painter, how'yer doing?'

(This to a short, chubby youth who wore white, paint-stained overalls.)

'Yo, Axeman.'

(That one had me fooled until I saw the kid's eyes close up as he claimed a drink at the bar.)

'Right, lads, sort yourselves out,' Ivy was saying. 'There's juice for the drivers. How many more pints?'

'Hi, Scooter, did you bring your arrows?' said Melanie towards the door.

'Of course I have, you foolish female. Prepare to be thrashed.'

I turned my head slowly, though nobody was looking at me, to get a good look at Scooter. He was my height but Mel's age, with a flop of blond hair over one eye, which hopefully got in the way when he threw the heavy metal darts he was brandishing. His whole body language said he was the leader of the pack and the others parted to let him get to the bar first. I noticed he was clipping a Nokia mobile on to his belt and wondered if he had just made a call.

'Where are Chip and Dale?' Mel asked him.

'Right behind us. Don't worry, the gang's all here.'

Scooter reached into the pocket of his jeans and produced a wedge of notes, peeling off a twenty for Ivy.

'How's my favourite landlady?' he asked, dripping with charm.

'The better for seeing you, my dear, but I'd settle for you being ten years older and me being ten months younger,' cackled Ivy.

The gang laughed along, as did Mel.

Dan took a few seconds to work it out then joined in.

I let myself smile but over the laughter I was straining my ears.

Scooter had left the door to the pub open and from the car-park came the distant but unmistakable sound of breaking glass. Just the sort of sound you get if you feed empty bottles into a bottle bank.

I thought it might be a good idea to stick around.

But what did I know?

10

If there was such a thing as a final exam for private detectives, then one of the papers – or at least forty per cent of practical course work marks – should be dedicated to the Hanging Around In Pubs unit of the curriculum. You find out so much so easily, and some of it is probably true.

Just by listening to their smalltalk and observing their body language as they played darts with Melanie, it was obvious that there were differences within the 'boffins'.

Combo, Ginge, Elvis (Costello) and Painter were all of student age and almost certainly contemporaries of Scooter. One of them, Ginge, had a battered paperback edition of Marcuse's *Eros and Civilisation* in the pocket of his jacket, which was a bit of a give-away, as was his total inability to score accurately at darts. But there were other clues, such as their constant references to daytime television, especially children's programmes, and up-and-coming bands still flogging around the campus circuit.

The two Mel had referred to as Chip and Dale were the same age as the others, but not in the same peer group. They wore anoraks and had tried to grow beards and they sat to the side of the darts players rather than joining in, drinking orange juice and not talking. After a while, Chip (or it might have been Dale) produced a small travelling chess set from a deep pocket and they began to play. I would bet my own money they were vegetarians.

Axeman was the odd one out and in more ways than one. He was older than the others for a start and certainly not a student, now or in the past. He kept himself apart from the group, back to the bar, watching them – and especially Melanie – with wide, flashing eyes. He was thin and twitchy and his eyes really did bulge, which suggested he had a hyperactive thyroid. Either that or he was a heavy drug user.

I couldn't work out where he fitted into the group. If he was a software programmer, then so was I.

I offered to buy Dan another pint and asked for a tomato juice for myself, hoping that Ivy stocked such exotic cocktails.

'You driving tonight as well, Roy?' she asked and I almost missed the look the Axeman flashed me.

'Yeah, I've got the car,' I said without thinking anything much of it. 'And I'd better go after this one, find myself some supper.'

'Stay here, my dear. I'm doing my specials for the lads so you might as well. One more won't make any difference and I've got the water on.'

How could I refuse? If I had she would have flayed me with her pearls.

113

'If you're sure . . .' I said hesitantly.

'It's no bother.'

She disappeared through the back of the bar into her living quarters. At my side, Dan chuckled quietly.

'You're very lucky, yer know. To get offered one of Ivy's specials.'

'She's a good cook, then?'

Before he could snigger a reply, Ivy's head appeared in the bar again.

'Plain or spicy, Roy?'

'Er . . . spicy, thanks.' In for a penny.

'Good choice,' hissed Dan, his shoulders heaving.

'Should I send out for pizza?' I asked him.

'You haven't time,' he said smugly. 'It'll be ready in three minutes.'

He was almost spot on, perhaps twenty seconds out, but then that is as long as it takes to boil an egg. Or about sixteen eggs to be accurate.

'Who ordered spicy?' Ivy shouted. 'Haven't you got the spoons out yet, Melanie?'

Ivy appeared clutching a huge tray on which were eight double egg cups complete with boiled eggs and two plates of toast which had been cut into strips an inch wide. One plate had buttered 'soldiers' and the other had been spread with Marmite. Plain or spicy. It all made sense.

'You know I can't get behind the bar these days, Ivy,' Melanie was moaning. To illustrate the point, she drove her wheelchair at the gap where the bar flap was open and juddered to a halt. Her chair was about an inch either side too wide for the gap.

'No wonder you haven't had to change the vodka recently, Ivy,' Scooter piped up and the others, all except Axeman, giggled politely.

'You watch your lip, Mr Scooter-Computer. Now where's the salt?'

Boiled eggs, Marmite soldiers and salt; what a feast.

'It's the only thing she knows how to cook,' Dan whispered in my ear.

'That'll be £2.50, Roy love,' said Ivy, holding out her hand.

I wondered if Amy had finished her pudding wine by now.

* * *

114

I drank my drink and dipped my toast soldiers into the yolks of my eggs and when I had finished I realised I was still hungry, stone-cold sober and had run out of things to do.

Ivy was washing glasses and polishing them with a tea-towel. Dan was thinking loudly about the chances of me buying him another drink. The 'boffin' gang had sat in a group to eat their boiled eggs, except for Axeman, who had pulled out a much-folded copy of *Exchange & Mart* and was scouring the small print without tiring his lips too much. Melanie wheeled herself in and out of them, collecting their glasses and plates like a demented mobile waitress. She seemed to have forgotten I was there.

'Well, better hit the road,' I said to no one in particular. 'Thanks a lot. Goodnight.'

'Take care, my dear,' Ivy said. 'Drop in and see us again.'

'You bet,' I said, hoping she wasn't a gambler.

I nodded to Dan and he nodded back, glumly resigned to having to spend his own money.

I walked across the bar until I was behind Melanie's wheel-chair and leaned over her shoulder.

'Thanks for the darts lesson,' I said softly, noting that the 'boffins' around the table had gone silent. 'Hope everything works out for you. And next time you ride in a pumpkin coach drawn by six white mice, fasten your seat belt.'

She smiled and her eyes twinkled.

'Thanks, I'll remember that, but quite honestly, I've had it up to here –' she held her hand flat in front of her stomach – 'with mice.'

I chuckled politely at that, then nodded to the students. The one called Scooter nodded slightly in return, studying me with his right eye only as his left was covered by his drooping shock of blond hair.

I waved to Ivy as I moved to the door and stepped out into the night. Before I had closed the door behind me, I heard three or four of the students burst into laughter. Whatever they had thought of me, one of them had now said out loud. I wasn't worried, the feeling was mutual.

Once out of the door, I strode purposefully as if heading for the Gents' toilet until I knew I was out of sight of the pub's windows. Then I skipped between two tubs of flowers and I was close enough to the beehive Bottleback bins to smell the stale beer.

It was at that point I remembered that I didn't have a torch or a match or a cigarette lighter and I just knew that the two old dears on the Dover cliffs would have come better prepared, with X-ray cameras and infra-red and such like.

Tentatively, I pushed in the rubber cover plate over the port-hole opening and put my hand in. It didn't have to go far before making contact with something, but at least it was something cold and unmoving, made of glass. Using my fingertips I pulled until I could make out the shape of a 25-centilitre bottle, a 'dumpy', bearing a label saying it had come from the St Omer Brewery in France. That didn't mean much in itself, but the fact that my hand had only had to dip about two inches into the Bottleback bin told me that it was almost full and that the dumpy bottle had a few hundred friends in there keeping him company.

As I walked to the BMW, I checked the other vehicles in the car-park, the Jeep, a Renault estate car and a Mazda flat-back pick-up, noting their number plates without really knowing why I was doing it. I did realise that it would be a tad obvious to stand there with a notebook, so I was glad I didn't have one. But I did have Amy's Grundig dictaphone in my emergency over-night bag which I retrieved from the boot of the Beamer before climbing in and starting the engine. With the headlights on, no one from the pub could have seen me anyway, which covered my fumbling with the Record button until I could commit the three numbers to tape. At the entrance to the car-park, I stopped and signalled left, even though there wasn't a hedgehog on the road for miles, then slowly pulled out and headed away from the village, roughly south-west towards the M20, Ashford, Maid-stone and then the bright, safe lights of London.

In fact I drove about a mile down the road until I found a gateway to a field where I could turn around and head back towards Whitcomb, driving on sidelights only. When I came to the bend in the road around which lay the Rising Sun, I pulled over close enough into the hedge to scratch Amy's paintwork and killed the engine. I reckoned that if any of the boffins came out of the pub car-park and turned my way, I had enough time to get moving and dazzle them enough so they didn't know it was me. (I had always been scathing about the BMW's dipped headlights, but on full beam they were pretty impressive.)

But they had all approached the pub from the other way, the village end, so I thought I was safe enough and settled down to wait.

This was the bit of the private eye's examination which I would fail. In fact, unlike the Hanging Around In Pubs paper, I wouldn't even bother to turn up for the practical. I had the radio for company but I couldn't read, there was nothing to look at except the hedgerow and the night, and I couldn't even tempt myself with a cigarette as my emergency packet and trusty Zippo were in the glove compartment of Armstrong back in Hampstead. There was nothing to do but sit there and focus on the single weak light which illuminated the sign of the Rising Sun. I looked at my watch to see it was 9.50 p.m. and thought how slowly time passed in the countryside. Amy was probably on the Armagnac and *petit café* by now, or in a club boogying along to French rap music. There didn't seem much justice in the world.

At 9.57 p.m., I turned off the radio and lowered the window to discover that sound travelled further in the country. In London you'd be hard pushed to hear a scream from the next street but out in the sticks I could hear traffic humming along the M20 at least four miles away. Then, suddenly, much closer, I heard a cow baying at the moon (or whatever it is they do) and it looked as if that might be the highlight of my evening.

Until 9.59 p.m., that was, when I was grateful for the fact that sound carried out here.

I heard the door of the pub slam shut, an unintelligible bit of shouting and then one, then two engines start up.

I could see two sets of headlights circling towards the car-park entrance as I started up the BMW, ready to gun it if they turned towards me. They turned right out of the car-park, back to the village, as I had guessed they would.

Feeling very smug with myself I pulled out to follow them. This private eye business was really just too easy for words.

As I passed the Rising Sun, I checked the car-park and the only vehicle left there was the Jeep, which I guessed was Scooter's. So I was following the Renault estate car and the Mazda pick-up.

Was being the operative word. Within 200 yards of the pub, I had lost them both.

It was not possible, but the two cars had vanished without trace in the middle of a one-pig village with one road in and one road out. I know, because I followed the road out for half a mile beyond the end of the village until I hit a straight stretch which I knew came out eventually on to the A2 near a village called Womenswold. Sure, the road dipped and rose over the edge of the North Downs, but there was no way I could have missed their headlights or tail lights.

I put the Beamer through a three-point turn and headed back down into Whitcomb, without meeting or seeing another vehicle. Once in the village I slowed to kerb-crawling speed and checked both sides of the main – the only – street. I could see houses, some with lights on trying to persuade me they were inhabited, and some had garages which might account for the fact that there was not a single car parked on the road. But I just couldn't see anywhere where the pick-up and the Renault could have gone.

I couldn't see, but perhaps I could hear.

Once again, I pulled over, killed the lights, lowered my window and turned off the ignition.

To my amazement, I got a result: engines, at least two. I looked in the mirror and saw nothing behind me so I strained my ears and tried to concentrate, putting the sound somewhere over to my right and getting closer.

Then I saw the first beam of headlights coming out on to the road from behind a small thatched cottage 150 yards down the street on the right. For a minute the lights just stayed there, shining into the street, then I saw the Mazda pick-up emerge and, thankfully, turn right away from me and head off back towards the Rising Sun at the other end of the village.

The Mazda was followed by the Renault and then another pick-up truck, which might have been a Ford S-100 but was moving too fast for me to tell.

I reached for the ignition key but didn't turn it as there were still beams of light coming out on to the road. They remained stationary for maybe half a minute and then yet another pick-up emerged, turning right and heading off into the night.

I started my engine and moved off on sidelights only, looking

118

to my right to try and spot where the cars had come from. I thought I caught a glimpse of a five-bar gate but it was there and gone in an instant and the red rear lights of the last pick-up were almost out of sight, so I didn't have time to hang about. Just before the Rising Sun came in sight, I flipped on the headlights and put my foot down.

In the textbook I was going to write one day on how to be a private eye, there would be a chapter on how much easier it is to follow someone at night without being spotted yourself. Unless, that is, the person you are following knows the road better than you do; the road in question is a narrow unlit country lane which goes up and down when it is not zigzagging around corners; and the road you are on is heading for a junction of a major road, a motorway and a tunnel leading to an entirely different country. Apart from that, it's dead easy.

I saw the lights of the last pick-up turn left at a crossroads and climb up a small incline. Then we were in a small village which a sign told me was called Etchinghill and we both slowed to (roughly) 30 miles per hour until we were through it and the wooded countryside closed in around us again.

There was no sign of the first three vehicles which had popped out of nowhere back in Whitcomb, but there was light up ahead, a dull orange glow flickering through the trees, and I knew it must be the Folkestone end of the motorway.

The road curved around a large pond and up to a roundabout where the Renault and the other two pick-ups were waiting. I slowed instinctively and reached to turn my lights off but there was no need. The pick-up I had been following flashed its lights to tell them he had caught up and all four pulled off, indicating right at the roundabout on to the A20.

I let them get well ahead of me, certain now that I knew where they were heading. Sure enough, the convoy looped around the A20 and almost immediately picked up the slip road on to the M20, hugging the left-hand lane marked Channel Tunnel Rail Terminal. I pulled out into the motorway proper, but hung back just in case they were looking behind them, waiting for a lorry to pass to give me cover.

If they spotted me, it didn't deter them. All four vehicles sailed on into the Cheriton Terminal as I shadowed them in parallel from the M20 until the approach road swung them out of sight, down towards the toll booths and the border controls. Their next stop would be France, perhaps on the Shuttle train which had just pulled in with its load of lorries in their protective cages. That, the fences and the security lights on high poles gave the impression that I was driving by a prison camp.

At Junction 12 I turned off the motorway and headed back along the A20, getting a closer view of the Shuttle and the Terminal which glowed like a volcano in the distance. There was no sign of my little convoy doubling back on me. Why should they? All the tobacco and beer bargains they could handle were twenty-odd miles away under the Channel.

It was tempting just to keep heading towards London, but I didn't exactly have enough information to fill out one of Veronica's do-it-yourself private eye report forms. (I was sure she had some.)

I had a bunch of darts-playing students with funny names, two of whom were environmentally conscious enough to put their empties in a Bottleback bin. They all seemed to be able to drive and they knew the way to France. I had three of their vehicles' numbers on my dictaphone. And that was just about it. The least I could do was try and find where they were based and I reckoned I could do that and still get back to London before some of the more interesting clubs closed. Thinking about it, as I turned off the A20 back towards Whitcomb, I realised that all the interesting clubs I knew didn't actually open until after 1 a.m., so that was all right then.

There were lights still on in the Rising Sun, but no cars at all in the car-park. There were no cars on the road either, but now I knew to keep an eye open for overtaking wheelchairs.

The lack of traffic was a bit of a worry. I had driven through the village more times that evening than was sensible for a non-local car trying to retain a low profile. The Major had probably already picked me up on his home radar screen and was ringing round the rest of the Neighbourhood Watch. So I picked a spot between the pub and the southern end of the village and squeezed Amy's BMW into the hedgerow again until the paintwork squealed. What the hell, she could afford it.

Unless a juggernaut came round the corner too fast, or a drunken Melanie wheeled up and rear-ended it, I reckoned it was safe enough while I took a swift moonlight stroll in the countryside.

Two problems emerged straight away. Firstly, the lack of street lights, the cloudy sky hiding the moon and the fact that I had left the only torch I possess in the boot of Armstrong, meant my progress was anything but swift. Secondly, the countryside was no place to go for a stroll in the dark without protective clothing and a mine-detector. A space suit and thick rubber boots could have kept me cleaner, the mine-detector might have spotted the strands of barbed wire which seemed to grow out of the bottom of the hedge as if planted there. After about thirty yards I gave up and walked into the village down the middle of the main road where there were only hit-and-run drunk-drivers to worry about.

Even so I almost missed it, spotting the thatched cottage only when I was right outside it and then having to backtrack half a dozen steps.

It was a five-bar gate, a heavy, rusted iron job held, between iron posts, by two hinges at one end and a leather loop which could have come from a horse's bridle at the other. Hardly hi-tech security; just lift the loop over the post and push.

Not that there seemed to be anywhere to push *to*. The gate opened into a field or a paddock which I guessed dog-legged round the back of the thatched cottage. Perhaps the students had just found some off-road parking. Without some light I couldn't see any other reason for them coming and going through that gate.

As if on cue, I was to get my light as I heard a car approaching from the north end of the village.

Rather than be caught in its headlights like a bemused rabbit, I grasped the top of the gate with both hands and vaulted over it, going into a crouch behind the gatepost. The car's main beams swept over the road, the gate and me and were suddenly gone and the light from them had not given me any time or opportunity to get my bearings before plunging me back into darkness.

But jumping over the gate had presented me with a clue. It was not exactly staring me in the face; in fact I was kneeling on it. What most people driving by and what most people living here would call grass, wasn't.

I was from Hackney. I could recognise Astroturf when I landed on it.

It didn't take me long to work out why someone wanted to lay a piece of artificial grass measuring, as near as I could estimate, three metres wide by ten metres long at the edge of a field in the middle of Kent. Under my feet I could feel the deep wheel ruts made by incoming and outgoing vehicles under the carpet of plastic turf and they were deep enough to have been made by regular trips over a period of some time, not just tonight. Somebody had put it down to cover up tyre tracks which showed the gateway was in use. Therefore there must be something through the gateway worth hiding.

I put my back to the middle of the gateway and walked in a straight line out into the paddock or field or whatever it was. Once the Astroturf ended, the ground was firm enough and I could make out tyre tracks and, to my right, a hedge about ten feet high.

My eyes were getting used to the dark and I followed the tyre marks around the corner of the hedge and suddenly there was light ahead.

About a hundred yards away was a single-storey building showing lights in two windows. From its outline, it was flat-roofed and could have been a barn, a large garage or the sort of pre-fabricated service building which still dotted hundreds of disused airfields and RAF stations in this part of the world. I could guess even from where I was standing that it would have metal-framed windows. There was a Jeep parked outside and I didn't need to get any closer to read the number plate. I had it on tape already.

But I did get closer, in a shambling, crouching run. Close enough to confirm my guess about the metal window frames. Close enough to peep in through one.

They had venetian blinds on the windows but hadn't bothered to close them so I got a good view. So good it hurt my eyes.

Whatever the building had been, the walls and floor were now painted white, white enough to dazzle and I was on the outside. But students were tough, they could take it. They could take the harsh strip lighting and the cold stone floors as long as they had a camp bed (eight to be precise), a sleeping bag and an individual case of St Omer beer, and there were more than enough for one each piled casually around the room.

They did run to a few home comforts, though: a four-burner stove powered by a canister of Calor Gas, three giant space heaters, a CD-player and tape-deck with hundred-watt speakers, a large-screen television and video, and, naturally, a computer or two.

Four computers, actually, though only one was in use.

The student Mel had called Axeman was hogging the screen watched by two of the others as he began to interact with one of the porno sites on the Internet. From the reactions of the other two, Axeman's tastes clearly drifted on to the wrong side of sexuality street but they didn't stop looking over his shoulder.

Scooter on the other hand was more interested in plugging a video into the VCR under the giant screen television.

I moved along to the second window to get a better look, not worrying about any noise I made as I could hear the throb of the space heaters from outside, so they wouldn't hear me clumping about.

They didn't have to. They had already seen me, they just didn't know it.

Scooter pointed a remote at the VCR and pulled a chair over from one of the computer terminals. The screen flickered into hazy black-and-white life and I thought for a moment this was part of his PhD studies into silent Japanese cinema.

Then the picture became clearer as he paused and frame-advanced the tape and I knew what it reminded me of, the sort of footage you get on *Crimewatch* from closed-circuit security cameras. Probably cameras just like the ones Veronica sold.

But the tape must have been an old one to give such a washed-out picture with almost a greenish hue. I could just make out a road and some houses and then, as Scooter froze the frame, the outline of a car pulling into the side of the road and its lights going off.

That's when I realised that some form of light-intensifier had been used and the scene had been shot at night.

That night, about forty-five minutes earlier.

Up there on the screen, in dingy murky green, was Amy's BMW right where I had parked it on the main street of Whitcomb.

I made it back to the five-bar gate without falling over or bumping into a cow and walked briskly back to the BMW.

I wasn't paranoid, but I do admit to checking every roof, tree and telegraph post for closed-circuit cameras and I didn't see one. Maybe he only had them facing northwards, maybe they were motion-activated. Maybe he only turned them on when they were using the gateway, after all, he was watching a tape shot whilst he was down the pub so it wasn't continuous surveillance. Maybe I was worrying about Scooter too much.

In London I must appear on CCTV a hundred times a day, in car-parks, banks, department stores, even Mr Patel's 7–11. It was said that the cops had a video surveillance unit at Marble Arch which could zoom in on a pickpocket at Tottenham Court Road station the other end of Oxford Street. Why should I worry? These days your fifteen minutes of fame comes with *not* appearing on a screen somewhere.

But out here in the sticks it was unnerving. The only people who should be allowed to use cameras like that out here were the BBC's Natural History Unit and then only if they were on badger watch.

I unlocked the BMW and looked behind me for the last time. Nothing stirred. Good; keep it that way.

As I got behind the wheel I thought I heard the sound of a siren in the distance and thought that it would be just my luck if Scooter had reported me for trespassing or violating the Country Code on some account.

I turned the Beamer round in the road and focused on getting back to the big, safe city where you simply didn't notice sirens any more.

But this was one siren I could not ignore. It got louder and then up ahead I could see blue flashing lights turning across the road in front of me. Turning into the car-park of the Rising Sun.

The front door of the pub was wide open and all the lights

in the place seemed to be on to welcome the ambulance as it screamed to a stop and two paramedics piled out and began to unload a stretcher.

I could have driven on, gone home, gone clubbing, gone to bed.

Instead I drove up to the pub again.

And that was when it all started to go wrong.

11

'She was looking for a silver tankard and had to get a chair to stand on so she could reach. Said somebody was offering good money for them,' Melanie was explaining breathlessly. 'She dragged the chair behind the bar and she must have knocked the latch on the trap-door – the trap-door that goes to the cellar. The chair started to fall through and she sort of fell sideways on to her ankle.'

'There's no need for all this fuss. I might leave this pub in a box, but I'm not ready to go yet.'

I could hear Ivy but not see her. I presumed she was behind the bar, one of the paramedics leaning over her, the other kneeling under the open bar flap. Melanie was swinging her chair from left to right, trying to look over his shoulder. Dan was ashen-faced at the end of the bar, his fingers in a white grip around an empty glass. It must have been shock – and the prospect that the pub might close on time for once.

'You're not going anywhere on that foot, Mrs Bracegirdle,' said one of the paramedics, 'except hospital. We'll get you into the Royal Victoria and you'll be flat on your back for a week at least.'

Ivy laughed loudly and dirtily.

'Heh-heh! I haven't had any offer that good since VE Day!'

The kneeling paramedic turned and shot Melanie a killer look.

'Who gave her the brandy?'

'I did,' she said sheepishly, 'while Dan was upstairs phoning you lot.'

'I only went into Ivy's bedroom 'cos that's where the phone is,' Dan blustered as if anyone was listening.

'And you couldn't even remember the soddin' number,' shouted Ivy.

'I knew it was nine nine something,' Dan muttered quietly.

I thought that was hilarious but realised no one else was laughing.

'Don't you piss me off, Dan Dexter, I'm running out of places to hide the bodies,' the hidden Ivy retorted. 'Oooh! That hurts like fuck, as the bishop said.'

'I don't think the brandy was a good idea,' said the other paramedic.

'I don't think you gave her enough,' I said and they noticed I was there.

'Who's that?' shouted Ivy.

'It's me, Roy. I was just passing and wondered if I could help.'

I moved to the bar and leaned over. Between the bending heads of the two paramedics, Ivy was sprawled on the floor of the bar, her legs spreadeagled. They had put an inflatable neck-rest behind her head and the kneeling paramedic was holding her right ankle and tenderly feeling his way up her calf muscles. Her dress had ridden up almost to the knee.

''Ere,' she snapped, grabbing the hem of the dress, 'I don't show me knickers to complete strangers.'

'I was in earlier, with Ted and Marion and the Major,' I said quickly. 'And I played darts with Mel here.'

'Oh, that's all right then,' she relaxed. 'Actually I wouldn't mind another snifter, Roy.'

'No!' said both paramedics together.

'She'll only start singing in the back of the ambulance,' said Dan with a twinkle in his eye as he added: 'Like last time.'

'I'm sure Mrs Bracegirdle is going to behave herself,' said the medic who had been examining her leg. 'We'll get you on the stretcher and down to Casualty. I'm afraid that ankle's broken. You're going to be laid up for a while.'

'You're afraid? Who's going to run my pub for me?'

There was silence at that and the paramedics looked at Dan. Ivy followed their gaze.

'Oh no, not him. Anybody but him. Get a Methodist minister in, but not him.'

'Can't somebody just lock the place up for a couple of weeks?'

'What? You mean stay shut, as in "not open"? I'd lose my licence. The magistrates told me I had to be open every day to prove there was a need for the place.'

'That's 'cos you called them all Freemasons,' said Dan and we all glared at him.

'Where's Mel?' Ivy snapped.

'I'm here, Ivy,' Mel said from my side.

I looked down into her chair and noticed that the mobile phone that had been clipped on to the side was no longer there. I had wondered why Dan had had to go upstairs to ring for the ambulance. And there was something else about Mel which bothered me, but I couldn't put my finger on it.

'You can run the bar, Mel,' Ivy was saying, 'You've done it before.'

Because she was flat out behind the bar and Mel was in her wheelchair, Ivy could not see Mel's expression, which was probably just as well.

She twisted her face and gritted her teeth as she said: 'Not like this I can't, Ivy.' She slapped the palms of her hands on the padded arm-rests of her chair in frustration.

'We could rename it the Walking Wounded,' Dan offered helpfully.

'You can just fuck off and die, Dan Dexter!' Ivy bellowed. 'You'll not be walking straight if I get my hands on you.'

'Let's get her on the stretcher,' said the lead paramedic, then softly to the other one: 'Have the straps ready.'

They picked her up gently and manoeuvred her out of the bar on to the stretcher laid out in front of the dart board. Ivy kept talking.

'Oh, go on, Mel, you can manage. You know how to do the books and the VAT better than I do. Deliveries on Tuesdays and banking on Fridays, you know the score. You could do it.'

'I can't do the heavy lifting, can I, Ivy?' Mel said, desperation in her voice. 'I can't even get behind the bar in this thing.'

'Then I'm not going.'

Ivy put her hands on the floor and tried to lever herself up.

The paramedics nodded to each other and flipped a blanket over her and then two wide straps, securing them with the dexterity of magicians.

'Oi! What's with the strait-jacket? I'm lame, not fucking mad!' she screamed.

The senior medic came over to Mel and me and spoke under his breath.

'Look, can't *you* help out?'

I realised he was talking to me.

'Me? Run a pub?'

What would Amy say? *Get me a solicitor*, is what Amy would say.

'Just for tonight. Lock the place up, send everybody home.' He looked around, realising that there were only three of us and I didn't even have a drink. 'It's nearly closing time anyway. Just lock it up and make sure everything's secure. I'll tell the local police in the morning and they can clear it with the magistrates.'

'But I'm just passing . . .'

'I'll do it if Roy here will help,' Mel said, not looking at me but reaching out to take hold of my hand.

'Are you sure?' the paramedic asked as if genuinely concerned. Me, I might not have been there.

'I've done relief work here for years, since I was at school,' she said, 'and I still do the books for her. I'll cover for a week or so and I'll let the brewery know tomorrow so if it's any longer they can get somebody in. We can manage, can't we, Roy?'

She squeezed my hand.

'Yeah, 'course we can.'

What was I doing?

Mel let go of me and wheeled herself over to Ivy's stretcher.

'Don't you worry about a thing, Ivy,' she said sweetly. 'Roy can do the bottling up and changing the barrels, I'll keep an eye on the takings and make sure Dan and the Major behave themselves.'

'Don't take any bullshit from them, Mel my dear, and you keep a *sharp* eye on the money. The keys are in the till.' Ivy's panic attack had suddenly vanished. 'Will I get a private room at the hospital?'

I would have said that was a safe bet.

The paramedic leaned into my ear and whispered:

'Do you know if she suffers from any sort of insanity?'

'From what I know, she doesn't suffer at all. She enjoys every minute of it.'

The three of us stood in the doorway of the Rising Sun as the ambulance's blue lights and siren faded into the night.

'There's a turn-up,' said Dan philosophically.

'Poor Ivy,' said Mel, shaking her head.

'Anybody fancy a drink?' I asked.

I awoke the next morning to the sound of a ringing bell, but I was too old and too wise to be caught out by that one.

I knew perfectly well where I was, I was on the couch in Ivy's upstairs living-room. I knew exactly what was wrapped around my legs, it was the eiderdown from her bed. I knew I had drunk too much brandy into the wee hours of the morning and as I knew I was going to have a hangover, I had been sensible and placed a bottle of mineral water next to the couch. And I knew that ringing bell was not in my throbbing head, but was really my mobile phone. No mystery, nothing to worry about.

Except that I had left the mobile in the BMW and the ringing showed no sign of stopping. Plus, the eiderdown seemed to have taken on a homicidal life of its own and I couldn't find my jeans.

'Roy? Roy? You up there?'

A voice replaced the ringing sound. It was Mel. I remembered her quite clearly. If only I could remember where I'd put my jeans.

'Yeah, yeah, down in a minute.'

I found them behind a chair, struggled into them and pulled my T-shirt over my head as I negotiated the winding staircase down to the bar barefoot and picking up splinters with every step.

Mel was in her wheelchair the other side of the open bar flap. She was holding a handbell by the clapper, tapping the handle on the palm of her other hand. (I had seen it, thick with dust, on the bar during the evening where it was supposedly used to ring

129

'Time'.) She had her hair tied up in a bun at the back of her head and wore a tight white cotton top and no bra. She looked an awful lot better than I felt.

I took a swig of mineral water and said:

'What's this, my alarm call?'

'I thought you might need one the way you were enjoying yourself when I left last night. Is there any stock left?'

'Loads,' I said expansively. 'I've found where everything is – Dan tested me on it – and I'm just waiting for the customers. Bring 'em on.'

'So you've sorted the menu for lunch then?' she asked with a smile. The sort of smile you might trust on a tiger, but never a woman.

'Lunch?' I said vaguely. I felt vague. 'Menu?'

'As in Dish Of The Day, our famous Chalkboard Special, Home Made In Ivy's Country Kitchen?'

'Kitchen?'

'I thought so,' she said smugly.

'Sorry.'

'And you didn't even lock the front door last night, did you?'

'Sorry.'

'And your flies are open.'

'Thank you for noticing.'

Actually, the whole indignant act about the lunchtime menu for the Rising Sun was a con. I should have remembered that the height of Ivy's culinary powers was boiled eggs and soldiers, but by the time I did I was in the kitchen up to my elbows in a sinkful of dirty dishes.

Ivy was, after all, the single parent of the pub and if she was serving behind the bar she couldn't be in the kitchen whipping up something off the *à la carte* menu. Therefore, the menu consisted entirely of sandwiches and in the kitchen was a hand-written list to prove it. It read: Egg, Egg Mayonnaise, Egg and Onion, Egg and Tomato, Egg Salad, Pickled Egg, Egg and Bacon (hot).

The preparation stage, which as any top chef knows is crucial, involved taking a loaf of bread out of the freezer and defrosting it in the microwave and then making sure that the butter was soft enough to spread.

'If there's a frying pan, I can do the Bacon and Egg, but what does she put in the Egg Salad?' I asked Mel, who was layering a pile of plates with paper serviettes.

'Mayo, onion, tomato and pickled egg,' she said.

'Oh, I get it,' I said, looking at the menu. 'Pickled egg?'

'The big jar on top of the fridge with those brown spherical things floating around. Ivy pickles them herself.'

'She's keen on eggs, isn't she?' I observed.

'Gets them free, that's why.' She looked up at me. 'You have fed the chickens out back, haven't you?'

I'd wondered what that noise was outside the bathroom window.

'Er . . . do it now. What do I give them?'

'Their feed is in that metal bowl on the end of the shelf.'

I had seen it when I had first found the kitchen to make coffee and had thought it was muesli. I had come that close to adding milk.

Out in the back garden of the pub I found myself confronted by hundreds of brown feathery prototype dinosaurs flashing their vicious beaks and complaining loudly until I threw corn on to their heads and backs. Some of them still weren't satisfied and just clucked on and on like a woman does when she knows you've got a hangover and your defences are down . . .

Oh my God. Amy.

I flung a pound of corn over the lead hen and ran back and through the pub to get the mobile out of the car.

'So let me get this straight,' said Amy as she lit a fresh cigarette from the butt of the last one. 'You come down here to check out a dustbin full of empty beer bottles and within twenty-four hours you're running a pub and a battery farm on the side. That's about the strength of it, right?'

'If you knew the circumstances, you wouldn't be so quick to judge,' I said, soaking up some passive smoke.

'I've found that snap judgements are usually the best when it comes to your little escapades, Angel, they save so much time.'

'Now, now, sweetheart, you're always saying I should get out more and develop my own interests,' I said smarmily, easing the BMW into the nearside lane for the turn-off to Whitcomb.

'Not if the interest is called – what was it? – Mel?'

'Amy, please,' I said, trying to sound shocked. 'Mel is a sweet girl, but she is very young and she's been very helpful to me. And she's also . . . disabled. She's in a wheelchair.'

'Oh,' said Amy, briefly subdued. 'What's wrong with her?'

'A traffic accident,' I said carefully. If I had told her that Mel had fallen off a EuroDisney float whilst dressed as a mouse, she would have slugged me. 'I don't think it's permanent.'

'How permanent is this pub thing, then?'

Time, of course, was money to Amy.

'A couple of days, tops. It's the perfect place for me to do my job for Veronica, just snoop about a bit more then write up a report for her. Call the brewery and tell them to put in a relief manager.' I took my eyes off the road to watch her face. 'Why not stay down here with me for a couple of days? You're ahead of schedule on the photo-shoot aren't you?'

I had met her off one of the Eurostar trains which stopped at Ashford, or Ashford International as they now proudly called it. When I had called her that morning, she had given me an earful about missed messages and then listened in eerie silence as I told her what I had been up to.

She hadn't said anything then, just filled me in on her Paris trip. Her photo-shoot with Nigel had been completed in one day rather than the three that had been scheduled. The three models employed – Neemoy, Sasha and Max – had been everything a fashion photographer could want: tall, beautiful, vacant and – added bonus – uncomplaining. There had been no tantrums (except from Nigel), the clothes had been in the right place at the right time and even the sun had shone for the outdoor shots with the Pompidou Centre in the background. Nigel had worked harder and faster than she had ever known and it was only in the evening that he had announced that he was taking a few days off for a romantic tryst in a new gay bar he'd been told about.

('Did he have friends there?' I had asked and Amy had said: 'Not yet.')

So Amy had taken charge of a bag of undeveloped film, just in case Nigel never made it home, and chaperoned the three models around Paris by night. That had put her in a bad mood as much as anything I had done. Well, you know what models are, always watching their weight, existing on a stick of celery a week or simply inhaling melon cocktail in restaurants with wine lists longer than *War and Peace*. Too tired to go clubbing, too paranoid to go drinking, always wanting to be left alone but really pissed off when nobody recognised them.

All they had going for them was their looks and long, long legs.

I could see they were beautiful and I knew they had long legs from the adjustments I'd had to make to the two front seats in the BMW. I was quite surprised the three of them had fitted in the back seat. I think BMW would be too and I considered writing to them to congratulate their designers.

'You see me as some sort of pub landlady?' Amy choked on her cigarette. 'This isn't some schoolboy fantasy of yours, is it? Sleeping with a woman who runs a pub?'

Sometimes her insights were frightening.

'No, nothing like that, just thought you might like a change.'

'Getting eight hours' solid sleep would be a change.'

'But I could use three barmaids.'

As I said it, I looked in the rear-view mirror but the expressions on the beautiful faces of Neemoy, Sasha and Max didn't twitch, just stayed beautiful.

Amy left it for a minute, then said: 'They are paid up until Friday.'

'And they could wear TALtops. They could be walking, working adverts for you.'

'I could get a photographer down,' she said, thinking aloud. 'We could try a few shots – country pub, barmaids . . . you don't have to be on a catwalk to model a TALtop.'

'Yeah, that's good,' I encouraged her.

'Could make the Saturday broadsheets, the lifestyle sections.'

'Yeah, lifestyle.'

'Is this pub photogenic?'

'There it is,' I said, turning into the car-park.

'Oh fuck,' said Amy.

'But it's very rustic inside,' I said quickly. 'And you'll be doing interiors, won't you?'

'I suppose,' she said hesitantly.

Then she turned in her seat and addressed the three girls in the back who so far had not said a word and may not have said a word from birth for all I knew.

'Listen, girls, we're going to rig another shoot here in ... in ... the country in a traditional country pub. It's a bit off the wall, like you'll have to look like you're working for a living, but it could just get you into the newspapers without having to show your tits.'

She was still talking as I pulled up outside the Rising Sun. I could see Dan's face pressed to one of the windows trying to make out who was in the car.

'I'm going to zip up to town to arrange a photographer, so while I'm gone, Angel here will be your boss.'

'Call me Roy,' I said, smiling.

Amy took it the wrong way and glared at me.

'It's important they call me Roy,' I said. 'That's what they know me as here.'

Amy exhaled loudly down her nose.

'Very well, *Roy* here is the boss. And you know the first rule of modelling, girls: don't fuck the boss.'

'You mean fuck *with* the boss,' said Neemoy, the tall, voluptuous one with the ebony skin.

'That too,' said Amy.

12

Amy surveyed the bar of the Rising Sun first with horror, then with muted disdain and finally just a sneer.

'Rustic, did you say, Angel?'

'Yes, *darling*,' I stressed, hoping Mel had not picked up on the 'Angel'.

Mel was zipping around collecting dirty glasses and banging them down on the bar as loudly as she could. There weren't many empties, but she was making the most of them. Dan was standing back at his corner of the bar staring open-mouthed at Neemoy, Sasha and Max. Two youngish men in suits drinking Coke and eating sandwiches, which I guessed were egg, were doing likewise.

'Are those tankards silver?' Amy asked, ignoring all of them.

'Not really. Mostly pewter, I'd guess. Maybe silver plate.' I could guess what she was thinking. 'A tie-in with the silver thread TALtop?'

'It's a thought. I'll see if that nice little man in the Silver Vaults will supply some.'

'I don't think they hire them out,' I said, but she wasn't listening.

'Does the pub do food?'

'Kitchen's closed,' said Mel, driving her chair so close to the three models that they all took a step back to protect their toes.

'No problem,' Amy said airily. 'I'll get something on the way back. You should let Sasha loose in the kitchen. There's nothing she can't do with tofu, is there, Sasha my sweet?'

'Lots of people don't eat meat these days,' said Sasha, looking at her fingernails.

'How about eggs?' I said automatically.

'Eggs are OK,' she said, bored.

Thank God for that.

'Let me see what I can fix up once I get back to town. I'll give you a bell tonight.' She held out her right hand, palm up. 'Car keys, please.'

'You're taking the Beamer?' I said stupidly.

'It's mine.'

'Technically. But I'll be without transport.'

'Not going anywhere, are you?'

Neemoy, Sasha, Max and I made sure we had all our stuff out of the BMW and we stood and waved goodbye as Amy gunned the engine and scattered gravel as she drove off.

I turned to my new bar staff to give them the pep talk I was sure they were expecting.

Sasha had her hands inside her large leather shoulder bag,

rolling a fat, five-skin joint from a pouch of Drum rolling tobacco and a bag of what looked like seeds and leaves in equal proportions. Neemoy had unwrapped a King Size Mars bar and was munching away ecstatically.

'She's not coming back, is she?' Max, the short-cropped blonde asked.

'Not today,' I said weakly.

'Good. This pub sells tequila, right?'

I had the awful feeling that I had just introduced the Barmaids From Hell to the Pub From Hell, but I was delighted to be proved wrong. Within half an hour, the girls were wiping down the bar, filling the dishwasher (I didn't know there was one), cleaning ashtrays, even lugging crates of bottles up from the cellar.

True, Neemoy was on her third packet of crisps, Max had discovered that vodka would do at a pinch as there wasn't any tequila and Sasha was singing quietly to herself as she counted the glasses on the shelf under the bar. She did it first from left to right, then started again, right to left. No one knew why she was doing it and no one asked.

'Doesn't look like you need me any more.'

Mel had parked her chair at the table where I was enjoying a late breakfast. I had made myself some fresh coffee (instant) and an omelette with some dried herbs I had found in the kitchen. They were so dried they were dust and I knew I could have soaked more flavour out of whatever Sasha was smoking. It was only made palatable by the view I had of Neemoy leaning lengthwise over one of the long tables with a cloth and a spray gun of all-purpose cleaner.

'Hey, look, I'm really grateful to you covering for me at lunchtime like that. Did you manage?'

'Had to. Dan helped out behind the bar, so I slipped him a tenner out of the till. I did the lunches. You took about £23 in wet sales, just over sixty in dry.'

'Excuse me?'

'Drinks as opposed to food. I've left you £10 float in the till, the rest is in the safe.'

'There's a safe?'

'In the kitchen under the sink. Do you want the keys?'

'I'd rather not have the responsibility,' I said.

'Comes with the job.'

'What job?'

'Running the pub. You'd better do a stock check, prepare the order for the brewery and you'll have to go to a cash-and-carry or somewhere to get the basics in, bread, milk, stuff like that. I'll talk to Ivy when I see her, find out if there are any bills need paying or if she's expecting her area manager, anything like that. Keep an eye out for Trading Standards officers doing spot checks to see if you're selling watered-down whisky or short pints. Don't serve any kids and don't let the one smoking dope anywhere near the kitchen.'

'In case what?' I asked, catching on. 'In case we get an inspection by the Food Standards Agency?'

'No,' Mel said seriously, 'because there are sharp knives in there.'

'Anything else?'

'The local police might turn up if they hear Ivy's in hospital, but they won't bother you if you're running an orderly house. If the VAT inspectors turn up, just plead ignorance. Pretend you don't know where the cash books are.'

'I don't.'

'That's for the best. I'll keep the safe keys then, but I'll look in tonight after I've been to the hospital.'

'How are you getting there?' I asked, realising that I didn't actually know where Ivy was.

'My mother will drive me when she gets home from work.'

'She's got a car?' I said without thinking.

'No, she tows me behind the lawn mower.'

'Could she give me a lift if I sat on your knee?' I asked innocently, just to show I could handle sarcasm.

'I don't think so, it's only a small car and the chair takes up the back seat. Where do you want to go anyway? I thought your . . .'

'Yeah, my partner took the car but now it looks like I'm going to have to go shopping, or so you said.'

'And leave these three to run the pub?' she said loudly.

'Is that a problem?'

'Not for me, I'm out of here.'

'I'll come with you, for the walk. I need a break.'

I looked around at Neemoy dusting the pelmet above one of the windows – although sadly she was tall enough to do it without standing on a chair – and at Max carefully cleaning the optics under the spirits bottles and then at Sasha who was manhandling a vacuum cleaner down the trap-door into the cellar.

Everything seemed to be going swimmingly in the pub. It was time to go back to my proper job.

I didn't even offer to push Mel's wheelchair down the lane towards the village, just walked alongside her in the road.

'How about one of your dart-playing boffins?' I suggested.

'What about them?' she replied, staring straight ahead.

'Would one of them lend me a car for a few hours?'

'I'm sure they would. Hey fellas, this guy who was hanging around the pub last night, the one you've never seen before in your life, just hand over your keys, will you?'

'Bit thin, you think?'

'Just a bit.'

'How about a lift into Folkestone or Dover, then? Just to do a bit of shopping.'

'You could ask, I suppose.'

I supposed I could, if she was going to be so selfish that she wouldn't ask for me. I mean, they were her friends after all.

We were round the bend in the road from the Rising Sun now, approaching the five-bar gate near the thatched cottage where I had gone exploring last night. The main street of Whitcomb was empty again, not a sign of a car or a pedestrian. I was getting the impression that I had left the Barmaids From Hell running the Pub From Hell in the Village Of The Damned.

'I haven't seen any buses round here,' I wheedled, 'and I wouldn't give much for my chances of thumbing a lift. Does anybody actually live in this village?'

'Oh yes, a few,' she said in a prickly sort of way, 'but they're mostly retired, like the Major, or they work somewhere else, like Dover or Folkestone or Ashford or even Canterbury. There's no work here in Whitcomb any more.'

'Except your friends the computer boffins.'

'You seem very interested in them.'

She put her hands on the rims of her wheels to brake herself, then she swung round to face me.

'I'm just looking for some transport, that's all. I guess I feel a bit stranded without my wheels.'

Even as I said it, I knew I should be biting my tongue.

'You should try mine,' Mel said.

'I'm sorry.'

'Aw, what the fuck, I've heard worse things said when people were trying to be sympathetic. And I suppose I owe you one for offering to run the pub for Ivy last night.'

I remembered her holding my hand when the paramedic had mentioned telling the local police.

'I didn't seem to get much say in the matter,' I said ruefully. 'Come to think of it, I've been running the pub for over twelve hours now and I haven't pulled a pint in anger, not for an actual customer, that is. You seem to have done most of it. You should be running the place.'

'Oh sure, you can just see the brewery letting me run the place. I can't even get behind the bar in this thing.' She gripped the arm-rests of her chair and shook them violently.

'But you live here, you know Ivy. You've worked there before.'

'Yeah, and you're a man and you've got two good legs. If you're a man and you can whistle and pee at the same time and you don't have a criminal record, you can run a pub.'

I decided not to ask her for details about the 'criminal record' bit.

'Look, can I give you some money? Get some flowers for Ivy and tell her for Christ's sake to get well soon before I bankrupt her.'

'I think you did that last night buying drinks for me and Dan.'

'I did?'

'Don't worry, I put an IOU in the till for you. If you ask me, you want to make sure your three barmaids do the same before they eat and drink Ivy out of house and home.'

'The thought had occurred. I'll put it on my Things To Do list.' I took my wallet out of my back pocket and pulled out a

139

£20 note for her. 'But I really could use a lift to find some shops. There's stuff I need, like a toothbrush and a razor and deodorant. I wasn't planning on an extended stay down here.'

She nodded at that and pushed her chair along. We were now opposite the five-bar gate.

'Well, you can always ask Scooter. He can only say no.'

She stopped her chair again and pointed at the gate.

'Soft Sell work out of the old hop farm, over there.'

'Soft Sell?'

'That's the name of Scooter's company. They do software for computers. Just walk through the paddock and you'll see the old hop sheds. That's where they are.'

I leaned on the gate and looked over the paddock. There wasn't a sign of a building from this angle, but I already knew they were dog-legged off to the right. From the gate the paddock sloped up to a wooded hillside which disappeared over the Downs.

'In here?' I tried to inject the right note of disbelief into my voice.

'It's just a short cut. We let them use our paddock as a short cut to the pub. They're not supposed to as there's no right of way but the real entrance is over the hill, off the old Roman road to Canterbury, miles away.'

'So this is their back door? The tradesmen's entrance?'

'I don't think they encourage tradesmen,' said Mel. 'To be honest, they don't encourage visitors. I think some of the things they do are sensitive, commercially sensitive.'

'Do they export much?'

'I suppose so, they're always coming and going at all hours. But that's why a lot of software companies have moved down here to Kent.' She laughed suddenly. 'One or two of them have always got French beer on hand and duty-free cigarettes, but they don't let Ivy see them when they're down the pub.'

I bet they didn't. The torrent of obscenities would have had them reaching for their dictionaries.

I made a play of crouching and stroking the carpet of Astro-turf which peeked out from under the gate.

'What's with the artificial grass?'

'Scooter put it down to stop the gateway getting churned up in winter. Me and Mum thought it was a good idea.'

'You and Mum?'

'It's our paddock, we live here.' She pointed to the thatched cottage a few feet away. 'Hop Cottage. But we haven't used the paddock since I had a pony when I was a kid, so we don't mind Soft Sell using it as a short cut.'

And why should they? It wouldn't have occurred to them that one man's short cut was another man's escape route.

I watched Melanie wheel herself up to the front door of Hop Cottage and reach up to push a Yale key into the lock. She waved at me as she pushed herself into the house and out of sight.

I clambered over the gate and trudged down the paddock for the second time, but this time I could see what I was doing. The hedge to my right must have been the border of Hop Cottage, and once at the end of it I could see what was left of the hop farm as I approached it from the rear.

The nearest building was the one I had spied on and this afternoon it had the Jeep, two Volvo estate cars and three pick-up trucks parked outside. Whoever these students really were, they seemed to have more vehicles than the average Ford dealer.

There were three other single-storey buildings about a hundred yards away and a large corrugated iron barn, a bit like an aircraft hangar with sliding doors, beyond them. A single track road ran by the buildings and disappeared into the distance in the wooded hills. To either side of the track were grubbed-up fields gradually filling with grass and weeds and littered with hop poles and trellis wires, giving the impression of a World War I battlefield.

I didn't get much time to get my bearings and I was still fifty yards from the first building when the doors opened and out stepped Scooter, flanked by the staring-eyed Axeman and the one I think Mel had called Painter.

'Can we help you?' Scooter called out. 'You're not lost, are you?'

'No, it's you I was looking for,' I called back, marching on straight towards them.

I never gave a thought to be frightened of them. It wasn't just

141

because they were younger than I was; I'd been scared by twelve-year-olds before now. And it wasn't so much the setting – broad daylight in a field in Kent just couldn't hold a candle to 1 a.m. in the Tottenham Court Road for scare factor. (Broad daylight in the Tottenham Court Road come to think of it.) It was just that these lads didn't *look* the violent type; they were trying to look cool, not threatening, although I had to give the benefit of the doubt to Axeman. He *did* look like a psychopath, but I put it down to genetics, not malice.

'You found us,' said Scooter, leaning casually on the bonnet of the Jeep, waiting for me to make my pitch.

'I seem to have sort of inherited the pub down the road,' I started.

'We heard,' said Axeman, but I ignored him.

'Ivy the landlady had an accident last night and was carted off to hospital. Somehow – and I'm not too sure how – I was left in charge and now I'm without a car.'

'Somebody's stolen it?' Scooter asked without even trying to look interested.

'No, the car wasn't mine. It had to go back to London, so I'm kind of stranded and I need to go shopping.' That sounded a bit lame so I added: 'Get some provisions in. For the pub. For Ivy.'

Scooter looked at me, his head tilted so that his shock of blond hair fell over his left eye. He still didn't look violent but he didn't half irritate me.

'And so?' he drawled slowly, opening the palms of his hands towards me.

'So I was looking for a lift to the nearest supermarket.'

Axeman let out a giggle which was almost a squeak.

Scooter flicked his head and his hair and dug a hand into his jacket pocket to produce a set of keys.

'Is that all?' He patted the windscreen of the Jeep. 'Jump in.'

I was in the middle of the aisle which had fabric conditioners and washing powders down one side, household cleaners, bleaches and disinfectants down the other when I used my mobile to ring Nick Lawrence at Customs and Excise in Dover.

I reckoned it was the geographical centre of the supermarket Scooter had driven me to. He had said he would wait in the car-park for me, but just to be sure I picked a spot where there was no way he could see in from the outside.

I switched the phone on and pressed for the memory. When 'HMCE' came up, I hit the Send button.

'Lawrence,' he came through after three rings.

'It's Roy Angel, remember? Working for Murdo Seton's brewery.'

'I can remember yesterday, if that's what you mean. You still on the case?'

'Up to my neck,' I said, smiling as a woman with a young child in her shopping trolley glided by. It looked like there was a special offer on lean mince somewhere in the shop. 'Can you check out car number plates for me?'

'I can have them checked out,' his voice crackled in my ear, 'but whether I'll tell you is another matter. Where the hell are you?'

Above my head, a tannoy was announcing double saver points on items marked with a red sticker.

'Never mind. Got a pen? Take these down.'

I pulled a beer mat from my pocket and read out the numbers I had recorded last night and scribbled down before leaving the Rising Sun. I knew the plate of Scooter's Jeep quite well by now, having ridden in it, and I added the two Volvos I had seen at the hop farm, hoping I remembered them correctly.

'You opening a garage or something?' said Lawrence. 'I'll see what I can turn up, but don't hold your breath.'

'Fair enough. I'll call you, don't you try and ring me.'

'Why would I?'

'I might have something for you.'

'Oh yeah? Well, I won't hold my breath.'

He hung up but I kept smiling into the phone as another trolley pushed by a vivacious redhead in a very short miniskirt overtook me.

'Don't worry, darling,' I said into the dead phone, 'I won't forget the whipped cream. It's on my list. Yes, the sort in the spray can.'

The redhead didn't look round, but I saw her ears blush.

Later, in the car-park, she saw Scooter helping me load my carrier bags bulging with bread, frozen pizzas, butter, baking potatoes, family packs of lean mince (I couldn't resist, it was a bargain) and tins of non-genetically modified tomatoes into the back of his Jeep.

As she unlocked her VW Golf and packed her own shopping away, I could tell she was thinking: *I knew he was gay.*

13

Scooter wasn't gay, or at least I don't think he was. I never got to to know him that well, but then as he was still short of his twenty-third birthday I suppose you could say that nobody knew him well.

When he drove me to the supermarket that late afternoon he wasn't giving anything away. It was as if it was the most natural thing in the world for a complete, or almost complete, stranger to turn up at his place of work (in the middle of a field in Kent) and ask for a lift to the shops.

He started up the Jeep, waited whilst I clicked in my seat belt and then slipped a Blur CD into the player on the dashboard. Then he reversed the Jeep beyond the edge of the first building and swung left, changed into first and drove slowly alongside it. He was clearly not going to use the gate I had climbed over even though I knew he had used it last night, and I had a good idea that he knew I knew. Perhaps he was waiting for me to mention it.

'This is where you work then?' I said cleverly, to divert him.

'For the moment,' he said, turning the Jeep on to a single track concrete road leading to two smaller one-storey buildings of similar design.

'Melanie said you were in software.'

'That's right. Know anything about computer programming?'

'Square-root of bugger all.'

'That's the way I like it.'

'Business good, then?'

As I spoke I noticed, now I was nearer, that one of the other buildings was virtually derelict and open to the elements. No way were they programming anything in there.

'As long as people have computers but know bugger all about programming them, business'll be good. There's a lot of work around, it's just a question of finding it.'

'And you found it *here*?' I gestured to the windscreen. We were passing the large aircraft hangar building and the road was dipping down between the churned-up fields littered with poles and coils of wire. Ahead, the track turned into a line of trees. It was like a scene from *Dr Zhivago* except somebody had forgotten to order the snow. 'What is this place?'

'It's an old hop farm which went bust a couple of years ago and they grubbed up all the hop bines. They used to grow up those poles supported by wires, ten, twenty feet, something like that.'

'And that makes it an ideal place for you to program computers?'

The Jeep was going uphill now, into the trees, leaving the brown, gutted fields behind.

'All we need is a building we can keep reasonably clean and some electricity.' He turned his shock of droopy blond hair at me. He used it like a gun. 'Companies hire us to reprogram their computers or upgrade them, memorywise. Most don't like it done on the premises so we bring the kit here. With things like shops and small offices, we do it overnight or at the weekend. It's a good system. This way they don't get to see how easy it is.'

He stopped the Jeep at the junction with a B-road and signalled left. There was a wooden signpost at the side of the junction with a carved picnic table and an oak leaf, signifying a nature reserve of some sort. A road sign opposite said that Folkestone was the way we were heading, Canterbury was the other.

'You don't advertise much,' I said, trying not to look as if I was mapping the route in my head.

'We go to customers, we don't expect them to come to us. What about you?'

145

I had been expecting this and was rather surprised it hadn't come before.

'Me? What about me?'

'What do you do when you're not running a pub? Didn't Melanie say you were a fashion photographer or something?'

'Oh no, not me. I'm just driving one around at the moment, or I was. I'm a driver, that's all.'

'So how come you're running the Rising Sun, then?'

'Dunno. Just lucky, I guess.'

On the way back, once we had loaded my shopping into the back of the Jeep and avoided the smug stare of the redhead with the VW Golf, he brought it up again.

'So what sort of things do you drive?'

'Anything. Trucks, stretched limos, minicabs when times are hard. I'm in a drivers' pool and we'll turn out for anything. The company's called Duncan's. Heard of it?'

'Can't say I have.'

Good. Neither had I, but I did have a friend called Duncan, better known as Duncan the Drunken, possibly the best motor mechanic in the world, who could get hold of any sort of vehicle short of a tank if you asked him.

'No matter. I'll be glad to get back to work, though. I'm not a good passenger.'

'How did you end up here in Whitcomb?' he asked as we turned off the motorway. He wasn't a bad driver himself; a touch heavy on the gas pedal but careful with it.

'Pure chance. I had to bring somebody's car down here to meet them off the ferry but then their plans changed and they got the Eurostar to Ashford this afternoon instead. By that time I was lumbered with running the pub so the boss lady took her car home. Guess I'll have to thumb a lift back to London once Ivy gets back.'

'What if she doesn't come back?' he said, flicking his hair at me.

'What do you mean?'

'Well, she is getting on in years, you know, and maybe the hospital wants to put her in a twilight home or similar.'

146

A maximum security one from what I knew of her, I thought.

'I haven't burned that bridge yet,' I said, 'but I suppose we'll have to call the brewery and get them to put a relief manager in.'

He didn't give much away did young Scooter, but I saw his hands tighten on the steering wheel at that, though I couldn't think why.

'Couldn't you run things? Get a temporary licence or whatever they call them?'

'Er . . . no. I don't have time, don't want to hang around this backwater – no offence – and the last thing I want to do is present myself before Folkestone magistrates pretending to be an upright citizen. There was a publican in the pub last night, a Ted something-or-other, friend of Ivy's. I've got his card. I'll give him a ring, see what he says. If it comes to that.'

'But you're OK for a couple of days?'

'End of the week, tops. Depends on my new staff.'

'Staff?'

'I've conned three of the girls from the model agency into helping out. Their boss is considering doing some photographs in the pub, but that may or may not pan out. It just means I've got some cheap labour for tonight and tomorrow. It's not fair to lean on Melanie, though if she hadn't had her accident, she'd have been the natural choice to cover for Ivy. She's a good kid.'

He pointed the shock of hair at me again. I still wasn't sure how much he could see through it.

'Yes, she is,' he said in a neutral sort of way.

'Known her long?'

'Since university. I heard about her accident and when I knew we'd be working down here, I looked her up.'

'Moved in next door, in fact.'

'Yeah, as it happens.'

'And now your guys are part of her darts team?'

'There's not much else to do round here and all our work is short-term, odd-hours stuff, so the pub's convenient. Mel said it could do with the customers as well.'

We were rounding the bend towards the Rising Sun and had a full view of the car-park. It struck me for the first time that the

147

pub also offered an excellent view of the road approaching Whitcomb from this, southern, end. But that was no more than a fleeting thought because something more peculiar was nipping at my brain.

The car-park was full, or appeared so. There were certainly twenty or more cars there, including a couple of pick-ups which could have been the ones I had seen parked outside Scooter's Soft Sell works on the old hop farm.

I looked at my watch; it was six thirty.

'Do they hold car boot sales here?' I asked as we turned in towards the pub.

'No,' said Scooter and he wasn't smiling. 'It looks like your business is booming.'

It was. The pub hadn't seen so many paying customers since VE Day, or so Dan said and he would know.

Dan had at least claimed his traditional place at the corner of the bar. The Major was trying to mark his territory by huffing and growling every time he was jostled on the shoulder or rocked on his bar stool. Two of Scooter's boffins, the ones called Combo and Painter, were trying to play darts without putting anyone's eye out. The spooky Axeman was leaning up against the bar. The rest I didn't know, although two of them were the pair who had been in at lunchtime when I had turned up with Amy and the girls. They must have told their friends, or at least all their male friends for there wasn't a female in the place this side of the bar.

It was the three females *behind* the bar that were important, behind a bar that was so small they couldn't help but bump into each other as they tried to serve drinks to the assembled throng. That in itself seemed to make most of the customers more thirsty, although it might have had something to do with the fact that all three were wearing red TALtops pulled to reveal maximum cleavage (what I had once described to Amy as 'Danger Mode'), very short skirts and suicidally high heels. For Neemoy, who didn't need heels to be impressive, this meant that she had to stoop every time she walked under the tankards hanging from hooks in the roof beams. When she hit one, it cannoned into the next in line like an off-key peal of bells.

148

I struggled through the crowd, two carrier bags of shopping in each hand, shouting, 'Coming through! Mind your backs!' and suchlike until I could station myself by the kitchen door at the side of the bar.

The Major nooded grimly at me and flexed his moustache. Dan grinned broadly.

"Evening, Roy. Now this is what I call under new management!' he jerked a thumb at Neemoy who seemed to be able to reach every drink in the bar without moving her feet. 'And I wouldn't mind getting under her.'

I was about to tell him not to think about fighting out of his weight class when the opening chords of 'Walking On Sunshine' by Katrina and The Waves boomed out from the other side of the bar accompanied by a loud cheer from most of the customers.

The three girls behind the bar broke into spontaneous applause and several voices yelled to 'buy that man a drink'. A figure in an anorak, blushing bright red, was pushed towards the bar into the arms of Max who was leaning forward to give him a hug. It was Chip – or it might have been Dale – from Soft Sell and if he didn't make contact with Max's bosom quick, there were others ready and willing to step into his shoes.

'Lad fixed the jukebox,' said Dan in my ear above the music.

'I didn't know we had a jukebox,' I shouted back.

'Neither did I,' he said.

Sasha spotted me and focused her disappearing pupils on my face.

'It's Roy – right?'

I nodded, suddenly tired. I had been out shopping all afternoon while they had been enjoying themselves.

'This is fun, isn't it? Do you want a drink?'

I finally got the door to the kitchen open.

'No thanks,' I said. 'I've got to get on with the dinner. But call me when the lap dancing starts.'

'Lap dancing,' she said to herself, but I could read her lips above the music. 'Cool.'

Over by the dart board I spotted Scooter remonstrating with Combo, even poking a finger into Combo's chest to make a point. Now didn't seem the time to thank him for the lift. And out of the corner of my eye I saw that Axeman was not taking either of his protruding eyes off Neemoy, not for a second. That, I was sure, would end in tears before bedtime.

The kitchen was a haven of peace and sanity if you didn't count the sprinkling of cannabis seeds which Sasha had left on the main food preparation area. They popped as I plonked my bags down on them and began to unpack my shopping.

I heard a door open and a burst of music as Max came through the back of the bar and the small storeroom and into the kitchen from the other end.

'Got any ice in here?' she asked.

'Try the fridge,' I said. I was, after all, a private detective. 'Isn't there any on the bar?'

'Nope.'

She opened the freezer compartment of the large fridge and tentatively poked in a magenta fingernail.

'You coping out there?'

'Yeah, we're enjoying it. We don't often get to talk to people face-to-face.'

'The novelty'll soon wear off. How did you draw the punters?'

'Dunno, really.' She had located a plastic tray of ice cubes. 'A couple of guys appeared and we chatted them up and they got on their mobiles and some more turned up. They all seem really nice, except for the spooky one who won't stop clocking Neemoy. You know, the one who looks like he's from the Addams Family. Called Alex or something. He's creepy.'

'Yes, he is. You watch him. Tell me when he goes, will you?'

'OK. What'll you be doing?'

'Staying out of the way mostly,' I said truthfully, 'and getting something to eat. I'm starving. There's pizza or pasta or one of my homemade cheeseburgers if you guys want to take a shift break.'

'Oh, we're fine at the moment,' she said lazily, 'we're just playing the field, seeing how the evening pans out, checking out the local talent.'

'Isn't this all a bit tame for you guys?'

'No, it's great. With Amy gone it's like being off the leash.' She looked at me. 'Oh, sorry, no offence.'

'None taken,' I said. 'I know what you mean.'

She finally cracked the ice tray, removed one single cube and replaced it in the freezer, closing the door.

I looked on open-mouthed, my arms full of frozen pizzas, as she delved inside her TALtop and began to rub the ice cube over her left, and then her right, nipple.

'I've got a bet on with Neemoy that I can distract her pop-eyed stalker.'

If Axeman didn't have a thyroid problem already, he soon would have.

I let them get on with it while I heated and ate a pepperoni pizza, working on the basis that they were selling more beer than I could and anyway, things would calm down as the evening wore on, but I was wrong about that.

I did a couple of circuits out into the bar, nodding to customers and collecting glasses as I went like I had seen publicans do for real. I might as well have been invisible as all eyes were on the Terrible Trio. By eight o'clock they had a routine worked out where they did a sort of static line dance behind the bar to Bobby McFerrin's 'Don't Worry, Be Happy'. The game was to put the song on the jukebox and then order a vodka and tonic. Max would fill a glass with ice (there was an ice bucket on the bar), fling it to Neemoy, who would jiggle it under the vodka optic while Sasha juggled a bottle of tonic water. A few more turns to the music and the drink was slammed down in front of the customer, most of it slopping on to a grimy bar towel. They charged £3 for this, not including the jukebox, but no one seemed to be complaining. We were going to need more vodka.

On my first wander round, I noticed that Scooter and the boffins from Soft Sell had gone, although the Axeman remained, rooted to his spot at the bar which ensured he was never more than three feet from Neemoy. He had switched to drinking vodka and tonic too.

I would have expected that to have emptied the pub and things to have quietened down, but more cars arrived – and more pick-up trucks – and the bar continued to heave. I identified at least six youngish guys who could have been part of the

Soft Sell set-up from the way they acknowledged Axeman, but I had seen none of them before.

As soon as it was dark I left the pub by the back door and, careful to avoid stepping on a chicken, made my way to the gate which opened into the car-park for a closer look at the pick-ups.

I had Amy's dictaphone with me and began to read their number plates into it. There were two Fords and a Mazda and all were empty and shouldn't have been at all suspicious except I had been seeing quite a lot of pick-up trucks in the past twenty-four hours and this, after all, was Kent not Texas.

But it was beginning to look like it, as the headlights of another one swung in to the car-park.

Instinctively, I dropped into a crouch behind the Mazda until the new pick-up had parked and killed its lights. Two figures got out and crunched across to the pub.

'We ought to log in our load,' one was saying, 'before we do this.'

'With Scooter on a blitz? No way. He'll have us doing another run. I want to see all this crumpet they've got down . . .'

The rest was lost to me but as soon as I heard the music level rise as the pub door opened, I scuttled across to their vehicle, another Ford. This one was full, very full. I could tell by its silhouette that it was low down on its axles and a quick peek into the back showed why. The whole of the flat bed was covered, three deep, in cases of '33' French beer with a loosely tied tarpaulin thrown over them in a half-hearted attempt at concealment. They were either very confident or very sloppy smugglers.

I bent over to read off the rear number plate into the dictaphone and something struck me as odd about it. It was a white plastic job and I knew there was something strange about it but I couldn't put my finger on it, until, that is, I actually did put my fingers on it and found I could bend it.

I was starting to form an idea about what Scooter and his students were up to, but I needed another look at the old hop farm just to be sure. The time seemed to be right and I guessed nobody in the pub would miss me for an hour or so. The question was how to get in there, knowing that Scooter had at least one night camera trained on the village street and I had to assume he had another on the gate into Mel's paddock. In any case, that would be the entrance they would be using if they were running across to France tonight.

The real entrance off the old Canterbury road, which Scooter had used that afternoon, hadn't appeared to be guarded by any security devices but then again, could I find it in the dark and how did I get there? This was the crazy thing about the countryside: no tubes, no taxis, not even a night bus.

But Dan had a bicycle, parked as usual against the wall of the pub near the front door. Very gently, I picked it up and carried it round to the side of the Gents' toilets.

I walked back through the pub, picked up a few more glasses and worked my way to where the Major was still muttering under his breath and Dan was flushed with Seagrave Special Bitter and testosterone in equal measure. I put my arm around his shoulder.

'I'm going to put my head down for an hour or so,' I shouted in his ear as the girls started their 'Be Happy' routine again. 'If the beer needs changing or anything, will you go down into the cellar?'

'Oh, I don't know if Ivy would like that,' he said, not taking his eyes off Sasha.

'She won't mind, don't you worry. And don't spend too much time down there looking up the girls' skirts.'

I let the thought sink in and knew I could rely on him. It didn't seem worth mentioning the bike.

In the kitchen I unwrapped one of the items I had bought at the supermarket which hadn't been stuffed into the freezer, a rubberised torch complete with batteries. I made sure it worked then stuffed it inside my leather jacket, zipped up and left through the back door again.

Amazingly, the lights on Dan's ancient boneshaker worked though I wasn't too sure about the brakes. Still, riding a bike was like making love to a woman. If you've done it once, you can do it again. Just remember not to fall off.

I fell off twice before I got out of the car-park, but I put that down to pot-holes. Once on the road proper I found I could get up a fair head of steam, fairly flying along behind the saucer of yellow light from the flickering headlamp, and I found the B-road which flanked the village easily enough, turning right and heading north.

It might have been a straight road – the Romans liked straight lines – but I had forgotten about the hills and the Roman penchant for going up and down them. By the time I got to the top of the second one, my legs were screaming and the night air rasping at my lungs. I was shattered, I was out of condition, I was dying for a cigarette.

But then I thought I saw something through the darkness and I stopped and pulled out my torch to light up the wooden sign for the nearest picnic site, the marker I had been heading for. Just further up the hill was the turning Scooter and I had come out of in the Jeep.

I flashed the torch around the entrance but couldn't see any cameras, pressure pads or tripwires. Not that I could see much with the trees blotting out what little light there was from the moon and stars.

I freewheeled down what had been the farm road, not looking to the side at all in case I saw what was making those strange rustling noises in the underbrush. And then I could see lights in the distance, which must be the buildings of Soft Sell down across the old hop fields.

On the edge of the wood, I stopped and turned off the bike's lights, laying it down behind a tree just in case anyone did use the road, and began to trot down the track through the field using my torch only when I stumbled and using the lights from the furthest building as a navigation aid.

The first building going this way was the huge aircraft hangar which loomed out of the gloom. It was dark and deserted and so I pressed on up the hill towards the single-storey buildings.

Half-way there I saw a flicker of light on my horizon, which I guessed was the paddock at the back of Hop Cottage where Mel lived. Then the light solidified into a beam pointing to the sky and I realised it was a set of headlights coming through the gate off the main street in Whitcomb. Allowing for the driver to stop and close the gate, I had no more than ten seconds before he reached the Soft Sell bunkhouse and his lights picked me out, standing panting in the middle of an open field.

The aircraft hangar was the nearest cover – the only cover before the wood up the hill where I had left the bike. No competition. I legged it off the road and across rough ground, tripping over discarded bundles of twine and spools of wire, sliding in mud. And then I reached the cold metal side of the hangar and almost hugged it in relief.

The headlights were over the hill now and beaming down towards me, so I edged around the front of the hangar, crouched low, until I got to the far corner and was able to slide around the far side.

I put my head and back to the cold wall and tried to get my breath. I could hear the engine of the car now and pressed myself even further into the hangar as I realised it wasn't stopping at the Soft Sell building, but coming straight for the hangar.

Whatever it was, it stopped no more than ten feet from the hangar, its main beams lighting up the front, the light spilling around the corner where I was hiding and bleeding off into the field.

I heard doors open and slam and then, even with the engine idling, I heard footsteps on the concrete and *whistling*. Whistling in stereo, or almost. Two people, both slightly out of tune, whistling the same song: 'Don't Worry, Be Happy'.

Then I heard a loud clicking noise, which I worked out must have been a padlock, and a long screeching metallic scream as the hangar door was slid open. As it hit its stop buffers, it rattled the wall I had my head pressed against.

One of the whistlers stopped and said: 'That pub has *definitely* gone up in my estimation.'

'Too right. Trust that tight-arse Scooter to pull us out,' said the other one. 'What say we stash this lot double quick and get back there before closing time?'

'Sounds good to me,' came the answer. 'Three runs is enough for one day.'

A car door opened again and the engine revved and the headlights swung away so I risked a look round the corner of the hangar.

It wasn't a car, it was a Ford pick-up, the one I had seen loaded with beer in the car-park. The driver swung in a circle and then put it into reverse and began to back into the hangar.

Lights suddenly came on inside the hangar, followed by a clang of metal and then another one. The pick-up disappeared and then I heard one of the voices shouting: 'Left, left, straight, straight, keep it there, straight, straight, you're on.'

And then the engine cut out and I heard footsteps clumping on metal this time.

I gave it a minute or so and then edged carefully around the front end of the building, pressing my palms against the open sliding door until I reached the edge.

They had reversed the Ford up two iron ramps into the back of the trailer of a gigantic articulated lorry. The trailer was static on its hydraulic legs, its cab and engine unit, a new DAF 97, parked neatly at its side.

The driver of the Ford and his mate were removing cases of beer from the pick-up and stacking them in the body of the trailer. Even from where I was I could see it was more than half full already with a solid wall of cases of French lager, but it still had room for the Ford.

I had found what we expert detectives in the bootlegging business called the Mothership.

14

The two guys from the pick-up finished loading the Mothership, drove back to the Soft Sell building, took a shower, shaved, got changed, squirted on deodorant, splashed on aftershave, put some folding money in their back pockets and got in the pick-up again. And they still made it to the Rising Sun with enough time to down two beers before I did.

Then again, they didn't have to sneak along the side of an aircraft hangar and across a churned-up field in the pitch dark, locate a bicycle without walking into a tree trunk more than once and then push it without lights through a forest transplanted from Transylvania, before discovering that the gears no longer worked properly, at least not uphill.

This country living was going to be the death of me. Eight hours without a car and I was getting withdrawal symptoms, so much so I began to urge Dan's boneshaker on by shouting at it, christening it 'Cold Turkey'.

And because I was high on adrenalin from the fear of being seen, filthy from falling over so many times scrambling across the hop fields, and in agony as every tendon in my legs twanged as I pedalled, cars began to pick on me. I hadn't seen a car on the road all night, but suddenly, when I was most vulnerable, it was rush hour. On the road into Whitcomb I was buzzed four times by overtaking cars and twice almost clipped into the hedgerow. I had no idea where they were all coming from, but I soon discovered where they were all going.

For the first time since Mr Mercedes or Mr Benz (whoever) ran over a hedgehog, the car-park of the Rising Sun was full to overflowing and I had to get off Dan's bike and wheel it through the maze of cars.

Every light in the place seemed to be on and the jukebox was pumping out something at full volume. I couldn't tell what it was but I guessed it would be something from the mid-Eighties, which seemed to be the last time the man from the music company had called.

I replaced Dan's bike against the front wall by one of the windows without being noticed. No one in the pub was looking out and although it was only a trick of the light, I swore that the walls of the pub were bulging outwards.

The clientele were not exclusively male, just mostly. There were half a dozen women there, dressed for a night out and looking rather bemused as to why their partners had brought them here. Every seat in the place was taken, some of them twice, and the shutters on the dart board had been closed to discourage anyone from playing, which was just as well otherwise the local ambulance would have been on its way by now.

As it turned out, I could have saved time by ringing them then had I only known how the evening would pan out.

I dipped round the back of the pub to the back door and as I passed the Gents' toilet I heard the distinctive sound of someone thumping on an empty, echoing condom machine and moaning softly, 'Oh no, please, no.' Still, I suppose it was better to travel hopefully than to arrive.

The hens squeaked in protest as I disturbed them again and then I was in the kitchen and sneaking upstairs to Ivy's private living-room and, as far as I could tell, I hadn't been missed.

In Ivy's bathroom I washed and cleaned as much of the mud from my jeans and shoes as I could, ran my fingers through my hair, checked my smile in the mirror and went downstairs prepared to play the genial host.

'Where the fuck have you been?' Max hissed at me as I entered by the door at the side of the bar.

I leaned in to her ear so she could hear me above the music and the throb of chatter and laughter.

'Doing the books, creating a business plan, stocktaking, thinking up a new marketing strategy, that sort of stuff. How's it going?'

'We keep running out of things but Dan the Man seems quite happy to go down into the cellar for supplies. Poor Neemoy's got him looking up her skirt half the time and the psycho at the bar looking down her top full-time. He's an indecent assault just waiting to happen, that one.'

I scanned the bar and silently agreed with her. The one they called Axeman was slumped against the other end of the bar near the bar-flap opening, his shoulders drooping and his mouth fixed in a lopsided grin. It was difficult to tell, given his condition, whether his eyes were glazed.

'One of his mates had a right go at him half an hour ago,' said Max, 'and it looked like he wanted him to go home but he just told him to piss off. I think he's got just the one thing on his mind.'

I looked at Neemoy's chest straining the stitching on her TALtop.

'Maybe two,' I said.

'Coming up!' somebody shouted and I leaned over Max's shoulder to see Dan climbing out of the trap-door from the cellar.

He had two bottles of vodka wrapped in his arm, a red flush in his cheeks and a dreamy look in his eyes. He climbed up the ladder slowly, inches away from the back of Neemoy's long black legs, then pulled the hatch up and secured the bolt. He patted Neemoy on the backside and did a little pantomime telling her to be careful of the door and the bolt.

'I think we've made an old man very happy,' I said to Max.

I scanned the bar, checking out the faces through the fog of smoke. There was no sign of the Major, which didn't surprise me, nor of Scooter. Some of his boys were there, in fact quite a lot of them – the ones called Combo and Painter and the two anoraks, Chip and Dale, and the two who had almost illuminated me out at the aircraft hangar. It got me thinking that if he still had pick-ups on the road ferrying beer off the Shuttle, just how many did he have on his payroll in total? And that wasn't counting the mad Axeman, although he didn't seem to be one of the regular drivers. At least he had not been involved in the previous night's beer run and tonight he wasn't able to find his wheels let alone France.

I spotted Melanie in a corner, sipping delicately from a bottle of Beck's, staring lovingly into the eyes of a young man sitting across the small round table from her. He wore the only three-piece suit and the most expensive haircut in the building and had a glass of orange juice in one hand. With his other he occasionally reached out and stroked Mel's arm as he talked. She nodded and smiled at everything he said. You didn't have to be a psychologist to tell she was in love. We publicans tell you things like that for free.

I pushed my way over to her, picking up some empty glasses on the way to make it look as if I knew what I was doing.

'Hi, Mel, how's Ivy?'

It took her five seconds to realise someone was talking to her but eventually she tore her eyes from the guy in the suit and looked up. I realised it must be worse than I thought.

'Oh, hello ... Roy,' she said eventually.

I could see her thinking: *What was the question?*

'Ivy, the landlady. Hospital?' I prompted, but sarcasm was wasted on her.

'Oh, yes. Christian drove me there. And back.'

She had no idea how goofy she sounded.

'You must be Christian,' I said, 'the chauffeur.'

The suit made to stand up and offered his hand to shake. He had the best set of manicured nails I'd ever seen on a man – and quite a few women.

'I don't mind driving Melanie around,' he said smoothly as we shook, then looked down into her eyes. 'I've offered to do it on a permanent basis.'

Christian smiled, Mel blushed, I felt nauseous.

'Your friend Ivy's going to be laid up for quite a while, I'm afraid,' he said. 'Bones get very brittle at her age and she has got a break, but it's a clean one.'

'Christian's a doctor, you know,' said Mel soppily. 'Actually, a consultant in private practice.'

He didn't look old enough to be a medical student to me but perhaps that was a sign of me getting older, when the consultants start looking younger.

'How long?' I asked him.

'Three months, perhaps longer, before she can even think of coming back here unless she has someone to look after her and she certainly won't be able to run a pub single-handed. I've told Mel to tell her she really should think about retiring.'

'I'm not going to tell her *that*,' said Mel sharply, snapping back to reality.

'Me neither,' I agreed. 'Look, I'll have to ring the brewery tomorrow and tell them. Let them put it to her. I'm sure they'll want to send a bunch of flowers or something anyway.'

'I'm sure that's the best way,' said Christian, dripping with concern. 'Does she have private medical insurance?'

Mel and I both shrugged. Behind me a cheer went up as somebody put 'Be Happy' on the jukebox again and the girls behind the bar went into their routine.

Christian looked at the Rolex on his wrist.

'We ought to going, Mel dear. I really must get back to town tonight.'

Mel immediately placed her beer on the table even though it was still half full and pulled her jacket around her shoulders.

'Ready when you are,' she said obediently.

'Let me see you out,' I said, dumping the glasses I had collected on their table. So much for my career as a pot boy.

Christian positioned himself behind Mel's chair so he could push and I stepped in front of her and acted as a crowd marshal, touching people on the shoulder, asking them to give us room to move.

Once in the car-park, Christian wheeled Mel towards a

top-of-the-range Mercedes and he bleeped the remote locking from ten yards away.

'Could you get the passenger door, please?' Christian asked me politely.

As I did so, he picked Mel up out of her chair – the classic bride-over-the-threshold pose – and they gazed longingly into each other's eyes. For a moment, I thought Mel was starting to drool.

Christian placed her carefully in the front passenger seat and even clipped her seat belt in for her. Then he pushed her chair to the back of the car, opened the boot and folded it with practised ease so that he could pack it away.

'Goodnight,' he said with a wave before he climbed into the car and started the engine.

Mel didn't even look at me let alone wave. She only had eyes for the driver as the Mercedes pulled smoothly away.

I memorised the number plate and made a mental note to add it to my next report to Nick Lawrence, just for the hell of it.

My watch told me it was ten minutes to eleven and that seemed as if it should somehow be significant. Then I remembered, that was closing time or at least 'last orders'. I had been a publican for a whole day almost and still not pulled a pint for a real customer. The least I could do was ring the bell on the bar and shout at them, asking if they had homes to go to.

The punters, though, showed no signs of wanting to go home as I elbowed my way through them to get to the bar. By the time I got to the bar flap it was exactly eleven o'clock.

'There's a bell somewhere,' I said to Neemoy. 'Let's tell 'em it's chucking-out time.'

I made to lift the bar flap but it wouldn't move. A leather-jacketed forearm was resting on the edge, holding it down.

I did say 'Excuse me' but there was a lot of noise and perhaps I did jerk the flap up rather hard. Whatever, the arm was dislodged but so too was its owner who took a pace backwards as lager from the glass in his other hand missed his mouth and soaked the front of his T-shirt.

It just had to be Axeman.

'Sorry, mate, you're blocking the bar exit. Health and Safety at Work Act. They could have my licence for that,' I waffled, moving quickly behind the bar.

With superb timing, Neemoy found the bell and began to ring it, almost decapitating Sasha who obviously thought it was the start of some bizarre form of karaoke.

Neemoy and Max yelled: 'Time, ladies and gentlemen, please! Can we have your glasses?' in unison, like they had rehearsed it, with Sasha following about two beats behind them. Neemoy rang the bell a final time and Sasha finished: '... your glasses?'

To my amazement, people started to pack up and leave. It was like the climax of *The Wild Bunch* where an entire Mexican army starts to surrender to the four heroes, but then that didn't go to plan either.

'You spilled my beer,' slurred Axeman, steadying himself by holding the edge of the bar.

'Sorry about that, sir. Get you one tomorrow. We're closing now.'

I was being nice to him, I really was, though I refused to make eye contact.

'You don't fucking treat me like that!'

He was getting louder but there was still music on and glasses clashing and chairs being scraped so nobody took much notice.

'I want another lager!'

'We're closed.'

I looked around for something to do to ignore him. Sasha swayed by me to open the flap on her way to collect glasses. Axeman grabbed it and held it open.

'Get me a fucking top-up drink!' he snarled. His eyes were near to bursting and a vein on his nose began to throb.

Neemoy, well aware of the situation, squeezed in front of me so I could hide behind her.

'Come on, lover, it's time to call it a night. I need my beauty sleep, you know.'

She had a cloth and was wiping the bar in front of Axeman. Smoothly, she lifted his pint glass to wipe underneath and somehow just forgot to give it back to him. She swung away and poured what was left of his beer down the sink, putting the empty glass in the open dishwasher, then turned back to him with a big smile.

It was the smile that defused things. Axeman had to smile

back, even though it looked as if it was being wrenched from an intestinal tract.

'See you tomorrow?' Neemoy asked him sweetly.

'Yeah, oh yeah. Definite.'

He began to step away from the bar, zipping up his jacket over his soaked T-shirt, trying to look cool, making for the door as if he'd planned to leave that way all along.

I put an arm around Neemoy's waist. In the cramped conditions behind the bar I was surprised it hadn't happened before.

'Thanks,' I whispered into her ear as she leaned back into me. 'I thought you were going to have to get down and dirty with him.'

She laughed, put her head back even further and said: 'He wouldn't like me when I'm angry.'

Unfortunately, he didn't like her when she was being friendly, or at least not with me, for that was the moment he chose to stop and turn round and catch us in what must have seemed a compromising position. (And to be honest, I'd seen porn movies with less sense of direction.)

'Oi! Don't you fucking touch her,' he growled as he stomped back towards the bar.

The pub was emptying and I looked around frantically for any of the other 'boffins' from Scooter's set-up but they had all disappeared. None of the remaining customers seemed to have noticed anything untoward and none seemed likely to rush to my aid.

'I said don't touch her like that!' He had his finger out like a gun, stabbing the air as he said each word.

'Now calm down, lover boy,' said Neemoy.

'Let her go, you shitarse!'

I presumed that was meant for me as I somehow still had my arm round Neemoy's waist and it must have looked – *looked*, mind you – as if I was keeping her in front of me as a human shield.

'Hey, no trouble in here, OK?' I said over her shoulder.

'I'm having you,' he snarled and lunged for the open bar flap.

He was less than a yard from me when I pushed Neemoy to the right and moved as far as I could, which wasn't far behind that bar, to the left feeling behind me for the bell or a bottle or a baseball bat or Neemoy's handbag. Anything to hit him with.

As he came through the bar flap, he bunched his hands into fists and pulled his right back and up. One more step and he couldn't miss. I could almost smell his breath. I could certainly see the whites of his eyes. They were huge.

I slid my right foot forward and kicked the bolt on the cellar trap-door. The trap fell open inwards and Axeman, shuffling sideways through the bar flap, probably couldn't have stopped himself even if he had been looking down rather than straight at me.

He didn't make a sound as he disappeared downwards as if in some invisible elevator right in front of me, but there was a hell of a crash as he bounced off the ladder and sent goodness knew what flying once he hit the cellar floor.

Even old Dan heard the noise of breaking bottles and clanging metal barrels being knocked over and he leaned over the bar in case he missed anything.

'What's going on?'

Neemoy and I peered cautiously over the edge of the trap-door. Axeman was spreadeagled on his back on the cellar floor, his head resting against a steel keg of lager. He wasn't moving but he was breathing.

'One of Neemoy's friends dropped in to see her,' I said, then winced as she playfully backhanded me in the stomach.

'Is he all right?' asked Dan anxiously. I didn't think he would ever forgive me for making his life so interesting.

'You remember where the phone is?' I asked him.

''Course I do.'

'Well, you know the number.'

It was the same two paramedics as the night before. We were getting to know each other quite well.

'You haven't given this one a brandy as well, have you?' one of them shouted up from the cellar.

'It wasn't me that gave Ivy brandy,' I protested. 'Anyway, this one didn't need one.'

'You're not kidding,' said the paramedic wafting a hand in

front of his nose. 'If I gave this guy mouth-to-mouth, I couldn't drive the ambulance.'

'Mmmm, mouth-to-mouth,' Sasha said dreamily from behind me. She was sitting on the bar, legs dangling over the inside, rolling a joint between forefingers and thumbs.

'No smoking this side of the bar,' I reminded her primly, so she swung her legs round, giving Dan a great view, until she was facing the other way.

The paramedic standing over the trap-door shook his head slowly.

'Can you still be charged with "running a disorderly house" these days?' he asked me.

'Dunno,' I said, 'but I've got a feeling we could find out by the end of the week.'

'How long has he been unconscious?' the one in the cellar shouted.

'He was out for about ten minutes,' Neemoy told him as she ripped open another packet of crisps. 'Then he came round and started swearing and then I think he just sort of passed out.'

'How much had he had to drink?'

'Seven pints and two vodka and tonics,' Neemoy said without hesitating. When everybody looked at her she shrugged and said: 'What? What?'

'There doesn't seem to be any ID on him,' the medic shouted up. 'What's his name?'

'Alex something, we think,' I said.

'Where does he live?'

'No idea,' I said, glaring at Dan so he wouldn't say anything.

'Is he a regular?'

'He might be, but we're not,' I said. 'We're just the temporary management.'

'You're not kidding there,' said the other paramedic.

They carted Axeman off strapped to a stretcher just as they did Ivy and I had a twinge of sympathy for him in case he woke up in the bed next to her.

The three girls and Dan made a fair fist of cleaning up the

pub while I counted the night's takings. If we stayed on here, Ivy was going to have to get a bigger safe.

Then we had a nightcap together and then another one and finally, around half-past midnight, I insisted that Dan went home and I locked the front door after him though he was still protesting that I shouldn't have to face a night in the pub with just the three girls ('fashun modals' as he called them) for company.

Unfortunately, they had decided something along the same lines amongst themselves.

Neemoy had disappeared upstairs and returned with an armful of cushions and a pair of what looked like army-issue blankets.

'Sasha and I are taking the big bed upstairs,' she said, all businesslike. 'Max'll sleep it off on the sofa in the living-room.'

'And I . . . ?'

She pointed to the bench seat under one of the windows near the dart board in the corner of the bar, then she dumped the cushions and blankets into my arms.

'Fair enough,' I said. 'I've been here before.'

In fact the arrangement suited me well, not because I didn't trust myself with the three girls and thought I should suffer a monastic penance by sleeping on a hard wooden bench, but because I had one final bit of detecting to do that night.

While the girls were settling in upstairs, I crept into the kitchen and removed a pair of yellow rubber washing-up gloves from under the sink. I pulled them on with a thwack, wishing I'd remembered to steal some talcum powder from Ivy's bathroom.

Armed with my torch, I locked the back door after me, pocketed the key and disturbed the chickens one last time as I sneaked round into the car-park.

There was only one vehicle left there, a battered Ford Mondeo which had seen better days. The keys I had taken from Axeman's pocket when I had insisted on being the first down the cellar to examine him fitted perfectly and the engine turned first time.

I wasn't too worried if the girls saw or heard me. Sasha was on another planet, Max would be out of it by now and Neemoy

166

was probably organising a midnight snack. So I hit the lights and pulled out of the car-park, turning right into the village.

At the five-bar gate next to Hop Cottage, I left the lights on full beam as I climbed out and opened it, driving the Ford over the fake grass then getting out and closing the gate after me. Then I sat behind the wheel again, took a deep breath and drove round the corner up to the front door of Scooter's place of business.

A face appeared at one of the windows as I parked and turned off the headlights. The single-storey building was lit up but most of the windows had blinds down. Further down the fields I could see a vertical line of light which could only be the doors of the aircraft hangar. Someone was busy loading up the Mothership again.

I took another deep breath, peeled off the rubber gloves, got carefully out of the Ford, leaving the keys in just in case, and walked to the main doors, pushing them open and striding in.

I recognised the ones called Combo and Painter before it dawned on them who I was. Both held Play Station joysticks and were staring at a monitor. A radio played softly somewhere, the only sound in the main room which was much bigger than I had imagined from my previous snooping through the windows.

Scooter was sitting at one of the PC consoles scanning what looked to be spreadsheets and did not look up. Beyond him, half the room was in darkness and I could make out the shapes of camp beds, some of them occupied with figures in sleeping bags. The place stank of stale beer, cigarette smoke and old curries.

'Where the fuck have you been?' Scooter said without looking up.

That was twice in one night; a record, even for me.

I pulled my hand from my pocket and flipped a plastic-coated document on to the keyboard in front of him.

It was a Heavy Goods Vehicle licence made out in the name of one Alex Steven Hayward.

'You're gonna need another driver,' I said.

15

That got his attention.

'What the fuck have you done with Alex?'

He looked at the licence, not me, but he made no move to pick it up or touch it. The other two shuffled closer, but it was so they could see what I had thrown down, it wasn't to threaten me. Unlike the missing Axeman, they didn't really scare me at all.

That was one of the things I had thought about and weighed up before I had come there. In fact I had been thinking about it since I had seen them in the pub the night before, when I'd had time to look them over one by one. Scooter was too intelligent to get violent, Axeman was too strung out not to. The rest had struck me as ordinary, middle-class students veering on the wrong side of nerdy. Mel had called them 'boffins' but not in the white-coated mad scientist sense. She had picked up on the current playground slang of 'boffs' or what a previous generation would have called school swots. She'd probably heard it while she was a mouse at EuroDisney, entertaining the kiddies.

To the majority of Scooter's gang, I must have looked ultra cool – the guy who could take over a pub, staff it with supermodels and get rid of Axeman all in the same day and then calmly walk into the middle of their bootlegging operation. At their age I would have thought I was God.

'I haven't done anything with Axeman,' I said, perching one buttock on the edge of Scooter's desk, 'except help him into an ambulance. He had an accident down the pub, getting a bit too keen on one of my barmaids.'

'The tall black one . . .' Combo said under his breath before he could stop himself, then he blushed as Scooter glared at him.

'She's unlikely to press charges,' I said with absolute conviction, knowing that the thought had never crossed her mind. 'But Axeman's going to need collecting from Folkestone hospital when he comes round and sobers up. I brought his wheels back.

Could be there for a few days, though. It looked like he had things broken.'

'What happened exactly?' Scooter was trying to stay cool, still not looking at me.

'He took the quick way down into the pub cellar. He bounced once.'

'Who pushed him?'

'Probably me. He was well out of order.'

'That I can believe.' Then he looked at me and for once he didn't bother to flick the shock of blond hair in the irritating way he had perfected. 'I suppose you want his job,' he said and it wasn't a question.

'You got anyone else can drive a forty-one ton, tri-axle rig?'

If that took him by surprise, he hid it. In fact, he was scoring quite well on the cool-ometer.

'Nope,' he said calmly, shaking his head slowly as if he'd had to give it some serious thought. 'Can't say I have.'

'Thought not,' I said with a smile.

Axeman had always been the odd one out; the toughest nut among them but also the weakest link. The loner not in with the student crowd socially. The one who wasn't worried about drinking orange juice or leaving the pub early because he wasn't on a beer run to Calais. Once I had seen the Mothership in the hop farm hangar I had guessed that must be his job, the once-a-week big delivery somewhere, and the HGV licence in his wallet had confirmed it.

The key question, of course, was where that delivery was made. If I could find that out I could present a report to Veronica which would knock her pop socks off, prove to Amy that I wasn't a total waste of space, get me a medal from Nick Lawrence and the Customs and Excise boys and probably earn me free beer for life from Murdo Seton.

That's what I would call a result.

I should have quit whilst I was ahead.

'How much do you think you know?' Scooter asked.

It was a fair question and I would have asked it in his place.

'Bits and pieces,' I said, wishing I had a cigarette. That would have given me the edge in the cool stakes and probably made me forget how much the edge of Scooter's desk was cutting into my buttocks.

'You're running beer through Le Shuttle, putting small vans and pick-ups on the train rather than using the old Transit van on the ferry route which everybody knows about. You do it mostly at night, so I'd guess you get a good deal on the crossing rates.'

'Cuts three ways,' said Scooter as if answering a curious child. 'Pick-ups and small vans get charged the same as private cars, not like Transits or small trucks. Then you get a fifty per cent discount if you go after 6 p.m. Plus you can also buy your duty-free allowance going and coming back and prices on Eurotunnel are very competitive. Some things are cheaper than they are duty-paid in France.'

'The papers say that duty-free is going to be abolished.'

'So what?' He shrugged his shoulders, but not enough to crease his denim shirt. 'It's a nice addition to our margins while it lasts.'

'You seem to have it well sorted,' I said.

'I've tried to cover all the bases. No one load is so big that it attracts suspicion but *everybody* buys over the limit. If you're stopped, you say it's for a friend or a party or a wedding and – oh, dear, am I over the limit? So you offer to drop a few cases because you're only a student and you can't afford to pay the excess duty. Most times they wave you on. Most times they don't even stop you. Fuck, it's only a bit of beer after all. It's not like it was drugs or tobacco. And you're not a regular runner because they've never seen you before and you'll not do it again. Or at least not until the Customs boys change shifts.'

'So you have a big pool of drivers, then?'

'You know how much the average student loan is these days?'

'But not many students have HGV licences?'

'True,' he agreed, almost philosophically. 'That's why we had to bring in Axeman. It was always a risk. He wasn't exactly stable.'

'But you needed him to drive the Mothership?'

He smirked at that.

'Yeah, the Mothership. I thought that one up one night in the student union bar.'

I might have known, but I said nothing.

'It was just a question of logistics. I had lots of drivers in small vehicles bringing in relatively small quantities so the chances of them being pulled were remote. But they made their profit by doing lots of trips, three or four a day.'

'And they couldn't do that if they had to drive up to London to unload,' I added.

'I see you've thought it through,' he said.

'Some. London's still the main market, isn't it?'

'Yeah, though Manchester's coming on strong. But you're right. By the time a small pick-up delivered in London and got back here for another run, the numbers just didn't work out, not to make any decent money. So I thought of the Mothership – and that's exactly what I called it, though the original concept was too off the wall to work. I planned on having it driving up and down the M20 and my guys driving their cars up into it to unload. Up a ramp, like without stopping. Got the idea from a film.'

'*The Italian Job,*' I said automatically.

'You've seen it?' said the one called Painter with wonderful innocence.

'Hasn't everybody?'

I despair about modern youth sometimes. Then another thought struck me.

'You all use these daft nicknames, don't you? Scooter, Painter, Chip, Dale, Axeman. That's so you don't know anyone's real name and you can't grass them.'

'I didn't know Axeman was called Alex until now,' said Painter sadly.

'You got that from *Reservoir Dogs*, didn't you?' I shook my head. 'Jesus, how have you lot survived so long?'

'We've got security,' said Combo petulantly.

Scooter was sucking his teeth, happy to let us squabble. It wasn't a good move to give him too much thinking time.

'A video camera which points one way and some fake grass to cover tyre tracks? I found you easy enough.'

'But you were looking,' said Scooter suddenly. 'How come?'

'I saw two of your boys recycling French beer bottles down the pub. You all drive pick-ups. France is twenty-two miles that way. It didn't need Sherlock Holmes. In any case, Sherlock Holmes doesn't need a driving job which pays cash and is tax free. And don't forget, I saw how much cash there was in Axeman's wallet.'

I hoped Scooter didn't register the 'was' as significant, even though it was absolutely accurate.

'Three hundred,' he said, suddenly coming to a decision. 'Two drops, south London, tomorrow and the day after.'

'Whereabouts?'

'You'll find out when you get there. One of us'll go with you.'

'Five hundred, each drop.'

'O-kay,' he said slowly.

Then somebody else said, 'Time's it?' from the darkened end of the building and a light came on, an Anglepoise bedside lamp, but at ground level.

'You'd better wake 'em up,' Scooter said to Combo, looking at his watch. 'One more run tonight and we'll have a load for our new driver.'

'Scooter . . .' Combo started, unsure of himself.

'We've not got a lot of choice in the matter, but it's an acceptable risk,' said Scooter, all businesslike. Then to me: 'You sure you can handle Axeman's rig?'

'I'd like a closer look at it, but if it's got wheels and a full tank I can drive it.'

'Then let's do it now. The midnight shift'll be here soon. Painter, get the new plates and meet us down at the shed.'

He reached down and opened a drawer in the desk, taking out a rubberised torch and a bunch of keys which he flipped to me and which I managed to catch one-handed. So far, so cool.

'You'll need those, Roy. Do I call you Roy? Is that your name?'

'If we're all on code names, you can call me Angel,' I said, feeling ridiculously pleased with myself.

So far it was all going smoothly to plan.

It couldn't last.

I was grateful for the light of Scooter's torch once we were outside as there was no sign of a moon and rain in the air. I let him lead me down to the hop field and the hangar while Painter, with another torch, stumbled off to our left to the other building which I had thought was disused.

'What goes on there?' I asked him.

'That's where Painter makes up false plates for us, so we can use the same vehicle more than once a day.'

I remembered the one I had touched in the car-park of the Rising Sun.

'What's he got? Some sort of heat sealer?'

'Yeah, that's right. He knocks them out on the word processor and then seals them with acetate. Same principle you can make place mats out of photographs, or seal maps so you can pin them on the wall. Every school's got one these days.'

'And they're good enough to fool the video cameras?'

'So far. He usually just changes the odd letter or two, so P321 OLG on one run becomes R321 DLG on the next. DLG doesn't exist, by the way, but by the time anybody's checked, we're long gone.'

Behind us I heard engines and I stumbled as I turned to look and see headlights, three sets of them, coming in our direction.

Scooter ignored them and shone his torch on the hangar which loomed out of the darkness, focusing on the padlock on the sliding doors. I saw him reach into his shirt for a key on a chain around his neck.

'What was this?' I asked him.

'A stripping shed,' he said as he inserted the key into the padlock. 'They used to cut the hop bines and bring them in here to string them on a moving pulley to go through stripping machines which ripped the hops off them. A conveyor belt would shake them and sift them and dump them in a truck at the other end. It's ideal for us now all the machinery's gone. Two big doors. We just drive in one end, load up and drive the artic out the other end. Roll on, roll off, just like the Dover–Calais ferry.'

'Is that where you got the idea, or was it in a movie I haven't seen?'

He ignored that and put his shoulder to the door and rolled it back as the first set of approaching headlights picked us out.

173

Once the door was open, he stepped inside and clicked a switch to illuminate the interior.

The last lot of loaders hadn't even bothered to close the doors of the articulated trailer properly and had left the metal ramps in place ready for the next delivery. Cases of beer, mostly French bottled lager but some well-known British names too, were stacked the entire width and most of the height of the trailer. I guessed it was full to about eighty per cent of its depth of around fourteen metres and there wasn't room left for a pick-up to drive up into it any more. I was looking at an oblong block of beer about eight feet wide, twelve feet high and forty feet long.

I was impressed.

'How much can you get in there?'

Scooter pulled the metal ramps away and let them clang to the floor, then pulled the trailer's doors fully open. He made a circling movement with his right hand and the Ford pick-up which was now right outside the door began to turn and reverse into the shed. Two more pick-ups bounced down the hill and waited in line, turning off their headlights.

'The big brewery fleets reckon one of these will take twenty-two pallets,' Scooter said, casually waving the reversing Ford up to the tail of the trailer. 'But we can't bring pallets over intact, so we buy in advance and then split them into smaller loads. It means we have to handball the cases in once we get them here, but it makes the guys feel they've earned their money.'

'How many in a pallet?' I said, finding myself trying to count the cases in one visual line, but quickly losing track.

'Fifteen cases per layer, nine layers.'

Two figures climbed out of the Ford, its rear lights now up against the trailer. I had seen neither before but a wild guess would have put them as first-year medical students as they already had bags under their eyes.

'Who's he?' the driver asked Scooter.

'He's Angel,' Scooter said deadpan. 'He's replacing Axeman for the last two runs.'

'Oh, we'll miss *him*. Fucking psycho.'

I was right about them being medical students; you could always tell a professional diagnosis.

174

'Start handballing, guys. Sooner you're done, sooner you can sleep.'

The two students untied a canvas secured across the flat back of the pick-up and rolled it back to reveal cases of St Omer and Bière 33. They climbed into the back with the beer and began to 'handball' – to gently throw each case from one to the other and then on to the trailer.

'That's 135 cases,' I said out loud, pleased with my maths. 'At twenty-four bottles per case, that's over 5000 bottles per pallet. And how many pallets did you say?'

'Twenty-two. Well, that was what the breweries told me when I rang them.'

He must have seen the expression on my face.

'I told them it was part of my project into distribution costs in modern industry,' he said, allowing himself a little grin.

'So, twenty-two times . . . shit! That's over 70,000 bottles.'

'No, it'll be more than that as we don't have the pallets taking up room, so we can stuff more in even though it increases our labour input and turn-round time.'

'If they're quarter-litre bottles . . .' Why hadn't I packed a calculator? '. . . Then that's nearly 18,000 litres, which is like over 30,000 pints . . .'

Or about the amount of beer needed to keep a pub like the Rising Sun going for four months. More to the point, if Scooter was buying in those quantities he was getting a good price and selling on the London black market, he could be making £3 a case profit. Therefore each trailer load was making him around £9000 gross profit. He'd have his overheads and expenses – like me – but he would have worked out his margins carefully, as part of his degree studies. He'd probably get course credits for it.

'This bit's not your problem,' he was saying in my ear. 'That is.'

I followed him across the shed to where the tractor cab was parked neatly alongside the front end of the trailer, which was propped up on its retractable dolly wheels. I unlocked the driver's door and climbed up the steps into the cab.

It was a new rig, a DAF 95XF, but the cab stank of stale smoke and spilled Coca-Cola. Behind the two main seats was the padded cot bed running the width of the cab and on it a threadbare sleeping bag which I didn't want to have to examine too closely.

'Axeman sleeps in here sometimes,' said Scooter looking in, his face level with my feet.

'I guessed,' I said, checking over the dashboard and trying to remember the last time I had driven one of these beasts. 'Is this his rig?'

'No, it's leased.'

'Like the computer gear?' I tried.

'Just tell me you can drive this thing or not,' he said impatiently.

''Course I can.'

It was a tri-axle tractor, six wheels in all, the third set dropping down when you had a load on. That was supposed to spread the weight and stop the lorry beating the crap out of the road surface, which was why they were taxed at about half the price of the old two-axle rigs. The DAF had a 430 horsepower engine, with an eight-gear, sixteen-speed gearbox so you could work a range change and go up or down in 'half gears'. It also had cruise control which would cut out at 85 kilometres per hour (the speedo was primarily in kilometres) or 54 miles per hour, unless you were going downhill that is. And it had switches for a differential lock, which you put on if the going got rough or in wet and slippery conditions, the same as you would switch to four-wheel drive if you had it on a car.

'Piece of piss,' I said, jumping down and almost knocking Scooter over, forgetting how high up the cabs on these things were. Professional drivers always come out backwards and slowly.

'Know how to connect it up?' he asked me.

I strolled round to the back of the tractor unit, with him at my shoulder.

'That's the fifth wheel,' I said, pointing things out as I spoke, 'which isn't a wheel at all, but that's what locks the trailer on. The red air line releases the brakes on the trailer, the yellow one connects the brakes to the whole unit. The other one is the Electric Suzy which connects up your electrics for lights and indicators and so forth. Don't ask me why it's called an Electric Suzy; maybe some trucker knew a girl called Suzy who struck sparks, I don't know.'

He looked convinced. But then, I had almost convinced myself. I didn't like to mention that it had been over five years since I'd driven a truck this size and that was for a very bad (but very loud) touring Heavy Metal band where nobody really gave a damn.

'So, I get the job?'

'Tomorrow,' he said. 'Combo'll go with you.'

'Go where?'

'London.'

'That doesn't narrow it down.'

'Dartford. Combo'll show you. Aim to leave about five o'clock.'

'I hope you don't mean a.m.' My watch now showed 1.45 a.m.

'No, five in the afternoon's fine. That way you hit the rush hour going out and you come back after dark.'

'And both those things are good?'

'Rush hour going towards the Dartford Tunnel and you think the cops are going to pull over a truck like this and search it?'

He had a point. The traffic police's priority would be to keep traffic moving, not block off a lane for a weight check or a search and create a thousand cases of road rage among the commuters trying to get home.

I didn't get a chance to ask why it was important to come back in darkness as Painter appeared with a huge sports bag slung over his shoulder.

'What do you fancy on this one, Scooter?' he asked as he handed a set of plastic plates to the driver of the Ford pick-up.

Scooter turned to me.

'Any requests?'

'What do you mean?'

'For the back of the trailer,' said Painter cheerfully. 'It's less suspicious than a totally anonymous truck. Got to be something British as well, something domestic. Nothing to suggest the truck's been across the Channel.'

He dropped his sports bag on the stone floor and it spilled open to reveal a stack of acetate stencils of letters and numbers and about two dozen cans of spray paint.

'So what do you want? A name?' I asked.

'A company and a place. You know, something like 'Smith's of Salford' or 'Harrogate Haulage'. I just make up a phone number to go with it.'

'I get the idea. How about "Angel's Home Removals, You Can Trust Us With Your Valuables"?'

They both stared at me with dead eyes.

'I kinda like that,' I said.

16

I drove Axeman's Mondeo back to the Rising Sun because nobody said I couldn't and crept round the back and into the bar on tiptoe so as not to wake the girls. I should have worried. Two of them (and I don't know which two) were snoring loud enough to rattle the tankards hanging behind the bar.

I laid out my monastic pallet on the bench seat by the dart board and kicked off my shoes. Then I thought of one of the perks of the job and walked round the bar – stepping carefully over the trap-door which had swallowed Axeman – and reached up to help myself to a shot from the brandy optic.

I took a swig and put the glass down whilst I unzipped my jeans and reflected that this detective business was really quite hard work. I don't remember finishing the brandy. I don't remember lying down or pulling a blanket over me. I do remember thinking there was something else I should have tried to find out from Scooter, but I couldn't remember what it was.

I awoke in hell and this time I couldn't blame alcohol.

Oh yes I could, the smell of it at least. There was that stale beery stench which all pubs have in the morning before they open the doors for an airing and on top of that, there were fumes from the unfinished brandy still in a glass balanced precariously on the edge of my bench seat bed about two inches from my nose. And if that wasn't bad enough, somebody had started an industrial fan on the other side of the bar and somebody else was banging on the window from the outside, trying to get in.

It was all too much for me, so I closed my eyes again to make the smells and the sounds disappear but they stubbornly refused to go.

'Cease fire!' I shouted but nothing happened, so I took drastic action and stood up, just as another smell assaulted my nostrils: frying bacon.

I took in the scene gradually. It was the only way my brain could handle it.

Max was behind the bar, leaning on it and pouring three small bottles of orange juice into a straight pint glass filled with ice. She kept her elbows on the bar to steady her hands and she had an unlit cigarette between her lips. Behind her, in the doorway, stood Neemoy. She was wearing a white T-shirt and eating a thick sandwich made with two doorstep-sized slices of white bread. I could tell it was a bacon and egg sandwich, partly from the smell coming from the kitchen and partly because she had dribbled egg yolk down her cleavage. Most bizarrely of all, Mel was there, in her wheelchair, pushing a vacuum cleaner across the floor in front of her. When she saw me standing up, she reached down and switched it off.

As the whine of its engine disappeared, the only sound in the place was the chink-chink of ice in Max's glass as she raised it unsteadily to her mouth, remembering at the last minute to remove the cigarette.

I surveyed the scene and nobody spoke.

Then the battering on the window started again and I turned round to see a bespectacled face, a hand at the forehead, pressed up against the glass trying to see in.

'And who,' I said with as much dignity as a befuddled, trouserless man could muster, 'the fuck *is that*?'

Mel shook her head. Neemoy shrugged her shoulders and pushed more sandwich into her mouth. Max replaced the unlit cigarette in her mouth and just stared at me from under droop-ing eyelids.

'If you want something doing . . .' I muttered, striding towards the door but halting with my hand on the lock. 'One of you is missing,' I said.

'Sasha's having a bath,' said Neemoy. 'I'm next.'

'Then me,' snarled Max.

'We'll see about that,' I said primly, opening the front door, but all they did was snigger. I knew I should have put my jeans on.

The window-peeper was waiting for me on the doorstep, holding out a business card. He had a natural stoop, like a pecking bird, and some of the thickest lenses I had ever seen in a pair of glasses. The card read: TONY REDSTON: FLEET STREET FASHION FOTOS.

'Hello,' he said in a sing-song voice, 'I'm Tony, your photographer for the day. I'm guessing you're Mr Angel. Your wi –'

'Come in, Tony, come in,' I said quickly. 'Make yourself at home. You're going to fit right in.'

I hadn't exactly forgotten what Amy had said, it was just that I had had to prioritise things. I introduced Tony to Mel, Neemoy and Max while I put my jeans on and then offered to accompany him to his car, an old Volvo 940, to help unload his gear.

Photographers and Heavy Metal bands share the same mantra: *you can't have too much equipment*, and Tony had enough lights to do a *son et lumière* on Dover Castle. As we pulled metal box after metal box out of the Volvo, I asked him:

'Just remind me what Amy's brief was for the shoot. Did she say she was coming down here, by the way?'

'Never said anything about coming along,' chimed Tony. 'Seemed in a bit of a rush actually. Just said, "Tony, I trust you. Get your arse down to this pub at the back of beyond and make the girls look like barmaids." She couriered a parcel of blouses over for them to wear. It's on the front seat.'

'Any message for me?'

'No. Oh yes, "Check your fucking messages." Does that make any sense?'

'Perfect. Did she say anything about some silver tankards?'

'No, she didn't, but a guy called Reuben Sloman rang from something called the Silver Vaults – is that another pub? Anyway, he said there was no way he was lending out his stock to people like you, but you were always welcome there.'

I squared up to him.

'Tell me, Tony, do you have an extra truth gene or something which stops you letting people down lightly?'

He pushed his glasses back up his nose with his forefinger.

'Never thought about that. Shall we kick some perfectly formed butt?'

'Why not?'

Let's see how far you get with the three Attitude Queens, I thought.

But he had them under his thumb within seconds, and I shouldn't have been surprised. He was a photographer, they were models. Mere mortals can't interrupt that equation.

Once inside the bar with his gear, Tony transformed. He peeled off the grubby dark blue trenchcoat he had been wearing to reveal a vicious pink shirt and a tie which looked as if it had had a lamb biryani pre-spilled down it. He clapped his hands three times.

'Come on, girls, get down here. Let Tony see what you've got – but you can keep your knickers on for now,' he shouted.

They trooped in from the back room and stood in a line in front of the bar, Max taking deep breaths and exhaling down her chest so we didn't get the fumes, Neemoy trying to sponge egg yolk out of her T-shirt with a damp tissue and Sasha wearing only a bath towel and dripping all over the floor.

Tony put his left hand on his hip and the palm of his right hand across his forehead.

'*This* is what I have to work with?'

'You're on your own, son,' I said.

'And what time does this pub open?'

'Twenty minutes ago,' said Mel and she smiled up at me, all innocence.

'Right, get these on.' He threw the parcel of TALtops at Max. 'I'll set up and we'll concentrate on bar shots. The customers'll just have to work around me. There will be some customers, won't there?'

Max had opened the parcel of TALtops – an experimental batch where Amy had used her interwoven silver thread technique – and selected a black one. She pulled the regular one she had been wearing yesterday over her head and threw it on the floor, then held the new one out in front of her to examine it before starting to pull it over her head. She wasn't wearing a bra.

'I think we'll get a few,' I said.

At my side, Mel snorted in disgust the way only women and cats can.

'Have you thought about the lunch menu?' I asked her, keeping one eye on Sasha, although she gave no sign of letting her towel slip.

'Me? Why me? You're supposed to be in charge.'

'That's as may be. You're the one who knows what they're doing, though. And remember, you're doing it for Ivy. Now get into the kitchen. Don't worry about the vacuum cleaner, you can put that away later. And if you've got a minute, I could go a bacon sandwich myself. I mean, it's not like I've had breakfast or anything. There is some coffee on, isn't there?'

By this time I was behind her, pushing her chair into the kitchen.

'Wait a minute!' she snarled over her shoulder. 'You're expecting me to run the pub while those three play at supermodels, aren't you?'

'They *are* supermodels, Mel, that's why I need you to supervise them and you have to promise to use only small words.'

'And where will you be when the work's being done?'

I spun the chair round so I could face her, my sincere expression turned up to 11 for maximum effect.

'I've got things to do, Mel, including a very big favour for your friend Scooter.'

'Is it something to do with Axeman? I heard he had an accident.'

'Where did you hear that?'

'From Sasha. She said she was sorry I had to leave early last night because I missed the magician who disappeared right in front of her eyes.'

'Yeah, right. Just say I'm helping Scooter out of a big jam, because I feel a little bit responsible and anyway I'm that sort of guy. And I promise I'll go now and ring the brewery and tell them to send a relief manager to run things. With a bit of luck they could have one here tomorrow. I'll go and do that right now. Just as soon as you've made my sandwich. Don't worry about the coffee, I can manage.'

* * *

182

After a bath, a shave, something to eat and three mugs of coffee, I felt up to the trials ahead.

Upstairs, from Ivy's private sitting-room window, I could see that the car-park was about half full and they were all quality cars, no tatty pick-ups or vans. The mobile phone networks had obviously been busy; as mine ought to be.

I dug my mobile out of my bag, noting that I had run out of clean underwear and socks and making a mental note to do something about it, and checked my messages. I had two, the first from Veronica simply asking how I was doing and would I give her a call sometime.

The second was from Amy telling me that she had a problem with one of her suppliers so she couldn't make it 'down to the country' – as if someone was listening. But she was sending Tony to take some photographs. 'He might come across as a raddled old queen, but he does know his aperture from his anus and he won't take shit from the zombies.' (Amy had been known to refer to models as 'Zombies in frocks' when the mood took her.) She ended by saying she wanted the girls back in London tomorrow. She didn't express an opinion about when, or how, I should return.

I punched in the number of the brewery, which I didn't have to remember as it was printed on three ashtrays, a calendar and a water jug in that room alone.

'Seton and Nephew, Seagrave's Seaside Ales. Good afternoon.'

I remembered the receptionist back at the brewery, Beatrice or something. The one who dressed like something from *The Glenn Miller Story* from the waist up and *The Story of O* from the waist down.

'Murdo Seton, please.'

'May I ask who is calling?'

'Roy Angel, he knows me.'

'I'm sorry, but Mr Seton is tied up with the other directors at the moment. Could I give him a message?'

'Just say I called and that I have almost finished down here in Whitcomb and I should have a full report for him tomorrow. Oh, and tell him he'll need to get a relief manager for the Rising Sun.'

'Is that everything?'

'That'll do until I can talk to him, thanks.'

She said goodbye ever so politely and I envied Murdo Seton. He seemed to have no trouble getting decent staff.

I hit the Memory button for where I had filed Nick Lawrence's number under 'HMCE' and then Send. He answered on the second ring and sounded as if he was eating a sandwich himself. Something in a baguette, I guessed.

''Waurence,' he said, or that was what it sounded like.

'Roy Angel. You were checking out some car numbers for me.'

'Oh, them. I might have,' he said grumpily. I could hear him chewing. Now that's something they don't advertise when they try to sell you a mobile phone.

'And I might have found out something *you'd* be interested in.'

I could play hard to get too. Not often, but I could.

'Go on then, baffle me with your brilliance.'

'You show me yours first.'

I heard a deep sigh followed by a rustle of papers.

'The numbers all check out bar two, M 606 VRR and A 454 THG simply don't exist. The rest are all legit but they're registered to people all over the place. There's no pattern to it. What did you do, go round collecting numbers in a car-park?'

'Give me a few examples, especially the R-registered Jeep.'

'Hang on. Here we are. That's down to a Brian Anthony Scoular, S-C-O-U-L-A-R, of 23 Regiment Road, Guildford. The others are private cars registered to citizens in Cardiff and Salford, two in Birmingham, and a couple are company vehicles, both building firms, one in Somerset and one in Suffolk. Nothing stolen, all legit as far as we can tell. Mean anything?'

'Probably not. I've got one more for you, grab a pen.'

I gave him the number of the Mercedes driven by Mel's boyfriend Christian. I had no particular reason for doing so, but if you had access to that sort of info, why not use it?

'Okay, got it, see what I can do,' he said. 'Now, what you got for me?'

'The Mothership,' I said smugly. 'An amateur ring of bootleggers, very professionally run by a real whiz kid called Scooter, or Brian Anthony Scoular as you have him. He's got a couple of dozen students working for him.'

'Students?'

'Students. They skip a few lectures, nip over to France on Le Shuttle and bring back a load of beer. He's got them working almost round the clock, but mostly at night.'

'Hang on, what sort of quantities are we talking about here? Is this a few students earning pocket money or what?'

'That's probably why they're doing it, but they fill an articulated lorry which gets delivered to London two or maybe three times a week at somewhere around 18,000 litres a pop. Is that impressive enough for you?'

'Sounds like it's organised,' he said grudgingly. 'Must be going to someone with contacts at the retail end.'

'Either that or somebody's stocking up for one hell of a party,' I added helpfully.

'You any idea where it's going?'

'Not yet, but I might have something for you tomorrow.'

'Where's the base?'

'Right here in Whitcomb, on an old hop farm. The front is a computer programming company called Soft Sell.'

'And where are you right now?'

'You remember that pub I told you about, the Rising Sun?'

'Yeah, like in the song.'

Well, that dated you, I thought.

'I'm sort of running it until the brewery –'

'Have you told Murdo Seton about this?' he interrupted.

'Not yet, I haven't been able to get hold of him.'

'Leave that to me until I've checked things out. I'll contact you at the pub.'

Then he cut me off. No 'thank you', no mentioned-in-dispatches, no nothing. He didn't even ask for the phone number of the pub. He had no intention of getting back to me. If there were any Brownie points to be earned from this business, he was going to claim them all.

I dropped the phone and the dictaphone in my bag and wandered down to the bar.

Tony had transformed the girls by toning their make-up down a notch so that they looked like believable barmaids. Every time they pulled a pint or reached for a tankard or served a lunch, he was there, snapping away.

'Only doing chest shots, darling,' he confided, 'to show off the product.'

He had ringed the bar with lights, hoisting the temperature up way above normal, and the girls took ages serving a drink so he could get his angles right. Half the food they served – preceded by a very bad-tempered 'Ready!' from Mel in the kitchen – must have been stone cold by the time the customers got it as Tony insisted on it being presented to them at least three different ways. Funnily enough, none of the customers – mostly male – seemed to mind.

'Tony seems to have everything under control,' I said to Neemoy. 'I'm just nipping out to do a bit of shopping. Back in an hour. Don't tell Mel I've gone until I've gone.'

Before she could argue I was out of there.

I drove Axeman's Mondeo into Folkestone and found a Marks and Spencer's where I treated myself to underwear, socks, deodorant, a black polo-neck shirt, black leather gloves and a slice of lemon cheesecake. (I have a weakness.) Then I wandered down the Marine Promenade to take in the sea view, or rather the view of the sea fret and the rain heading inland. As the rain started in earnest, I bought a stick of Folkestone rock to take back to Amy and some genuine Folkestone fudge for Fenella, then ran for the car.

Back at the Rising Sun the trade had thinned out, leaving only a couple of cars outside and no more than six genuine customers inside.

Tony was packing his lights away, two salesmen in suits were chatting up Sasha at a corner table, Max was nursing a glass of something clear and medicinal and Dan was on his bar stool by the kitchen door, peering over the bar as Neemoy bent over to steal another packet of crisps from the box on the bottom shelf of the back bar. All seemed right with the world.

'I'm offski, outa here,' Tony griped as soon as he saw me. 'It's like working in a madhouse. Gawd knows what Amy'll say when she sees the contacts.'

'They'll be brilliant, Tone, relax.'

'Can we go home now?' asked Max.

'Tomorrow. Promise.'

'Mel's quit,' said Neemoy. 'Went off in a right snit.'

'Bound to happen. Surprised she stuck it this long.'

'And they've sold off the family silver,' Dan chipped in.

'Come again?'

'This American couple called in for lunch,' said Neemoy. 'Really sweet they were. Said they were interested in antiques and silver tankards so I let them have a look.'

She raised her eyes to the tankards hanging like bats from the beam above her.

'And they gave you £250 for one, right?'

'Yeah, how did you know? Dan said it wasn't anybody's in particular and we thought the landlady could use the money. I got the cheque made out to the pub.'

'Show me,' I said.

Neemoy pulled open the till drawer and handed me an American Express sterling traveller's cheque. The signatures on it were for a Joseph M. Maron.

'Did I fuck up?' she asked me.

'You're not alone. I've got to ring somebody about this. Listen, if Mel's not around, Dan here'll help you get ready for tonight, won't you, Dan?' He nodded enthusiastically. 'Just hold the fort for one more night and the cavalry will be here in the morning.'

'It sounds like you won't be around,' Max said with only a slight slur.

'Got a job to do, but I'll be back before closing time,' I said confidently.

Tony was snapping the locks on one of his camera boxes and I crouched down to whisper in his ear.

'You didn't by any chance get a shot of these two American tourists who bought the silver tankard, did you?'

'Might have.' He thought about it. 'Yeah, think I did, when they were talking to Neemoy. Why?'

'Can you knock off a print overnight and get it down here for tomorrow morning?'

'Courier? Cost a bomb.'

'Amy's paying.'

'No problem.'

Upstairs again, I changed my shirt, socks and boxer shorts and tried on my new gloves. I had no intention of leaving my fingerprints on a truckload of illicit booze but if I had worn the yellow washing-up gloves, I would have been pulled by any passing patrol car on the grounds of weirdness, not to mention being beaten up by real truck drivers for giving them a bad name.

I made two phone calls, one to Reuben Sloman at the Silver Vaults and one, when I had dug out his business card, to Ted Lewis, the landlord of the Old House At Home in Rye.

Then I pulled on my leather jacket, stuffed the gloves in the pockets and went down to the bar again where I changed a £5 note in the till for coins for the cigarette machine. There was so much money in the till I had trouble closing the drawer, so I decided Ivy wouldn't miss a box of matches and I picked one off the back bar.

'That'll be 10p,' said Max.

She was sitting in a window seat, her back to me, filing her nails.

'Put it on my tab,' I said, trying to work out how she'd known.

'I didn't know you smoked,' she said as I fed coins into the machine.

'Only in times of extreme stress, or when I'm bored, or after totally successful love-making,' I said as the coins dropped.

'That pack should last you then.'

I didn't dignify that with a reply.

I walked round to Hop Cottage and the paddock leading to the hop farm, leaving Axeman's car outside the pub on the grounds that it is always best to have one means of making a rapid getaway up your sleeve.

On a whim, I walked up to the door of Hop Cottage and knocked loudly, just to see if Mel was there and willing to make peace. There was no answer, although I thought I heard a thud from somewhere inside which made me crouch and peep through the letter box. All I could see was a small hallway and some stairs, which had been fitted with a disabled chair lift.

'Mel! It's Roy, from the pub,' I shouted, but there was no answer.

I gave it up and strolled around the front of the cottage to the five-bar gate where I pulled on my gloves, grasped the top rail and vaulted over in one smooth movement which amazed even me.

Still with a spring in my step, I rounded the corner of the paddock.

There were eight vehicles parked outside the Soft Sell building. I recognised three of them, but none of the number plates. Painter had been busy.

Then I heard an engine and automatically drew back into the hedge. The sound wasn't behind me, from the village, but from the other side of the hop farm buildings, down across the fields and the exit road through the woods.

It was Scooter's Jeep, probably in 4x4 mode, bouncing up the track by the stripping shed where the Mothership was hidden and eventually pulling in alongside the main building next to the assorted pick-ups and estate cars.

Brian Anthony Scoular, aka Scooter, was alone and I watched him climb out of the Jeep and open up the rear door. He was wearing green Hunter boots, caked in mud, which he proceeded to kick off and change for a pair of Reebok trainers from the Jeep.

I stepped out from behind the hedge and began to walk towards him. He made no sign that he was aware of me but he did suddenly look up whilst tying the laces of his Reeboks to his right. I followed his line of sight, over the back garden of Hop Cottage to the back of the cottage but saw no sign of life, just the windows of the kitchen and an upstairs bedroom.

'You're early,' he said, catching me looking where he had been looking.

'Can't wait to get to work,' I said with a smile.

He threw his muddy boots into the back of the Jeep and made to close the door before I got level with him.

I managed one quick glimpse and spotted a small shovel, the folding type which the Army uses, and something which looked like one of those strimmer things for trimming the lawn, what the Americans call a 'weed-whacker'. I didn't think much about it at the time. Maybe Scooter was a closet gardener.

'We're ready to roll,' he said as the Jeep door slammed. 'You wait here, I'll get Combo.'

I pulled the collar of my coat up as it began to rain again and shuffled my feet as Scooter pulled open the door to the Soft Sell building. From inside there came the sound of dull cheering and spattered applause. After a minute, Combo emerged, tucking a folded wedge of banknotes into the back pocket of his jeans.

'What's all that about?' I asked him.

'Payday. Always popular. Should be a good night for you down the Rising Sun, though it may be the last time for a while. You up for it?' He produced the keys to the DAF and flipped them at me.

'Let's go,' I said, catching them and falling into step beside him. 'What do you mean, *last time*?'

'A lot of the guys have done their last run today and Scooter's paying them off. I thought he'd told you there would only be this run and one other.'

'He did, sort of. I didn't realise this was the end of the business, though.'

'Needs must,' Combo said chattily as we approached the big stripping shed.

'How come?'

'Because of Coquelles.'

'*What?*' I thought the rain must have got in my ears.

'Coquelles. It's the place in Calais where Le Shuttle comes out of the Tunnel, the same as Cheriton is the Folkestone terminal.'

'And your point is what?'

'There's a French Customs post at Cheriton, right?' he said patiently. 'But it's never used 'cos the French basically don't give a shit. But there's a British Customs post at Coquelles, like a reciprocal deal. But it's never been manned until now. Well, next week actually. That means the Customs officers have two chances to get you now, once in France and once here. That'll scare off the odd day-tripper chancing their arm and make the chances of one of us getting pulled that much higher. Plus they're going to confiscate the vehicles if you're nicked and they can give you a driving ban. Scooter reckons the risks will be unacceptable, so he's winding things down.'

We were at the far end of the stripping shed by now where there was a large sliding door and padlock just as at the other end. Combo dug a key on a chain out of his pocket and unlocked the door, then put his shoulder to it and began to slide it open.

190

'How do you know all this?' I said to the back of his head.

'Scooter told me,' he said over his left shoulder.

'Who told Scooter?'

'Our buyer, the guy we're delivering to. He's very well informed.'

'Sounds like it. Who is it?'

'A real South London wide boy who fancies himself something rotten as a bit of a gangster. I think he's a bit of a psycho, myself. A big Jamaican ponce called Rufus Radabe.'

The door reached the end of its slide, revealing the DAF tractor unit and the trailer next to it up on its dolly wheels. I felt Combo turn to look at me.

'Are you all right?'

'Yeah, I'm cool,' I said.

But I kept my forehead pressed to the wet, cold metal of the shed while I took deep breath after deep breath; in through the nose, hold, one more sniff, hold, then slowly exhaling through the mouth.

It's what they tell you to do when you're having a panic attack.

17

I didn't know Rufus Radabe; nobody outside the police's National Crime Squad *knew* Rufus Radabe, but I knew *of* him. Anyone who had ever had any dealings in Brixton or Lambeth or Bermondsey or anywhere south of the river knew about Rufus Radabe.

He was said to have a finger in every dodgy pie going, starting from a base of minicab companies and a service for providing pubs with bouncers, or 'doormen'. There were the inevitable rumours about drugs and prostitution and protection rackets, most of which were probably legend rather than fact. But when the legend is more interesting than the facts, make an award-winning British film about the legend.

The one thing everyone who had crossed his path – and

I knew a few who had – agreed upon was that if you did cross his path, you kept on walking. Ideally, you never crossed his path. Preferably, you were on the other side of the street or, even better, on another street in a different town altogether. If Rufus was into bootlegging then he would be just the person to know where he could retail it and how to lean on the outlets, whether Domino Social Clubs in Brixton or off-licences in Hackney, to ensure they took a regular supply. He would have worked out his profit margins and risks, realising that the penalties were less for beer-running than for drugs or most of his other businesses. The one thing he wasn't was stupid. But then again, like most highly intelligent people with a large IQ, he was also a dangerously violent psychopath.

'You deal with Radabe himself?' I asked Combo when I had recovered the power of speech.

'Most times. He doesn't trust anyone else with the money.'

'So we're going to meet him tonight?' Combo nodded. 'Where?'

'He has a big warehouse near Dartford, behind that big new shopping centre. You can see it from the Dartford Bridge.'

'So there will be other people around?'

'Yeah, he employs ten or twenty guys there.'

That, at least, was something.

'You've been before?'

'Once, with Axeman, when Scooter couldn't make it. It's a strange place, man, I'm telling you. He only employs blacks – hey, nothing against that – but he plays music all the time, through speakers, like all over the warehouse. And it's not what you'd expect, it's not like gangsta rap or anything, it's big band swing. Cab Calloway, Benny Goodman, Count Basie, stuff like that. He makes them all listen to it.'

'Basie doesn't swing,' I said automatically.

'Huh?'

'Nothing. Something we used to argue about after the pubs closed.'

I had heard that story about Rufus before and that he called his most trusted heavies his 'Rhythm Section'. But there was no point in scaring Combo. I was scared enough for both of us.

'Let's get going,' I said. 'I'll pull the tractor out and you can watch me back up. I might be a bit rusty.'

In fact I did it first time. It must help to have something else on your mind, because without thinking I had the DAF fired up and the tractor unit out of the shed and was reversing it perfectly so that the 'fifth wheel' slid under the trailer.

'What about plates?' I shouted over the noise of the engine.

'Painter's supposed to have done them,' Combo yelled back, walking down the length of the trailer to check at the rear.

I jumped down from the cab and went through the motions of connecting the umbilicals from tractor to trailer, locking off the fifth wheel and clipping on the red and yellow air lines and the Electric Suzy. Then I jogged to the back end of the trailer unit to check that the rear lights were working.

'Looks good,' said Combo, but he wasn't talking about the lights or the plates.

He was looking up at the back doors of the trailer where Painter had been busy with some large stencils and a can of spray paint. The rig I was about to drive was now officially labelled:

ANGEL'S WINGS
DOMESTIC REMOVALS
OF SALFORD

There was also a phone number which, for all I knew, was a genuine Salford number.

'I just hope we're not followed by anyone thinking of moving house to the North-West,' I said to Combo. 'Come on, let's get it done.'

Stacked up near the door were dozens of cases of French beer which I had not seen from the other end of the shed.

'What's that lot?'

'Mustn't have been able to get it all in. It'll go in the next load,' said Combo.

That made me think of something I should have thought of before now.

'They have loaded this thing properly, haven't they?'

'What d'you mean?'

'I mean like somebody's spread the load evenly along the trailer. In fact, the bulk of the weight should be in the middle, between the axles. Too much weight at the back end and you could jacknife.'

Combo looked blank.

'Er . . . I think they just keep loading until they can't get any more in.'

'Oh, great,' I said, 'just great. Any other surprises coming my way?'

'Don't think so,' he said, but he was wrong.

We climbed into the cab and Combo settled himself in the air cushion passenger seat while I started the engine again, released the handbrake and selected fourth gear for moving off, something which always mystifies car drivers used to starting in first.

'Scooter says just stick to the concrete track and you can't go wrong. Down the field then up through the wood until we get to the road. Music?'

'He drove me down here yesterday,' I said, thinking, Was it only yesterday? 'What's the music?'

Combo produced a tape from his jacket.

'Smashing Pumpkins,' he said with a big grin.

'If you really must,' I said, concentrating on piloting the rig down the track and fumbling for the switch to turn on the three windscreen wipers.

In the gloom and the rain, the gutted hop field looked even more like a Flanders battlefield with the old hop poles standing like shattered trees and the disused bales of binding twine which tied the hop plants to them lying like abandoned coils of barbed wire. From the other side of the Downs the truck must have looked like one of the first tanks trundling up to the front line.

The track was wet and muddy, so I took it easy to test out how the loaded trailer would react, but I saw no need to put on the Differential Lock and the traction got a hold as we reached the end of the fields and began to climb the slope up towards the wood and the road.

In the giant wing mirror I could see the stripping shed, which we had left with its door open and the lights on, diminishing in the distance. It looked more like an aircraft hangar than ever, the light splaying out into the rain like a runway beacon.

'It's a sharp right once we hit the road,' Combo was saying, 'but it's a straight road so you can see a good way and there's not much traffic.'

That was just as well. Fifty feet and more of truck and trailer emerging out of a wooded nature reserve in front of you could unsettle the most experienced of drivers, let alone the local milkman on his float.

So I stopped dead with a satisfying hiss of the air brakes at the junction where the woods ended and the B-road ran left towards Whitcomb and Folkestone and right to Canterbury, the M2 motorway and eventually London.

I had been there twice before, once in Scooter's Jeep and once on Dan's bicycle in the middle of the night, but I'd never been there fourteen feet up in the air in a truck with powerful headlights. That's why I hadn't seen the broken sign which lay flat in the hedge by the junction before now.

It was obviously old, weatherbeaten and faded but from where I sat in the DAF's cab I could still make out the lettering: SETON'S HOP FARM, WHITCOMB and underneath, the by now all-too-familiar legend, Seagrave's Seaside Ales.

If it was a surprise for me, it was going to be one hell of a shock for Murdo Seton.

The B-road ran almost dead straight for three miles, which gave me time to get used to the truck's little quirks and satisfy myself that the trailer wasn't going to run out of control and attempt to overtake me going downhill. By the time we reached the A2 to bypass Canterbury, I was feeling confident and Combo had relaxed enough to take his foot off the dashboard where he had braced himself.

After we joined the M2 motorway I was relaxed enough to experiment with the cruise control and even sing along to Combo's tape. There really wasn't much to this truck-driving business, even when as out of practice as I was. All you really had to remember was that you had a better view of things than other road users, plus you were about eight times bigger than most of them so *they* had no excuse for not getting out of the way.

I sat back on my air cushion and held the wheel at arms' length, rolling my neck to ease the tension in my spine, thinking of myself as part of the machine and as long as I was in control, nothing could go wrong.

'When we get there,' Combo said out of the blue, 'it's best not to talk to anyone, Scooter says. Especially Rufus Radabe.'

'He'll be there, will he?'

'Yes, I thought I'd told you. He doesn't trust anyone else with the money, but we have to be careful.'

'Why exactly do we have to be careful?' I asked, not really wanting to know the answer.

'This Radabe character has been trying to find out where we keep the Mothership ever since we started delivering to him. That's why I've brought this.'

He held up a small, black electronic box not much bigger than the dictaphone I had borrowed from Amy.

'What's that? A stun gun?'

'It's a sweeper, a debugger. It bleeps when it finds a homing device. Hadn't you better watch the road?'

I realised I had been staring open-mouthed at Combo instead of straight ahead at the thickening traffic.

'Rufus tries to bug you?'

'He's tried twice. When we get there, we unhook this trailer and pick up an empty one, we don't wait for unloading, just get in, get the money, change over the plates and get out. But twice we've found transmitters planted on the trailers we've collected. We put one on a truck heading for Salford.'

No wonder this mob thought there was something intrinsically funny about Salford.

'Why would Rufus bug the truck if the truck's delivering to him in the first place?'

'Scooter says it's a great temptation for him to cut out the middle men, that's us, especially as we're coming to the end of our run. Think of his profit margin if he didn't have to buy the beer at all.'

'You mean, hijack it from the bootleggers?'

'Sure, then he's quids in. It's happened before. A gang of Czechs working the ferries got turned over earlier this year and lost their entire stock from three lock-up garages in Dover. They were pretty pissed off about it, but, fucking hell, they couldn't go to the police, could they?'

My neck suddenly hurt again and I realised I was hunched forward over the wheel, gripping it with white knuckles.

'What're you doing?' Combo asked.

I couldn't answer immediately as I was ripping the cellophane wrapping off the packet of cigarettes with my teeth.

'Falling back into bad habits,' I said.

It was fully dark and raining heavily when Combo directed me off the last exit of the M25 before the toll booths for the Dartford crossing (tunnel going north, bridge coming south). Rush-hour traffic reduced our speed to a crawl until we were off the motorway proper and heading for the warehouses and docking facilities which lined the Thames to the east of the bridge.

'That one,' said Combo.

A warehouse that big should not be that anonymous, but it was, sandwiched in between dozens of others equally grey, equally drab, identified only by a sign saying 'Unit 43' high up near the metal roof. It was perhaps six times bigger than the stripping shed at Whitcomb and this one would not have looked out of place at Heathrow. There was enough room in front of it to park a Jumbo jet let alone my rig.

There were two sliding doors, each having a regular door for people built into them.

'Turn and back in the left-hand door,' advised Combo. 'They'll have seen us on their security cameras.'

Sure enough, the door rolled open automatically as I completed the manoeuvre and edged my way backwards into the neon-lit interior.

A figure in overalls, a middle-aged Asian guy, appeared in my wing mirror. He took up position at the offside end of the trailer and began to wave me back, then over to the left, parking me next to another trailer unit on dolly legs which I assumed would be my empty load for the return journey. In my left side mirror, another Asian appeared and then I spotted two more off to the side, one climbing on and firing up a small fork-lift truck.

When I thought my trailer was level with the parallel empty one, I put on the brakes. The door in front of us began to roll shut, cutting off the comforting glow of street lights, the evening traffic and the lights of the Dartford Bridge.

The great metal cavern of the warehouse was split down the middle by a hanging curtain of plastic strips about a foot wide. They ran from ceiling to floor and were heavy enough to mask whatever was going on behind them although I could see figures moving around and another fork-lift truck zipping to and fro. It was the scene from the sci-fi movie where the visiting spaceship is isolated by the heavies from NASA. The only trouble was, the sound-track was wrong.

I turned off my engine and we could hear it quite clearly: fifty-year-old big band jive from the Swing era, belting out from a series of speakers hung from the metal rafters.

'That's him,' said Combo.

'I guessed,' I said, reaching for the door handle.

Our Rufus knew how to make an entrance, parting the hanging plastic strips as if he was coming through the curtains at the Cotton Club.

He was no taller than me, but wider in the shoulders, something accentuated by the white three-piece suit he wore, complemented by bright red leather shoes. His shirt was white and his tie was wide and gold, with a large gold tie pin in the shape of a saxophone. White suit, red shoes. I should have known he was a sociopath then and there.

As he walked towards us, his hips swayed and he snapped the fingers of both hands in time to the music. Even that minimal action showed that he had powerful biceps under the suit. The neon strip lighting reflected off his gleaming black, bald head, just as it did off the sun-glasses worn by a much larger black guy who walked one yard behind at his right shoulder. That one was dressed more conventionally in sweatshirt, baggies and trainers. He didn't need to show off his muscles but he did so anyway. I had him marked as one of Radabe's Rhythm Section, though I didn't think much of the dress code.

'Where's that little jive bunny Scooter?' he asked Combo, his accent pure South London.

Combo reacted like a rabbit caught in headlights. Rufus standing there in front of him, swaying to the music as the track built to a climax, was having a hypnotic effect on him.

'He's . . . he's . . . in . . . dis . . . indisposed.'

Rufus's eyes rolled, almost in time to the music.

'In. Dis. Posed. Good word that, innit, Yonk?'

The black bodybuilder behind him grunted and I noticed that Combo's legs were starting to quiver.

'He's got a problem with the regular driver,' I said, keeping my attitude as indifferent as I could. 'That's why I'm filling in.'

Rufus pointed a finger at Combo, then swung it on to me.

'Him I know, you I don't.'

'First trip here,' I said, bored, looking round, anywhere to avoid eye contact.

'You like my taste in music?'

The question caught me on the hop, just as the track was ending.

'Sure. It's Count Basie, 'One O'Clock Jump'.

He nodded slowly in appreciation.

'Try the next one.'

There was an uncomfortable silence and then the tape kicked in with a brash trumpet intro.

'Don't know the track, but that's Harry James.'

He seemed impressed.

'Very good. You know Harry James?'

'First bandleader to give Frank Sinatra a job.'

'Mmmm,' he mumbled, stroking his chin. 'Do I know you?'

'Don't think so. You want me to unhook this?' I jerked a thumb at the trailer.

'No bother, man, no bother.' He was giving me the once-over, so up close and in my face I could smell his toothpaste. 'Ali or Mohammed or Mustapha or one of them will take care of it.'

Even as he spoke, another four Pakistanis or Bengalis came through the plastic curtain, pulling on gloves, heading for the truck.

'Always hire Muslims in this business,' Rufus told me like I wanted to know. 'You get less breakages that way – if you know what I mean.'

'Wise move,' I said.

He screwed up his forehead and sighed at me.

'I *do* know you.'

I shrugged my shoulders. I could feel sweat running down my wrists and into my gloves.

'Well, I sure seen you around somewhere.'

'That's always possible.'

'Still, no never mind. You're a Swing man and that's neat, sweet and *reat petite*. Swing's coming back, you hear?'

'I hope so,' I said, just to be sociable.

'Trust me on that one.'

He turned back to Combo.

'Come with me if you want your money. Yonk here'll check the cargo, just to make sure we're getting what we're paying for, if you know what I mean.'

We nodded like schoolboys eager for praise and followed him across the warehouse and through the hanging gardens of plastic.

On the other side of the curtain, we were in Lilliput. Somehow we had been shrunk and placed in a massive off-licence. Pallets of beer towered above us and the towers stretched the whole length of the place, leaving a maze of corridors just wide enough for one of the small fork-lifts.

We followed Rufus's wide shoulders through the maze, dog-legging left and then right before coming to a glass box cubicle which seemed to be the office. I wondered if I should have unwound a ball of string as we walked so we could find our way back.

'Payment as usual, as specified by my good friend Mr Scooter,' Rufus said chattily, walking behind a desk and reaching down.

I took a half-step back, expecting him to come up with a gun. But then I was just jittery. He probably had nothing more dangerous than a Tommy Dorsey CD down there.

'These things are costing me a fortune,' Rufus grinned.

On the desk he placed a thin metal briefcase, flipped the catches and laid it down open. It was jammed full of piles of £20 notes.

'But if my friend Scooter specifies this sort of case, then it's the least I can do.' Rufus rambled on but I was still looking at the money. 'You wanna count it? You do and I'll have to get Yonk to count all the beer in your rig, and he don't count too fast.'

I sensed Yonk behind me in the entrance to the office. I certainly hadn't heard him arrive as the music tape had changed to Benny Goodman's 'Sing, Sing, Sing' and Rufus was miming the Gene Krupa drumbeat. There was another black guy with Yonk, much smaller and thin as a rake, dressed in motor-cycle leathers. They nodded in unison.

'Yonk and Fatboy here say your load is good,' Rufus shouted above the music. 'You happy with the money?'

'Yes . . . yes, that seems fine,' said Combo, reaching out with shaking hands to close the case.

'You guys attend to business,' Rufus said to his Rhythm Section. 'I'll see our friends out.'

He mimed some more drumming then paused, mid-beat, pointing an imaginary drumstick at my chest.

'I *do* know you, don't I?'

'Honestly don't think so,' I said, zipping up my jacket to give me something to do with my hands.

'Want a drink?'

He reached into a drawer in the desk and brought out a stack of plastic cups and a bottle of Wray and Nephew white overproof rum, 62.8 per cent alcohol by volume, all the way from Jamaica.

'It's very tempting,' I said and I meant it. 'But I'm driving.'

'Oh yeah, I forgot,' he said, pouring out a cup for himself but ignoring Combo. 'Driving all the way back to – where was it?'

'Kent,' I said. 'It's near France.'

He stared at me for what seemed like an hour but was no more than two seconds, then he downed the contents of the cup without choking, turning red or falling over, all of which are recognised medical symptoms following the ingestion of Wray and Nephew rum.

'It'll come to me,' he said.

18

Rufus walked us out of his office and through the beer maze back to the truck in case we got lost or decided to pocket a few thousand bottles on the way. I thought about what he would say if the police or Customs paid him a visit. Trouble was there wasn't much chance of that. Statistically speaking, the odds were on his side and he knew it.

'Stocking up for a party?' I said out loud, though I had in truth only been thinking it as one of a hundred lame excuses in the event of a raid.

'You're not wrong there,' he said to my surprise. 'Biggest party of them all. The Millennium, the Big Two Thousand. New Year's Eve this year starts a four-day party. Fuck, even a six-day, seven-day party. And I'm gonna have enough beer to supply all of South London, at prices you'll be amazed at.'

I had to admire his logic, and his nerve if he was going to sit on this much bootleg for eight months. The country was gearing up for an extended booze-up – or so the papers had us believe – stretching from Christmas Eve, right through to January 4th or 5th. A lot of pubs would close for the duration as their staff went home for Millennium parties and so would shops and off-licences. Even those who stayed open would have trouble getting deliveries as drivers and depot workers demanded time off.

If Combo's theory – and he'd heard it from Rufus – about Customs opening up a checkpoint on the French side of the Channel Tunnel was right, that would deter large numbers of amateur bootleggers trying to stock up at the last minute. By Christmas, the bootleg conduit under the Channel could be squeezed shut, so it made good business sense to build your stocks now.

'Listen.'

Rufus held the plastic curtain aside for us, but stopped in his tracks and held up a finger to my face. From the speakers came the soft vibraphone introduction to 'How High The Moon'.

'Lionel Hampton,' I said. 'Easy.'

I could have told him it was Nat Adderley on trumpet, but that would have been showing off.

Rufus stared at me again, trying to remember where he'd seen me before, but it just wouldn't come, and I could breathe again.

'Drive carefully,' he said.

I didn't need telling twice.

The Angel's Wings (domestic removals of Salford) trailer was already one quarter unloaded, the Pakistani warehouse crew unloading by hand on to wooden pallets balanced on the spears of fork-lift trucks. Someone had already set the dolly wheels and disconnected the power lines to the tractor unit, so all I had to do was drive away from under it and reverse on to the empty, unmarked trailer unit next to it.

'Can you change over the rear plate while I get hooked up?' I asked Combo.

He clutched the metal briefcase to his chest and stared at me as if I was talking Finnish. Then it sank in and he repeated 'Plates' to himself and nodded and headed for the rear of the trailer, still hugging the case. If he froze up like that when threatened with a Lionel Hampton solo, he was going to have a hard life.

I swung the DAF tractor unit out and to the left, then reversed under the empty trailer and got down again to lock off the fifth wheel and connect the umbilical pipes. Combo joined me back in the cab. He was shaking all over.

'It's done,' I said, 'and we're out of here.'

We were, once one of the Asians hit a switch to make the door slide open.

I inched the truck forward and out into the rain which was coming down in a steady sheet. I looked beyond Combo, shivering in the passenger seat, and in the nearside wing mirror I could see back into the warehouse to where Rufus Radabe was standing, supervising the unloading of his latest delivery, his left foot in its red shoe tapping to a beat I could no longer hear.

There was no sign of his Rhythm Section bodyguards, but I really didn't give that a second thought.

Then.

We were back on the M2 motorway, bypassing Chatham, before Combo spoke.

'Did he?'

'Did who what?'

'Radabe. Did he know you?'

'I've been around. He may have seen me around. I've heard of him, but I've never met him as far as I know.' I glanced at his ashen face. 'Honest.'

'That music, though, and the way he offered you a drink. You, not me. It was like he knew you and you knew him.'

'I know the type,' I said, but it didn't come out as comforting as it should have.

'I don't like his type.' Combo was staring out through the windscreen into the dark and the rain, talking to himself now, not me. 'I've had enough. Scooter was with me last time and I was still scared. The beer runs were a bit of fun at first. A nice little earner – isn't that what they say? – if you're trying to live on a student loan. And there was always plenty of beer to take back for parties. Made you dead popular.'

'I can see that.'

'But I can't hack it having to deal with people like Radabe, I just can't hack it.'

'Then don't. Quit. Walk away. Go home.'

'I can't go home, I've got exams this term.'

'What are you reading?'

'Law.'

'Most lawyers wait until they've qualified before getting a criminal record. I should quit whilst you were ahead. Go home.'

'I think I just might,' he said. 'Pull in at the next services, so I can do a sweep for bugs.'

'Why would Rufus bug us? He's expecting another load, or at least his trailer back, isn't he?'

'Scooter insists, so I'd better do it. It'll be the last time.'

A few miles down the motorway I pulled off into the lorry-park of a big service area which boasted a supermarket, a McDonald's and a games arcade. I parked as far away from the other trucks as I could and watched the mirror just in case somebody was tailing us and wondering why their electronic bug had stopped moving.

Combo got out his side and I noticed that he pushed the briefcase of money on to the floor of the cab without a second glance. Suddenly, he didn't want to know about the money and probably wouldn't have cared if I had driven off with it. He had had a spiritual conversion, and those were rare on the road to Canterbury these days.

I saw nothing suspicious in the mirror and Combo was back inside two minutes. He climbed up the steps of the cab but didn't get into his seat. Instead, he flung the debugging device on to the dashboard and reached for the metal case. For a second, I thought he was going to do the runner I had been thinking about.

'Give that back to Scooter, would you?' he said, putting the briefcase on the seat and clicking it open. 'Tell him the rig is clean, no sign of a bug.'

He took out a wad of notes and counted off what looked like about £200 worth of notes.

'And tell him I've taken my wages. I'm going back to college before I get ulcers.'

'How . . . ?'

'I'll thumb a lift with a truck driver,' he said with a grin as he closed the case.

'Haven't you got a car down there?'

'Yeah, my dad's old Volvo. Chip and Dale are using it. I'll bell them on their mobile, get them to drive it up to Cambridge. Tell Scooter goodbye and thanks for all the free drinks. Good luck with the pub and those barmaids.'

He made to jump down. Now that the cares of the world had lifted from his shoulders, I was warming to him.

'See you in court,' I said.

He froze, one hand on the cab door, registering alarm.

'Later, when you've qualified,' I explained.

'Oh yeah, right. But not if I see you first.'

'Good answer!' I shouted after him as the door slammed.

I fired up the truck and snaked back on to the motorway heading east and making good time as the nightly exodus from London had thinned out considerably. I checked my watch and found it was not yet eight o'clock. At this rate I could stop for a meal, get the truck back to Scooter and be in the Rising Sun well before closing if the girls hadn't smoked, eaten and drunk the place dry by then.

Alternatively, I could pull off the road into a quiet country lane, disconnect the trailer and let Rufus Radabe worry about it, drive the tractor unit up to London and dump it somewhere near the Elephant and Castle for Scooter to worry about. Then I could ride the Northern Line back home, pick up Armstrong and drive over to Hackney to stash the contents of the metal briefcase in the Stuart Street flat. Given that I'd worked out that

Scooter was looking at £9000 profit from the load, there could be as much as £18,000 in there. I'd even have enough to send a minicab down to the Rising Sun to rescue the girls. Murdo Seton could look after the pub; it was his after all. And Nick Lawrence and his Excisemen could take care of the rest.

It seemed like a plan; a good one, with no obvious downside.

Why didn't I listen to me?

I had to crawl down the old Roman road on the approach to the hop farm in order to spot the turning into the wood. The rain was slashing down now and I had the wipers on full speed. At least the straightness of the road meant that I could check the mirrors for headlights behind me for perhaps two miles and I found the inky darkness strangely comforting.

Once the rig was ten feet off the road and inside the wood, I began to relax, knowing that I was now virtually invisible from passing traffic. I eased the truck down the slope, conscious that now I had a trailer twenty-five or thirty tons lighter than the one I had taken out and it would react differently. I was also wary of the conditions as the concrete track up through the hop field was wet and smeared with mud leaking from the fields.

At one point I felt the trailer swing fractionally, so I changed down again and crawled uphill towards the stripping shed where the lights were still on, although the door at my end was only open about a yard.

I was tempted to give them a blast on the horn, but that would have scared the wildlife for miles around and probably stopped the hens at the Rising Sun laying for the rest of the year.

But there was no need. I could see in my headlights that it was Scooter himself who came out to slide the door open for me so I pulled up to the side of the shed and began the reversing operation. At the far end of the shed, cases of beer were stacked inside the other door to a height of about eight feet, so I aimed for them and managed to park without hitting them and, to my amazement, almost in a straight line.

The brakes hissed on and I killed the engine and the lights and climbed down from the cab. There was no sign of Scooter on my side of the rig, so I slid the door closed myself to keep out the rain and just in case a stray aircraft mistook us for a landing beacon.

I had opened the passenger door of the cab and was reaching in for the metal briefcase when I heard Scooter shout:

'What have you done with Combo?'

It was a fair question in a way. First Axeman doesn't turn up for work, then Combo doesn't come home from work, and I was always in there somewhere.

'He's quit,' I said, 'had enough. He's gone back to Cambridge.'

I grabbed the case and the electronic sweeper device and climbed down. Scooter was way back near the other doors, standing to the side of the pile of beer cases. I hadn't expected him to rush for a hug, but this was stand-offish to the point of rude.

'Where did you leave him?' Scooter's voice went up a notch as I walked towards him.

'I didn't *leave* him, he got out when we stopped at Medway Service Station. He said to tell you he had taken his wages out of this.' I held up the case. 'Rufus Radabe sends his regards.'

'Just put it down,' he said and for the first time I realised how nervous he was.

'What?' I was genuinely puzzled.

'Put the case down and don't come any closer.'

I stopped dead, about ten feet from him.

'What the fuck's going on, Scooter?'

'You tell me,' he said, petulantly like an angry child.

But before I could start to select a suitable lie, another voice said:

'Yeah, tell us about it.'

Mel's wheelchair appeared from behind the stack of cases of beer. It was being pushed by a middle-aged woman wearing trainers and a livid purple shell suit who seemed oddly familiar and I tried to remember where I had seen her before.

I didn't spend long doing that. I was more interested in the fact that Melanie had a double-barrelled shotgun across her knees and that she was swinging the business end of it up towards me.

'Hi there, Mel,' was all I could think of to say.

Once the wheelchair – and the gun – were clear of the stack of beer and facing directly at me, I placed the woman.

'Beatrice,' I said.

I hadn't recognised her with her legs covered, but I had talked to her since I had last seen her; that afternoon, when she answered my call with 'Seton and Nephew, Seagrave's Seaside Ales.'

'Stop smiling,' snapped Melanie, tucking the gun under her arm, the barrels aimed at my chest. If she fired it, the recoil would probably push the chair back over Beatrice's foot.

'Look, I hear you quit the pub in a bad mood, but this is a bit extreme, isn't it?'

'Shut up. What's your game?'

'Which?' I said reasonably.

'What? What do you mean?' She flashed a glance behind her up at Beatrice, whose face remained pale, pained and uncertain.

'Do you want me to shut up or tell you what my game is?'

She shook her head as if to clear it.

'Just explain yourself! Scooter, show him.'

Scooter reached into the inside pocket of his denim jacket and produced a mobile phone. My mobile phone.

'I found it in the Rising Sun,' said Mel.

'It's got HMCE – Customs and Excise – on speed-dial,' said Scooter. 'Why would that be?'

'Press Send and find out,' I said with a confidence I had no right to.

'No!' said Beatrice in a strangled soprano.

'Don't worry, he won't,' I said, 'but he might as well. All he'd get would be the Dover Customs' public information line. I was just doing a bit of research into bootlegging, that was all, to see what I was getting into. Size of the problem, how well Customs was dealing with it, all that public relations bullshit. Told 'em I was a journalist.'

I was gambling that Scooter wouldn't press the button. How the hell did I know if they had a public information line?

He pressed the button.

After about half a minute he turned the phone off without having said a word.

'It's Dover Customs all right, but it's just an answerphone,' he said to Mel.

'What do you expect this time of night?' I said, dead cool once more, thankful that Nick Lawrence was out bashing somebody's door in with his 'masterkey' somewhere. 'Anyway, Beatrice knows what my game is.'

The only sound was the drumming of the rain on the shed's metal roof as Scooter and then Mel turned to look at her.

'No, I don't! All I know is you're spying on me!'

She was chewing at her lower lip, holding back the tears.

'Now why on earth would ...' I started, then the penny dropped. 'Because this is the brewery's old hop farm, that's it, isn't it? You've rented it out to Scooter and his boys but nobody knows that back at the brewery, do they?'

Her silence meant I was on the right track.

'Who thought it up? It's brilliant. A gang of beer-runners working out of a base which is owned by the brewery that is investigating beer-running. Who would look here? Who suggested it to Scooter? I bet it was Mel – what, in the student bar one night? At a seminar on marketing and business administration? And who gets the rent? I'm guessing that Murdo Seton doesn't.'

'Some of it,' Beatrice said sulkily as Mel gave her an over-the-shoulder *I don't believe it* look. 'There has to be rental income on the books so we could get the water and electricity connected.'

'But Murdo doesn't look at the books too often, huh?'

She nodded.

Mel said: 'Muuum?' in the whining voice children reserve for when their parents embarrass them.

'Quite a scam,' I said, nodding in admiration, 'but not the one Murdo asked me to look into.'

'That was me, huh?' said Scooter.

'Only in passing. Everybody knows the stuff is coming in, just nobody knew where it was going. I do, now. Or at least

I know one conduit into London. That's enough for my report to Mr Seton. These are yours, by the way.'

I held out the briefcase and the sweeper device and he took half a step towards me. It seemed like ages since any of us had moved and I included the barrels of the shotgun in that.

'You're giving me the money?' he said, flicking back his lock of blond hair.

'It's not mine, apart from five hundred quid for doing the drop. I take it there won't be another trip this week now?'

He came towards me holding out my phone for the case and the sweeper and Mel waved the shotgun in my general direction as we exchanged.

'No tricks,' she said in her toughest voice. 'Don't make me shoot you.'

'Last thing on my mind,' I said.

'It would be,' she came back with style.

Scooter backed off and went down on one knee to open the case on the floor, flipping through the bundles of notes.

'It looks like it's all here,' he said to the two women.

Beatrice looked at the money open-mouthed. Mel hardly gave it a glance, keeping her eyes on me.

'Combo took his cut and, like I say, you owe me. In fact you should pay me double for having to deal with Rufus Radabe. Just seeing him brought on Combo's ulcers.'

Scooter looked up at me but held the lock of hair out of the way to show he wasn't being coy. In his other hand he held out a thick bundle of notes, much thicker than £500-worth.

'I'll pay you double if you take the trailer back to Radabe and dump the tractor unit somewhere far away.'

'Scooter!' Melanie was outraged, but unfortunately not angry enough to turn the gun on him. 'He was going to shop you to the Excise.'

Beatrice put a hand on her shoulder.

'We have to get rid of the truck, dear,' she said.

Go on, Mel, I thought, *listen to Mum*.

'You're shutting up shop, then?' I asked Scooter.

'Just a day or two early, that's all.'

'Leaving these two and your lads to take the rap?'

Now he was glancing towards Melanie, checking to see whether the shotgun barrels were moving in his direction.

'The guys have all gone, I've paid them off. Mrs Gibson and Mel here can say they were duped by a dodgy software company. They didn't know what was going on and anyway, there'll be no evidence.'

'Except that lot.' I pointed to the cases of beer.

'We'll load it into the trailer. You can sell it to Radabe, or give it to him. I don't care. It's an acceptable loss.'

'But you can't –' Mel started, but her mother squeezed her shoulder.

'It's the only way, Melanie. I'll help you load. If we can clear this lot out of here, there's nothing for the Customs to find and I can handle Mr Seton.'

There was something about the way she said 'Mr Seton' that made me wonder whether there had ever been a Mr Gibson and what had happened to him – married to a rock with a hard place for a daughter.

I reached out and took the money Scooter was offering.

'I'll dump the truck *and* the trailer,' I bluffed. 'That should buy you a couple of hours.'

'That'll do,' said Scooter and he began to close the case.

'Wait a minute!' Mel shouted, the shotgun waving around wildly. 'This isn't right. This just isn't *right* . . .'

She was pissed off because we weren't taking her and her big gun seriously and she was suddenly very pissed off because neither Scooter nor I were even looking at her.

Scooter had heard it first, over the beat of the rain on the roof.

His head snapped round, looking towards the sliding door behind me at the other end of the shed, and I automatically looked too.

'Oh, *Christ!*' he said softly.

He had heard the door being slid open.

The person sliding it was doing so with one hand. In his other he held a giant golfing umbrella to keep the rain from spoiling his white three-piece suit.

Things couldn't get any worse.

'Good evening, jive bunnies,' shouted Rufus Radabe. He nodded his bald head. 'And ladies too.'

Scooter looked down at the electronic sweeping device on the floor near his knee.

'Didn't you sweep the trailer?' he hissed at me.

'Combo did. Said it was clean,' I hissed back.

'I like to drop in on my suppliers from time to time,' Radabe was saying loudly. 'Just to boost morale, keep faith with the troops, that sort of thing. It's only good business sense, innit?'

He walked towards us, holding the umbrella in front of him, shaking the rain from it, then he lowered it and flipped his wrist until the fabric wound around the stem and he could fasten it. We watched in silence, fascinated.

'And how's my main man Scooter? Or should I call you Brian?' His face cracked in a smile. 'Nah, Brian's too uncool.'

Scooter rose unsteadily to his feet, leaving the briefcase where it lay. He seemed to be having trouble swallowing.

Radabe pointed his umbrella at me as he approached.

'And you – I still haven't placed you yet, but it'll come. You ladies – I don't know you at all.'

I took a step back towards the truck, thinking I might have to get under it at any moment.

Melanie tensed herself and held the shotgun as if willing the barrels to grow and hit Rufus in the stomach.

'Who the fuck are you?'

Rufus put the end of the umbrella to the floor between his red shoes and placed both hands on the handle. It looked like he was preparing to break into 'Puttin' On The Ritz'.

'I'm your customer, your buyer. I'm the payer-of-rent, the benefactor, the rewarder of honest labour. No, make that mostly dishonest labour. I am a lot of things in the world of business, but one thing I am not is an equal opportunity employer. I don't employ fools and I don't like having to rely on smart-arse white college boys. That's why I'm here. I've decided I need a better return on my investment and that means cutting out the middle man.' He nodded towards Scooter. 'Which is him.'

I took another step backwards.

'Shoot him,' croaked Scooter.

And then another.

'Now that's downright anti-social,' said Rufus, still smiling – but not with his eyes – at Scooter. 'It's just good business. Well, good business for me. Is that my money you're looking after?'

I pushed the wad of notes Scooter had given me deeper into the back pocket of my jeans.

'How did you find us?' said Melanie, her voice shrill, her chair shaking slightly, though that may have been her mother's hands on the pushing handles.

Rufus continued to totally ignore her and the gun, looking casually over her at the stack of beer.

'Is this my Friday load? Doesn't seem to be much so far.'

'Shoot him,' said Scooter again, and I wished he wouldn't.

'You weren't thinking of short-changing me, this being the last load of our contract, were you? Brian?'

'Get out of here!' shouted Mel.

'No, you wouldn't do that. You wouldn't dare do something like that, would you, Brian?'

'Leave us alone!' she screamed but still he didn't look at her.

'Do it, Mel,' said Scooter, shaking visibly now. 'Sh –'

He didn't get to finish.

Rufus Radabe stopped smiling. In one fluid movement he let the umbrella drop to the floor, reached inside his white suit jacket and produced a small silver revolver from his waist-band.

He swung his arm up and, with the gun on its side like you see in the movies these days, he fired once, the shot sounding like the crack of doom as it echoed off the metal walls.

Scooter staggered backwards on his heels, two steps, then three. His arms never left his side. There was a hole in his denim jacket but surprisingly little blood. Then his heels went from under him and his legs buckled and he folded to the floor.

As his head hit the concrete, it bounced and the forelock of blond hair bounced in sympathy.

'You fucking maniac!' Mel screamed, throwing the shotgun on to the floor in front of her chair.

The dull clang as it bounced, just like Scooter's head had,

was the only sound in the shed apart from the rain on the roof.

'It wasn't even loaded!' Mel shouted.

'He didn't know that,' said Rufus.

19

Mel began to sob, great racking, lung-bursting intakes of breath. Beatrice put herself between Mel and Scooter's body and leaned over her, throwing her arms around her and pulling her head into her chest. I took another step backwards and found my shoulder blades pressed up against the trailer. Rufus just stood there.

He still had the gun trained on the place where Scooter had been standing. It was a small, shiny, snub-nosed revolver. It looked like a toy, harmless. He began to sway slightly from the hips as if he had Basie's saxophone section playing in his head.

'Now why did he go and make me do that?' he said, shaking his head.

I had no intention of volunteering an answer but he looked at the two women and knew he wouldn't get any sense out of them. So he turned on me.

Two rapid steps and he was upfront and in my face and the gun was up against the side of my face and I felt cold steel against my cheek and could smell that Bonfire Night cordite smell.

'Why did he make me do that?' he asked me, almost reasonably. 'Why did he make me do that before he told me where the money was?'

He shook his head gently in disbelief at a world gone mad. Then he pulled back his gun hand and I thought that was it. The stubby barrel was going up against my ear and it would be Goodnight, Vienna.

But it didn't happen.

His hand came back and then flashed by the corner of my eye

214

twice as he smacked the canvas side of the trailer with the butt of the gun.

'Come on, you guys, wake up!' he shouted in my face. 'It's showtime!'

And there was I thinking it couldn't get any worse.

Rufus brushed past me, walking lightly on the balls of his feet to the back of the trailer. I heard the handles on the door click and then the door creaked open. Two lots of feet thumped down on to the shed floor. Rufus had brought his Rhythm Section with him.

Or rather, I had driven them here. No wonder there was no tracking device on the rig, Rufus had put a couple of stowaways on board to guide him in. But no, that wasn't right. How could they have known where we were going, stuck in the back of the trailer?

Yonk and Fatboy both carried pieces of timber, clean, white four-by-two inch pine about two feet long, weighing them in one hand and slapping them into the palm of the other. It was a sensible choice of weapon given the circumstances. If we had been stopped for any reason, they couldn't get out and run for it and two cornered black guys tooled up with guns or knives wouldn't have stood much of a chance. Handy pieces of timber, however, were just the sort of thing you'd find rattling around in an old trailer and if they got messed up, say with blood or fingerprints or anything, you could burn them.

'That what we heard?' Yonk asked Rufus, pointing his piece of timber at Scooter's body. Neither his nor Fatboy's face betrayed any emotion.

'Yeah, I guess I kinda lost it there for a minute.'

Rufus sighed, then tucked the gun back into the waistband of his trousers, smoothing down his white jacket in case there were any unsightly bulges.

'So whadda we do now, Big Boppa?' Fatboy's eyes roamed over Beatrice and Mel who were still sobbing in each other's arms, then they fastened on me. He looked no bigger than a jockey on a diet next to the body-built Yonk, but his dead eyes scared me more than Yonk's muscles, almost as much as Radabe scared me.

'Guess we'd better tell the Man,' said Rufus, or that was what it sounded like. 'Get his view on things.'

215

Using forefinger and thumb he delicately removed a small, fold-out mobile phone from the top pocket of his jacket, flipped it open and pressed one button. As he waited for it to ring he looked at me and raised his eyebrows as if saying: *Mobile phones, eh? Can't live with 'em, can't manage without 'em.*

'You'd better get in here,' he said into the mouthpiece, 'we've got a bit of a situation.'

He closed the phone and wagged it at me.

'Still haven't placed you, but it'll come, it'll come.'

'Maybe it was in a band,' I said, my mouth so dry I was surprised the words came out.

'A band?' He looked interested. 'What you play?'

'The horn,' I said, hoping that he had a thing about not shooting jazz musicians.

'What sort of unit?'

'Six or seven piece, mostly Trad jazz – pub jazz, student gigs, nothing fancy.'

'Swing's the coming thing, you know,' he said, tucking the phone away and leaning one-handed against the trailer, relaxing. 'I'm gonna own a big band one day, gonna get in at the grass roots of the revival. It's gonna be big, you mark my words.'

I wondered if he had a spare chair in the trumpet section but thought it best not to push it. I didn't get the chance to. The shed door began to slide open again and a figure holding his coat up over his head against the rain staggered inside.

He pulled his coat down and took in the tableau in front of him. The two women crouched over the wheelchair; Yonk and Fatboy holding their wooden clubs; Rufus leaning casually against the trailer, chewing the fat with me; me trying to look relaxed even though my shoulders felt as if they had been stapled to the side of the trailer; Scooter just lying there.

'What the fuck is going on?' said Nick Lawrence.

They hadn't needed to hide a transmitter on the truck because I had told them exactly where to come when I had phoned Lawrence that afternoon. It didn't make me feel any better knowing that.

Rufus strode over towards Lawrence, jiving his hips and clicking his fingers. He put an arm around Lawrence's shoulders and drew him towards the rest of us. Lawrence didn't look too happy about it, but there was no point in him glancing over at me for sympathy.

'You know I've always had a problem with Scooter's attitude,' Rufus was saying. 'That kid was just so sharp he was bound to cut hisself one day. I never did like dealing with him. It was like I always told you, Nicky, it was going to end in tears.'

'So you *shot him*?' The colour drained from Lawrence's face as he saw the hole in Scooter's chest.

'Somebody was going to someday.' Rufus looked at Scooter as well and the corners of his mouth turned down. 'Guess I was just a bit previous.'

'Did you find the money?'

What money? I wanted to scream.

'Not exactly yet,' said Rufus carefully. 'That's what I mean by me being a little previous.'

'Oh, shit,' breathed Lawrence. Then, as if for the first time, he saw Beatrice and Mel. 'Who are they?'

'Don't rightly know, but our friend Scooter tried to get this little lady here to shoot me with the old lock, stock and two smokin' barrels.' He nudged the shotgun on the floor with his red shoe and a lot of contempt.

'They're locals,' I said, trying to divert attention, 'just locals. They rented the place to Scooter but they didn't know what was going on here.'

Yonk moved like lightning and whammed his piece of four-by-two into the side of the trailer just above my head. I yelped, flinched, and my knees started to buckle.

'Somebody ask you?' he growled in my face.

'Now him,' Rufus was wagging his finger at me again, 'I'm sure I know from somewhere, but damned if I can place him.'

'He's called Angel,' said Lawrence. 'The brewery brought him in to keep an eye on the pub down the road. This lot couldn't have been too clever if he found them so quickly. He's the one called it in about this place.'

Rufus took his arm from Lawrence's shoulders and squared up to me.

'Then maybe he's the one who knows where my money is?'

I knew that if I didn't say something, however stupid, he would make eye contact with Yonk and I would be picking wooden splinters out of my skull.

'It's in the case, there, on the ground. It's all there apart from my cut.'

Rufus shook his head slowly.

'Oh no, no, no. Not *that* money, not *today's* payment. It's all the *other* money I've given Scooter over the weeks, that's what I'm looking for.'

'What money?' I said weakly, expecting a thumping.

'Listen carefully, man,' said Rufus, putting his hands on his hips. 'Scooter thought himself the big businessman, right? He comes to me with a plan, using nice white college boys to ferry my beer across the water 'cos he knows there is no way the Revenue Men will let people like me or Yonk or Fatboy there do the trip without being pulled. They see a black face in a car, car's gotta be stolen. They see a black face in a van, guy's gotta be a dope smuggler in a stolen van.

'Now all that's true and I know it makes sense to use Scooter's boys, but he didn't have to look so God-Almighty superior when he laid it out for me. That was just plain rude, man, just plain rude. So I made my mind up that I would teach the little shit the golden rule of business: take the goods in bulk, move 'em somewhere safe and then *don't pay for them*. Neat, huh? That's why I'm here. I've come for my money back. I like to think of it as the small print of our business agreement. Now, Mr Angel, you able to help me?'

'I don't know how,' I said, rather than saying 'No' and being thought rude. 'That case is the only money I've seen here.'

'There are eight of them,' said Lawrence.

'Nine,' corrected Rufus.

'Eight previous ones, then, plus this one.' Lawrence showed his irritation, which I didn't think was good personnel management, given the personnel involved. 'All metal cases, he insisted on that.'

'Maybe he took them to the bank,' I said, keeping one eye on Yonk.

'My very good friend the Revenue Man here thought of that.'

Rufus played up a cheesy grin and waved the palms of his hands in an 'over-to-you' move towards Lawrence.

'We planted known £20 notes in each payment and I circulated the numbers to every bank and building society in the area, but nothing's shown up,' he said.

'So we figure it's still here,' said Rufus. 'Now we can't ask Scooter any more and I guess I'll have to say that's down to me. You, Mr Angel, say you don't know nothing. Which leaves the two ladies here, don't it?'

'They're civilians, Rufus, they don't –'

That was as far as I got before Yonk slammed his wooden club into my stomach and I doubled over, sinking to my knees, gasping for breath. I splayed my gloved hands out on the floor in front of me and tried not to throw up.

The blood was pounding in my ears but I managed to make out Melanie's voice:

'He buried it. The money. He buried it at the bottom of the hop field. I've watched him do it.'

There was no sound in the shed except that of somebody sharpening a rusty saw and I realised that was me trying to breathe. Even the rain seemed to have stopped tattooing the roof.

'That would explain the metal cases,' said Lawrence.

'Wow! Buried treasure!' Rufus was bending over Mel's chair. 'And this little lady knows where to go treasure hunting.'

'No, she doesn't!' cried her mother. 'You leave her alone.'

'Hey, listen, older lady,' Rufus began to lecture her, 'no disrespect but you don't seem to get the picture here. If this little lady takes me to where Scooter buried his treasure, then I'll leave *you* alone. *That's* the deal, but it's not open to negotiation. It's what we entrepreneurs call a *done deal*. It's kind of a technical term you needn't bother your heads with.'

'Rufus, you're so full of shit sometimes,' said Lawrence.

I saw Yonk's feet move towards him.

'I'm not sure I can,' said Melanie, probably saving Lawrence from a smacking.

'What do you mean, little lady?' Rufus asked in a sing-song voice.

'It was mostly at night when he did it. I just saw the head-lights of his car down the bottom of the field, up towards the wood. It was only today when I saw him this afternoon that I realised what he was doing.'

'But, like, you know the general area, huh?' Rufus coaxed her. 'Where we could start digging.'

'For Christ's sake, Rufus, there are fucking fields out there and it's the middle of the night.'

Rufus looked at Lawrence as if giving him his second warning. Next sign of disrespect and he'd surely shoot him.

'I could show you the place where I saw him this afternoon,' said Mel.

She was patting her mother's arm, reassuring her that she knew what she was doing. She was buying time and I thought I'd better help her.

'Look in Scooter's Jeep,' I said and they all looked at me kneeling there on the floor. 'He's got a shovel and a metal detector in the back. Or he did earlier.'

'Now that's helpful,' said Rufus, 'truly helpful. You should take note, Lawrence. Mr Angel here is being totally positive. I like that. Fatboy, check the late Mr Scooter for some keys. Where do we find this Jeep of his?'

'It's up the hill by the office building,' said Beatrice.

'Thanking you, ma'am,' Rufus said with a flourish. 'You see, everybody's being positive. I like that.'

He picked up his golfing umbrella from where it had fallen.

'Now I'm going to escort this little lady out to my shiny new BMW and we're going to dig for buried treasure.'

'No, you can't!' Beatrice snapped, grabbing the handles of Mel's chair and pulling her backwards.

'Can do, will do,' grinned Rufus, then he put on a real hang-dog face. 'Oh, don't worry about her. She can hold the umbrella, she won't get wet. And while we're gone, you guys can get my beer loaded into my trailer. It'll be good exercise for you. Yonk here'll make sure you do a good job.'

'You don't mean me?' Lawrence pointed a finger at his own chest.

''Specially you – you're beginning to irritate me. Oh and

Yonk, make sure Mr Angel here doesn't strain himself too much. He's got some driving to do later.'

After about ten minutes of watching our feeble efforts, Yonk threw down his wooden club in disgust and began to hump cases of beer from the stack into the trailer himself. He was virtually doing them one-handed and was loading three to my one even before he got into his stride.

Rufus Radabe had pushed Mel out of the door and into the night and then we had heard a car engine start. Then another vehicle had roared down the side of the shed and we guessed that must be Fatboy driving Scooter's Jeep, on his way to the treasure hunt.

Apart from that, nobody had said much as we concentrated on our chain gang, passing cases of beer. Except we weren't as efficient as a chain gang and I made Beatrice climb into the trailer so she could push the cases deeper inside. She seemed grateful for the work as it took her mind off what might be going on between Mel and Rufus.

But it was Lawrence who broke first.

He slammed a case on to the trailer and turned to Yonk.

'I don't have to do this! Look, get on your phone, find out what that nutter is doing. He could be half-way back to London by now.'

Yonk just looked at him and flipped another case from the pile to the truck as if it was an envelope.

'With the money,' Lawrence added and that struck home.

Yonk was certainly not keen on being stranded way out here in the countryside with a dead body in the room. He pulled a small mobile from his back pocket and speed-dialled.

'Rufus? Yo, how's it going?'

He grunted a couple of times, then said 'Cool' and closed the phone.

'Looks like they've found something. They're starting to dig.'

He looked at us and nodded at the pile of beer. I could take a hint and I resumed loading and so did Lawrence.

'I shouldn't be doing this,' he said.

'No, you bloody shouldn't,' I said. 'You're supposed to be one of the good guys.'

'Screw that on what they pay us.'

'You're the one who told Rufus about the Customs post at the French end of the Tunnel, aren't you?'

I clumped another case down. We were getting ahead of Beatrice who couldn't cope pulling the cases into the belly of the trailer.

'That's right, Sherlock. It put a time frame on things and that was all to the good. Anything goes on too long and patterns emerge that even we couldn't miss. Anyway, I knew Rufus was a greedy bastard.'

'Did you do a similar trick on the Czechs in Dover? Let them build up a stock then hijack it without paying?'

'I told you he was greedy.' Then he lowered his voice. 'But he's not gone this far before.'

'Got any ideas?' I whispered, slamming down a case to cover my voice.

Lawrence shook his head and started to chew on his bottom lip.

It looked like it was all down to me again.

'Hey!' I said loudly to anyone and everyone. 'Has anyone given a thought to stacking this load right?'

The three of them stopped working but nobody said anything.

'Look, we don't have enough beer for a full load so this lot's going to rattle around like a pea in a drum unless we stack it properly. We should start at the back, near the wheels. Put most of the weight on the rear axles otherwise the whole thing could swing out of control.'

Or at least I hoped it would. From what I remembered about loading artics, you always started in the middle. Too much weight at the back can be dangerous.

'Okay, okay, I'll do it myself.'

I made a big deal of having to work with idiots and huffed and puffed as I climbed into the trailer.

'You just keep out of my way, woman,' I said to Beatrice,

staring hard at her. 'If I'm going to drive this crate I don't want any accidents.'

I think she got it, but I didn't have the time or energy to worry too much.

Facing out from the trailer, I began to stack cases two-wide as Yonk heaved them up to me, his biceps getting the sort of work-out he paid good money for down the gym. Lawrence continued to slam cases down to my left, pushing them towards Beatrice who was edging her way deeper into the trailer.

I had my stack two wide and six high when Lawrence said:

'Who's this Cartwright-Humphreys character anyway?'

Behind me I heard Beatrice take a sharp intake of breath.

'Who?' I said, taking another case from Yonk and placing it next to my stack so I could stand on it to pile the next two even higher. I glanced at Yonk. He was bending over to pick-up a case from a pile of three.

'That last car plate you asked me to check out. It's registered to a Christian Cartwright-Humphreys of Harley Street. What's he got to do with anything?'

'Nothing to do with this lot,' I said. Yonk was bending to pick-up the second from bottom case. My stack was now eleven high. 'That was a freebie. I needed a favour.'

'Thanks a bunch,' he said angrily. 'Do you know the hassle I have to go through to . . .'

Yonk was bending for the bottom case.

I jumped off the case I was standing on and positioned myself behind my stack, put my back to it and pushed.

I don't know how many cases hit Yonk. I think I managed to dislodge about a dozen and most of them seem to bounce satisfyingly off parts of his body.

'Shit!' screamed Lawrence, jumping out of the way.

Then, when he saw Yonk wasn't moving, he swung a foot at his head and shouted, 'Bastard!'

'Come on,' I yelled to Beatrice, grabbing her hand and jumping down from the trailer, careful to avoid broken glass. Beer was seeping everywhere. It was as if Yonk was bleeding beer.

Lawrence was making to kick Yonk again, just to take out his frustration on something that wouldn't kick back. He was actually clearing broken cases of beer away from Yonk's head to give himself a better shot.

'Is he dead?' Beatrice said.

'He deserves to be!' Lawrence screamed, pulling back his foot.

'That's enough,' I said.

Lawrence looked at me long enough to realise I was holding Mel's shotgun on him and lowered his foot to the floor. Beatrice looked at me wide-eyed and I prayed she wouldn't say something stupid.

'Find something to tie him up with.'

Lawrence looked at me sulkily.

'There are some old ropes in the trailer,' said Beatrice.

I looked in and found she was right. Yonk and Fatboy had tied four lengths of rope to the inner stanchions of the trailer to hang on to while they were riding in the back.

'Get it,' I told Lawrence, waving the shotgun at him.

He scowled, but climbed up into the trailer.

I climbed over the debris of smashed beer bottles, treading on one of Yonk's legs in the process, and moved a case of Kronenbourg so I could remove the mobile phone from his back pocket.

One of the cases had caught him on the back of the head and smashed his face into the floor. His nose was broken and bleeding freely.

'Hurry up, Lawrence, he won't be out for long.'

Lawrence was struggling with the knots on one of the ropes, cursing to himself and then producing a lighter, flicking the flame and burning it off.

'I want you to take the gun, Beatrice,' I said so he could hear, 'and keep an eye on both these two. I'm going to see if I can get Mel.'

I handed her the gun and she stuck her face up to mine and mouthed the words:

'It's not loaded.'

'They don't know that,' I whispered.

20

I ran the length of the shed to where the door was still open as Rufus had left it when he wheeled Mel's chair out, and peered out into the darkness. The rain had eased off but it still took me a minute to focus on the one source of light this side of the North Downs. Even then, I was too far away to pick out the detail of what was going on.

Down across the sloping hop field and half-way up the track towards the wood were two pools of light formed by the intersecting beams of two sets of headlights. Occasionally a shadow of movement would flit across the lights. As far as I could tell, the treasure hunt was still under way.

I jogged back down the length of the truck to where Lawrence was tying up Yonk under the two eyes and two barrels Beatrice was levelling at him. He had a five-foot length of rope and had put a slip knot in one end to form a noose around Yonk's neck. With the other end he secured Yonk's wrists behind his back. Still unconscious, Yonk lay there and let him do it. An inflating and then deflating bubble of blood from his nose told me he was still breathing.

'What are you going to do?' Lawrence asked.

'A deal – if I can,' I said.

'What about Mel?'

'She's part of the deal,' I said, but Beatrice didn't look convinced.

'I meant what are you going to do about me?'

Lawrence pulled a case of beer off the remaining pile and stood it on its end so he could sit on it. He picked up two loose bottles of beer, held one over the other until their metal tops locked and then flicked until the top came off the bottom one with a fountain of foam which soaked his trousers.

'You just sit there and take it easy,' I said, resisting the urge to make him swallow the bottle as well as the beer. 'We'll see what happens if matey-boy out there doesn't want to deal.'

'What if something happens to Mel?' said Beatrice through gritted teeth.

'Then I'll leave him,' I pointed to Lawrence, 'to you.'

He looked distinctly uncomfortable at that and I wanted to say *If they move, kill 'em*, but I didn't think Beatrice would get the reference and anyway, she had no ammunition.

'How are you going to deal with Rufus?' he said.

I showed him the mobile I had taken from Yonk.

'I'm going to give him a ring.'

I tried to guess how much beer we had managed to load into the trailer before I closed the rear doors. However much it was, it would have to do.

I jogged back towards the cab, tugging my gloves tighter and zipping up my jacket. At the back of the cab I stopped and disconnected the red air line which released the brakes on the trailer. With those out and whatever load we had stacked in the most unsafe position towards the rear axle, I had – I hoped – a highly unstable vehicle. I also hoped I knew what I was doing.

I climbed up into the cab and started the engine, letting it idle while I climbed down again and pushed the sliding door open with my shoulder. Back in the cab, I released the tractor brakes and edged the rig out of the shed, lining it up with the concrete track disappearing down into the dark field.

Then I hit all the lights, full beams, and the horn.

The mobile in my pocket rang within fifteen seconds.

'Yonk! My man! What the fuck's happenin'?'

'Hello, Rufus, I was just going to call you. Found your treasure trove yet?'

'Who the –?'

'Nobody you know, Rufus,' I said, anxious not to give him too much time to work out an edge. 'Straight deal for you. Take your money and let the girl go. We'll clean things up here.'

'You've still got some of my money,' he said, the instinctive businessman.

I had forgotten that the briefcase I had collected that afternoon was still lying on the floor of the shed near Scooter's body.

'Cut your losses,' I said into the phone. 'Go now.'

'Put my man Yonk on.'

This was taking too long. I revved the engine, hoping the noise sounded as threatening across the fields as it did in the cab.

'Can't do that, he's indisposed.'

'In. Dis. Posed,' he said slowly, like it was three words. 'That's interesting. Don't think Yonk's ever been that before. You're a man of talent, Mr Angel. You hurt him?'

'Not as bad as you hurt Scooter. Now let the girl go and get the fuck out of here.'

'And if I choose not the fuck to get the fuck out of here, what then?'

'Then I'm gonna run right over you,' I said. And hung up.

I gunned the engine, dropped into fourth gear and floored the accelerator.

As the truck moved forward, agonisingly slowly at first or so it seemed, I picked out the wet, mud-smeared track and basically pointed the wheels at it.

I was still too far away to see anything clearly, but I thought I could make out a blurring of the headlights of the cars up the other side of the slope and then, quite definitely, one set of headlights began to move. And they were retreating, back up the hill into the wood.

I hit the horn again as I changed gears, picking up speed. If I had been where they were, facing a charging truck lit up like a Christmas tree, I would have got the hell out of there.

Except the lights which had gone backwards were now coming forward, down the slope, aiming for a spot exactly where I reckoned my forty-one-foot truck would be in about ninety seconds.

Even worse, the headlights of what I could now make out was Scooter's Jeep were picking something up on the limit of their beams. Another vehicle in the middle of the track, going hell for leather downhill.

It was Mel in her wheelchair, pumping her arms like pistons. If the Jeep didn't catch her and kick her airborne, she would wrap herself around the radiator of my truck. There was no alternative and it was going to happen any second.

The phone rang.

'You want to play chicken? Let's play chicken!'

Rufus's voice was a distorted, metallic scream in my ear. I flung the mobile on to the passenger seat and moved my foot over the brake. My speedometer read 45 miles per hour and I could feel the trailer swinging behind me on the slippery surface.

'I'm gonna beat you!' Rufus shouted out of the phone. 'She's mine. Watch her fly, man! Watch her fly!'

Trouble was, he was right.

There was no way I could reach Mel before the Jeep and even if I did it would only be to smash her to pulp. My hand hovered over the Differential Lock switches. With those on I could risk swinging off the track as I braked and hope to get enough grip on the churned-up field to avoid totalling Mel, the rig and me.

'Here I come, little lady!' shouted the ghost voice in the cab.

Mel's chair had reached the bottom of the slope where it turned up the track I was speeding down. Rufus and the Jeep were yards away from her as the chair's momentum slowed. Feet away.

'Holy shit!' boomed Rufus's voice.

In an instant, Mel threw herself from her chair, landing on the track close enough for me to see her face in my headlights. She rolled over twice, like a commando in training, and then she was up and running with long, loping strides towards the hop field to my right.

'Keep running!' I shouted, though there was no way she could hear me.

The Jeep hit the empty wheelchair, booting it up into the air and on to the bonnet of the Jeep where it smashed into the windscreen. The Jeep swerved wildly and began to lose momentum, skidding sideways into my path.

I forgot about the Differential Lock, pounded the accelerator, swung the wheel to the left off the track and as the cab wheels took their first bounce on earth rather than concrete, I stood on the brakes.

The trailer, now out of alignment and travelling faster than the tractor unit, its wheels still on the slippery track, began to hang out and overtake the cab.

I had a birds'-eye view in my wing mirror. Rufus got an even better one as forty feet of badly loaded trailer jacknifed straight towards him; an unstable, unstoppable battering ram.

I think I was almost in a standing position, hanging on to the wheel for dear life when the impact came.

I was probably screaming as well, as the trailer smashed the Jeep off the track and right out of my line of sight.

I know Rufus was screaming up to the end. I could hear him.

I was lucky that the trailer had not smashed the Jeep into the cab. I was lucky that the cab unit was still upright, its front wheels buried in the mud of the field. I was lucky that when my head was going towards the windscreen at high speed I managed to get my forearm up to protect it. I knew drivers who had survived a jacknifing and walked away but never one who had deliberately jacknifed their rig. Lucky old me.

The first thing was the silence, then the disorientation as I was not sure which way the tractor unit was facing.

Then I heard an engine in the distance and turned my head slowly just to make sure my neck worked until I saw headlights up the hill. They swung around and disappeared, the sound of the engine dying away in the woods and the dark.

Through the fuzz between my ears I worked out that it must have been Fatboy disappearing in Rufus's BMW.

I fumbled the cab door open and looked over the wreckage of the trailer and the Jeep. Rufus himself wasn't going anywhere. The Jeep was on its side and only about half the width it had been when it left the factory. The trailer was crumpled and piled on top of it. There was beer pouring out of the buckled rear doors and an occasional pop as another bottle exploded.

It all seemed a hell of a waste.

'You okay?' somebody said breathlessly below me.

Mel was standing, legs apart, hands on hips, her chest heaving with exertion.

'Not doing as well as you,' I said. 'Nice line in miracle recoveries, I see.'

She gave me her hard look.

'You were trying to run me down! You were coming straight for me!'

'Aw, stop moaning! I knew you'd get out of the way in time.'

Her face softened.

'When did you guess?'

'First night, when you said you'd got Ivy a brandy after her fall. You have to stand behind the bar to reach the brandy optic. I know,' I said proudly. 'Plus today, when you found my mobile phone. I left it upstairs.'

'Bugger!' she said softly.

I had reminded myself and checked to see if my mobile was working. It was, but then I had another thought and leaned over the passenger seat to find the small fold-out phone I had taken from Yonk. Eerily, it was still on, the line to Rufus and the Jeep still open.

I switched it off and added it to my collection, the effort of straightening up making me dizzy. I shook my head to clear it and carefully climbed down the cab steps. Mel took hold of my arm to steady me.

'Was it Christian's idea?' I asked her, just to distract her from the wreck of the Jeep. 'Your Harley Street boyfriend, was it his scam?'

'Sort of. I did have the accident, it just wasn't that serious.'

'But you thought you could scam EuroDisney into a mega-bucks compensation payment?'

'Something like that,' she said quietly.

'Was your mother in on it?'

'No, she wasn't, she thought it was a genuine injury.'

'Going to be a bit miffed, is she?'

I took three or four steps to make sure my legs worked. Nothing seemed to be broken, so I wouldn't be able to do a deal with Christian myself.

'*She* didn't tell *me* she was ripping off the brewery, skimming Scooter's rent money,' Mel said grimly.

'I bet you didn't tell her you knew what Scooter was up to all along. You even came down to the pub to check me out for him, didn't you? I bet you acted as look-out for him.'

'Sometimes,' she admitted.

'Never mind, let's get back and see what we can sort out. What made you run, by the way?

230

'When we heard the truck's hooter, Rufus got on his phone. I kicked the other one in the bollocks as hard as I could and legged it.' She paused, then smiled. 'Well, wheeled it, really.'

'Did they find the money?'

'Four cases. Maybe there's more. We could –'

'No, we couldn't. See if you can find your wheelchair.'

'Why?'

'Because it's a long way back up this field and I'm knackered.'

The wheelchair still worked after a fashion, one wheel bent into an oval.

Beatrice and Lawrence were standing in the doorway of the shed as we approached. Beatrice screamed when she saw Mel walking, pushing the chair in a far from straight line. She propped the shotgun up against the shed door then rushed towards her daughter, arms open.

Lawrence was calmly smoking a cigarette. I pulled a crumpled packet from my pocket and he flicked me a light.

'That,' he said as I blew smoke into his face, 'was without doubt the most stupid thing I have ever seen in my life.'

'Then you can't be as old as you look,' I said.

'So what happens now?'

'You going to turn yourself in?' I asked.

I could see Yonk still hogtied on the floor by the remaining cases of beer at the back of the shed. I also saw Lawrence's eyes flash towards the shotgun.

'Doesn't appeal much,' he said, drawing on his cigarette.

'I'd think about it if I were you,' I said. 'You're already under surveillance. I saw them in Dover while you were talking to the Czechs.'

'Had to happen, I suppose,' he said, suddenly resigned to it all. 'There'll be lots of statements to make, coupla tons of paperwork and at the end of it, what? I took some bunce but all I was doing was help the bad guys steal from the bad guys.'

He dropped his cigarette and ground out the butt with his foot.

'And at least I haven't killed anybody,' he said calmly.

He had a point.

'In that case, you'd better be the hero.'

I handed him Yonk's mobile phone.

'You'll need this,' I said. 'Cut Yonk loose and give him and us half an hour, then ring the police or your own people. And you'll need an ambulance and probably the fire brigade. What the hell, ring everybody.'

Amazingly, it was still only ten thirty, and I had a pub to run.

I pushed the wheelchair and carried the shotgun round to Hop Cottage, Beatrice and Mel following, arm-in-arm, comforting each other. I told them not to hang about and made Beatrice back her car out on to the road whilst Mel found a pair of crutches which Christian had provided as potential props for when the insurance assessors called.

I folded up the wheelchair as best I could and stashed it in a cupboard under the stairs inside the cottage, then threw the shotgun in after it. I told Mel to dump the chair as soon as she could, and to either buy some shells for the gun or dump that as well. She said she couldn't do that as her mother had sort of borrowed the gun from Murdo Seton after the annual brewery pheasant shoot and she hadn't actually got around to telling him yet.

There was no point in worrying about it, I just resolved never to be around if those two decided to work as a team.

Beatrice drove us to the Rising Sun and as we arrived I scanned the car-park. There were a goodly number of cars there, but none I recognised from Scooter's operation. Even Axeman's Mondeo had gone. Somebody must have had a spare key or maybe it had just been stolen. Nothing was safe these days.

As we got out of her car, Beatrice fumbled between her feet then joined us, swinging a small handbag over her shoulder.

'I bet I look a right mess,' she said, helping Mel fit the crutches under her armpits.

'Forget it. Just remember we've been here for two hours at least and hope nobody notices us.'

As I opened the door for her, the cry from the bar was: 'Mel!'

But it was only Dan and the Major and the girls behind the bar. The rest of the customers were strangers or had been regulars only since Neemoy, Max and Sasha had arrived. There was no sign of any of the 'boffs'.

We joined Dan and the Major, pulling up a table and chairs to the end of the bar where they stood. Neemoy and Max seemed genuinely pleased to see Mel back and on her feet. I don't think Sasha had realised she'd gone anywhere.

'You can walk! I'll have what she's drinking!'

'Hey, I remember those legs!'

'Lost your licence for the wheelchair? Speeding again?'

There was a lot of banter like that, plus the Major saying:

'Beatrice, my dear, so nice to see you and you are looking quite lovely.'

Beatrice smoothed down her shell suit and ignored him. Then she opened her handbag and took out a fold of £20 notes, which somehow looked terribly familiar.

Automatically my hand went to the back pocket of my jeans, but that comforting bulge was still there.

'Anyone want a drink?' asked Beatrice. 'It must be my round.'

Anyone called Gibson who named her daughter Mel should be made to buy the first round by law, was my opinion. But we were well into the second round and thinking about a third when we heard the first sirens and blue lights flashed by the pub's windows.

The pub phone woke me the next morning at some unearthly hour just after nine. It was a woman, but not Beatrice, from the brewery telling me that a relief management couple, Mr and Mrs Coldstream, would be arriving to take over the pub at lunchtime. And that was fine by me.

I had just put my head back down on the bench seat by the dart board when my mobile went off. It was Amy telling me she'd sent a car for the girls and I could get a lift back to town with it if I wanted to. She left a big 'or not' hanging in the air.

My eyes had been closed for no more than ten seconds when somebody started hammering on the front door. I felt sure it must be someone in a uniform but it was a motor-cyle messenger with a cardboard envelope for me. I signed a chit, grunted thanks and shut the door in his face.

The envelope was from Tony the photographer and it contained three blow-up prints of a middle-aged couple talking to Neemoy. I stashed them behind the bar.

After that, I decided to get up and get dressed, turning the jukebox up loud to wake up the girls.

Just after noon, I was pulling a pint for money for the first time. There were about a dozen customers, including Dan, but no diners. I had decided to cancel the lunch menu as a treat for the girls on their last day.

Through the window I saw them park a Scorpio hire car and walk across the car-park hand in hand, although the man was carrying a Selfridges plastic bag. They were both in their mid-forties, smartly but loudly dressed as only Americans on holiday can be.

''Morning,' I greeted them as they ducked, as Americans always do in old buildings, on entering the bar.

'Good morning to you,' said the man. The woman smiled sweetly at me, eyes wide, head on one side. She was really rather attractive.

'And what can I get you? We've no food on today, I'm afraid.'

'That's okay,' he said, placing the bag on the bar. 'We're here to see the landlord if we could.'

'Sorry, he's not here at the moment,' I said, smiling back at his wife. 'Is there anything I can do?'

'Well . . . ?' He hesitated and looked at the woman.

'Go on, darling,' she told him, patting his hand. 'You know we should and our schedule means we won't be back this way.'

'Okay, I will.'

He opened the bag and produced a silver tankard which he placed on the bar in front of him.

'My name's Maron, Josiah P. Maron, and this is my wife Anna Lee. We called in here yesterday and purchased this tankard from one of your bar staff.'

234

'Josiah collects silver beverage vessels,' said Anna Lee and I tried to remain interested.

'There's a problem, though,' said Josiah.

'Is there? Like what? It's not genuine?'

'Oh no, quite the opposite. It's *too* genuine. Look down here at these silver hallmarks. See that? It's a "g".'

I screwed up my eyes.

'Yeah, I think so.'

'Now that letter indicates the year the silversmith made it, but they've been making silverware for like . . . ever . . . so they have to use the letters over and over again, but like different typefaces and sometimes with other marks.'

'Okay, with you so far.'

'Good. Now on this tankard I bought here, the "g" looks like the one they used in 1902, in which case, this is worth about £250. But when Anna Lee and I got back to our hotel I had a look under the eye glass and I see I made a mistake. It's also got a King's Head mark on it, really small – see it? Now there wasn't a King's Head used on British silver after 1838, when your Queen Victoria – you know, Mrs Brown – took the throne. And anyway, they stopped putting head marks on altogether after 1890. So this tankard couldn't be 1902, it had to be before then, and my guess is that "g" there refers to 1822, which makes this worth more like two thousand five hundred of your pounds, not two-fifty.'

'Wow!' I let out a whistle. 'Some mistake, eh? Thank you for bringing it back. I'd better refund you your money, hadn't I?'

'That would be mighty kind,' said Maron, beaming.

'Or would you just like your fake traveller's cheque back?'

I beamed at Anna Lee but she wasn't smiling back.

'I don't know –' he started.

'No, of course you don't, because they were always out when you called.'

Six of my customers had formed themselves in a semi-circle around the Marons.

'This is Ted Lewis, of the Old House At Home in Rye. That's Frank Jennings of the Cricketers in Deal. That's Tim – or is it Tom? – Hampson of the Horse and Groom in Folkestone. This is – oh, well, they'll introduce themselves . . .'

* * *

The couple who called themselves Nigel and Bronwen Cold-stream looked very young and fresh-faced. I hoped they were up to the responsibilities they were taking on. Running a pub was no game for amateurs.

'Was that a fight in the car-park as we arrived?' Nigel asked me after introducing himself as the relief manager.

'No, it was a local Licensed Victuallers' meeting. You'll like them, they're a friendly bunch.'

We had bundled the Marons into various licensees' cars, the plan being to take them into Folkestone police station.

In the boot of the Marons' hire car we had found another thirty tankards each labelled with the name of the pub they had 'bought' it from, covering an area from Brighton to Canterbury. We had also found books of American Express traveller's cheques, some with the ink still wet. And I had turned up a small hammer and a metal punch, about six inches long and well worn. It was a bigger version of the sort of punch you use to drive nails in flush, but it had the faded image of a royal head – George IV? – at the business end.

Ted Lewis volunteered to drive the Marons' car into Folkestone but he stopped off in the bar to welcome the Coldstreams.

'Good pub, this,' he said, shaking their hands. 'You'll be happy here until Ivy comes back. Well, you know what I mean.'

They nodded uncertainly.

'Thanks for the tip-off, Roy. How did you know about the dodgy cheques?'

'It had to be that. It was like the guy leaving the building site each day with a wheelbarrow and the foreman is sure he's nicking something so he keeps stopping him and searching the wheelbarrows which are always empty. In the end he takes him to one side and says look, I know you're thieving, but *what* are you thieving? And the guy says –'

'Wheelbarrows. Got ya. Thanks again and any time you're passing, there's a drink for you.'

'Don't say things like that, Ted, because I won't forget even if you do. Here, you'll need these.'

I handed him the phoney cheque Maron had left and Tony's photographs of them.

The Coldstreams watched him go in silence and if they hadn't been wondering what they had let themselves in for before, they certainly were when Neemoy, Max and Sasha came down into the bar, fully made-up, dressed to kill and carrying their bags.

'Car's here,' said Max, helping herself to a last vodka.

Neemoy smiled down at the Coldstreams, then said to me: 'Ready to go, Angel?'

'Yep, just put this in my bag.'

'What is it?' she asked.

'It's a nineteenth-century silver punch, probably Italian. They're quite rare, I'm told.'

Reuben Sloman had also said they were quite valuable.

Veronica Blugden did get a report – of sorts – and she passed it on to Murdo Seton and he seemed quite pleased as I was one of the first people in the country to receive a case of Seagrave's Millennium Ale. I still have it.

A month or so later, via Veronica, I got a cutting from the *Licensee and Morning Advertiser*, the publicans' newspaper:

FEUDING BOOTLEGGERS FOILED IN UNDERCOVER RAID IN 'WILD WEST' KENT
Exclusive by John Tomlin

Customs and Excise officials and Kent police were today claiming joint credit for foiling one of the best organised and most violent of the many criminal gangs which have moved into bootlegging near the Channel ports. Their enquiries also involve the deaths, described as 'suspicious', of two men named as John Rufus Radabe, 31, of Kennington, London and Brian Anthony Scoular, 22, of Guildford. On raiding a secret smugglers' headquarters, one Customs official described the scene as: 'Like something out of the Wild West . . .'

There was more, but I didn't need to read it.

A month or so after that, I was driving Amy through

Hammersmith in Armstrong when she leaned in through the glass partition and hit me on the shoulder.

'We're going the wrong way,' she said.

'Are we? You're not in a hurry, are you?'

'Not really,' she said reasonably. 'But you looked as if you were day-dreaming. You were miles away.'

'Sorry, maybe I was.'

I signalled to turn off towards Chiswick and let the truck I had been following pull away from us.

On the back of its trailer unit was the legend:

ANGEL'S WINGS

DOMESTIC REMOVALS

OF SALFORD

'There's a pub up ahead,' I said over my shoulder. 'Fancy a drink?'